THE RUNAWAY PROPHET

Also by Michele Chynoweth

The Faithful One
The Peace Maker

The Faithful One

"It often seems that the great characters of the Bible are so far removed from us. We sanitize them and dehumanize them. *The Faithful One* puts the character of Job into a whole new contemporary light. The story makes his struggles so much more tangible and relatable to today's audience. Kudos to Michele Chynoweth for helping us get a better handle on what Job may have gone through. It certainly makes my struggles seem much smaller!"

—**Gus Lloyd**, Host of "Seize the Day" on The Catholic Channel, Sirius XM 129 & Author of *Magnetic Christianity* and *A Minute in the Church*

The Peace Maker

"The race to The White House is set to be an interesting one. No one knows who may be the next one to claim the office and both Leif and Darren are extremely passionate about reaching that goal. Leif, the humble horse trainer from Kentucky, and Darren, the rich boy from New York, are pitted head to head. But there is more to this battle than meets the eye. Both Darren and Leif have things to hide in their past and they're determined to defeat each other, no matter what it may mean for them in the end. It's going to be up to Chessa, Darren's wife, to ensure that both of them are able to escape from the battle unscathed... *The Peace Maker* by Michele Chynoweth is the type of story that many young women have lived in one way or another. Many of us have been like Chessa, caught between the one we love and doing what's right, but how can you decide what's right when your heart and your mind are conflicted?"

—Five Star Review by **Samantha Rivera**
for Readers Favorite International Book Awards

THE
RUNAWAY
PROPHET
A NOVEL

MICHELE CHYNOWETH

New York

The Runaway Prophet
A Novel

Published in New York, New York, by Morgan James Publishing. Morgan James and The Entrepreneurial Publisher are trademarks of Morgan James, LLC. www.MorganJamesPublishing.com

The Morgan James Speakers Group can bring authors to your live event. For more information or to book an event visit The Morgan James Speakers Group at www.TheMorganJamesSpeakersGroup.com.

Shelfie

A **free** eBook edition is available
with the purchase of this print book.

CLEARLY PRINT YOUR NAME ABOVE IN UPPER CASE

Instructions to claim your free eBook edition:
1. Download the Shelfie app for Android or iOS
2. Write your name in **UPPER CASE** above
3. Use the Shelfie app to submit a photo
4. Download your eBook to any device

ISBN 978-1-63047-807-0 paperback
ISBN 978-1-63047-809-4 eBook
ISBN 978-1-63047-808-7 hardcover
Library of Congress Control Number:
2015915620

Cover Design by:
Rachel Lopez
www.r2cdesign.com

Interior Design by:
Bonnie Bushman
The Whole Caboodle Graphic Design

In an effort to support local communities and raise awareness and funds, Morgan James Publishing donates a percentage of all book sales for the life of each book to Habitat for Humanity Peninsula and Greater Williamsburg.

Get involved today, visit
www.MorganJamesBuilds.com

Habitat
for Humanity®
Peninsula and
Greater Williamsburg
Building Partner

"Those who cling to worthless idols
forfeit the grace that could be theirs . . .
Salvation comes from the Lord."
—Jonah 2:8-9

DEDICATION

- - - - - - -

To all my readers, from the critics to the fans and everyone in between—thank you each and every one for spurring me on to continue this challenging yet rewarding journey. I do it because I believe I am called to serve you. I hope I help not only entertain you but also help you hear God's message.

ACKNOWLEDGMENTS

- - - - - - - - - -

My profound thanks go to the following people who made this novel better: for his well-versed biblical perspective, Pastor Patrick "Bo" Gordy-Stith of Whatcoat United Methodist Church, Delaware; for his FBI consultation, Andrew P. "Andy" Black, Supervisory Special Agent, Federal Bureau of Investigation Office of Public and Congressional Affairs, Los Angeles Division; for his help with US Naval authenticity, Joe Potak, former crew member of the USS *Merrill, DD-976*; for their boxing and writing expertise, former middle-weight champion boxer Dave Tiberi and writer Mark Crouch; for his oft-visited experience with Las Vegas, Mike Leppert; for their sharp editing advice, Angie Kiesling and Janet Angelo; for their outstanding proofing skills, Judy Sweeney and John Styer; and for his unwavering support, my husband Bill Chynoweth.

PROLOGUE

Rory Justice covered his mouth and nose with his shirtsleeve as he opened the door to the hotel suite. The stench hit him squarely in the face like a two-by-four. The air in the room, laden with the smell of cheap perfume, foul body odors, stale beer, burned-out cigarettes, and day-old pot smoke made his stomach lurch, and he fought not to gag.

He stood in the huge living room of the suite and surveyed the damage: a table lamp overturned with the shade ripped . . . a few pizza boxes with the congealed remains of an uneaten slice that now attracted a fly . . . two dozen or more beer bottles and several empty liquor bottles of whiskey, vodka, gin, tequila . . . stains of various hues on the cream-colored carpet . . . couch cushions strewn about . . . cigarette butts randomly tossed and black burn holes in the upholstery. . . one of those life-sized, blow-up plastic dolls with the O-shaped mouth now partly deflated and slumped against a chair . . . various drug paraphernalia lying across a coffee table . . . and a jagged hole in the wall.

Rory hadn't seen the bedrooms or the bathroom yet, but he could hear a man's guttural snoring and knew it was his coworker and roommate Jim Smith, a three-hundred-twenty-pound pasty-skinned man prone to allergies, upper respiratory difficulties, and a whole range of other health problems due to his weight.

Things really got out of hand, Rory thought, assessing the damage with disgust. Anger welled up within him as he realized that his coworkers had made this mess in *his* hotel suite, and he would probably have to take some responsibility. *There is no way I'm paying for this.*

And then the memory of his part in it all surfaced as the fog in his brain lifted, and he cupped a hand over his mouth, stifling the nausea that rolled up inside, not just from his hangover, but from the sudden fear and regret that gripped him.

The woman. Rory slowly recalled, as if in slow motion replay, leaving the party with her, a bottle of cheap champagne in one hand, her waist in the other, headed for his coworker Chad Weeks's room, which he had asked to borrow for the night. He couldn't even remember her name, but the image of her appeared in his mind's eye—white-blonde hair, big pouty red lips, and huge brown eyes. She was curvy, some would say voluptuous—the opposite of Haley, his wife.

The woman had been invited to the party with the other young women. Everyone had eventually paired up, and he hadn't wanted to spend the night with her at first, but she had insisted, and he had felt much too intoxicated to resist. Besides, his marriage back home was a sham anyway.

What have I done? Remorse and anger, both at his coworkers from AdExecs and at himself, paralyzed him. *If only I hadn't listened to these guys and let them have the party in my room; if only I hadn't come to Las Vegas in the first place, none of this would have happened.*

Rory had worked in the advertising industry since graduating from Ohio State University, not because he particularly liked it, but because it seemed the easiest way to get a job with his marketing degree. He started out as a "go-fer" at the Columbus *Dispatch* where he had interned during his senior year, then worked his way up to senior account executive. During a meeting where he was pitching the *Dispatch's* latest media offerings to AdExecs, Rory met the advertising agency's CEO, Everett Major, known locally as the dean of marketing.

After visiting the agency's suite of offices in a sleek high-rise building and learning about some of the huge ad campaigns the company had conducted for several big-name clients, Rory decided to apply for a job.

"You look like a fine, upstanding young man," Everett told Rory during his job interview. "A little green, maybe, and very serious for a man in his thirties, but hang around with us for a while—you'll loosen up, and maybe learn a thing or two." The boss gave him a sly wink, but Rory wanted the job so badly that he didn't think anything of it at the time.

Rory had always been content working for the *Dispatch.* He had a loyal client list and didn't have to hustle to meet quotas or bring in new clients. If he felt he had a choice, he would not have wanted the position at AdExecs and all of the pressure and stress it would probably bring. But Haley encouraged him—well, if truth be told, threatened him at the time. She told him she wanted to cut back her hours as a paralegal and spend more time with their two school-aged children, and they desperately needed the money. "You're an idiot if you don't take the job," she said. So he acquiesced.

Their marriage had already started to crumble, before the trip to Vegas three years later.

Mr. Major and nine AdExecs associates made the four-day trip to the annual marketing convention that October, flying in from Ohio to McCarron International Airport. It was Rory's first business trip with the firm, and he had just been promoted from assistant account executive to associate.

When the airport taxi pulled up in front of Caesars Palace shortly after dusk that warm Thursday evening, Rory could feel his mouth hanging open as he took in the glittering lights of the casino resorts that lined the Las Vegas Strip from end to end, each one more magnificent than the next.

Entering the lobby, Rory was amazed at the gold and marble statues, the vaulted ceilings, the rows of high-end shops with haute couture, and the constant din of the slot machines that filled the sprawling casino. *It's everything they said it would be*, he thought, feeling like he had finally "arrived."

The next morning some of the guys went to take a dip in the resort's outdoor pools after breakfast. Since they had more than an hour before the conference was scheduled to start, Rory joined them, figuring he would swim a few laps. But the pool was more of a party scene, Rory realized, gazing at all of the bikini-clad women and fawning guys, drinks in hand, mingling in the water.

So he sat in a lounge chair in his swim trunks and polo shirt sipping a glass of orange juice, listening to his co-workers complain about their hangovers and losses from the night before, pretending to sunbathe but secretly wanting to be in the pool so that he could feel like he was one of the cool guys.

Rory had to pass the hotel casino several times a day on his way to and from his room to the conference halls where the seminars were held. He stopped once to watch out of curiosity as a man plunked down hundreds of dollars on a game of poker. *How could people throw away so much money? Haley would kill me.* Still, he did play the slots a few times. He was in Vegas after all.

The following morning, he took a half-mile walk to get some exercise and was approached on every street corner by men flicking cards with pictures of scantily clad women offering a good time if you called the eight hundred number listed or visited their website. Women in fishnet stockings and low cut tops shouted at him, saying they'd do him a few favors for a reasonable price. Rory felt a strange mix of excited curiosity and uneasiness, and hurried back to the safety of the hotel.

That final night, though, Rory wasn't able to hide from all of the city's temptations.

It was the company's annual big night out, Mr. Major's special way of saying thank you to his associates for their hard work all year. It was kept a surprise for first-timers like Rory.

It all started innocently enough with dinner at the Luxor, the pyramid-shaped resort with Egyptian lion statues at its entrance. A few of the guys who had been to the Luxor in the past laughed and chattered with anticipation.

Halfway into dinner, Rory figured out why his coworkers were so excited. The deluxe prix-fixe dinner package also came with tickets to the Fantasy show. In his naiveté, Rory entered the auditorium assuming it was some circus or magic show like the Cirque du Soleil acts he had heard were prevalent in Vegas. Instead, after having a large shot of sake that he had let them talk him into drinking, he found himself sitting in a front row seat watching topless women dance and strut across the stage to the blaring beat of disco music. Then, under the guise of going for dessert, he was duped into going with the guys to the hotel's famous and exclusive nightclub, Lax.

A tipsy Chad Weeks stood next to Rory in the shoulder-to-shoulder crowd waiting at the VIP entrance, the young new hire's face flushed with enthusiasm. "You have no idea how hard it is to get in," Chad whispered, pointing to the hundreds of patrons in the regular line waiting to gain admittance. "Those poor slobs will never make it. This is the chance of a lifetime. All the celebs come here. I think we have a private loft too. I hope to get some action tonight, if you know what I mean."

Rory felt embarrassed just listening to Chad's over-eager rants. He was wondering if maybe he should take a cab back to Caesars instead when Jim grabbed his arm, and he felt himself being pulled into the dark, narrow entrance.

It's literally like entering the gates of hell, Rory thought, trying not to worry where the night was headed. His head pounded with each loud, synchronized beat of music, and his heart raced with anxiety.

The entrance was made of black, wrought-iron gates. Inside, it was so dark he could hardly see a foot in front of him. An usher led them along a maze of dim corridors with a flashlight until a glowing red light loomed ahead, the inside of a cavernous club, where girls in six-inch spiked heels and tight, shiny dresses that barely covered their bottoms writhed around, some with male partners, some with each other. Rory's group was led upstairs to a dark red lounge with low, plush couches and recessed rooms and iced tubs of vodka. "All for us," Mr. Major said proudly, winking at Rory. "Fellas, welcome to the AdExecs private party."

Several young women seemed to appear out of nowhere, sidling up to them, and minutes later Rory found himself on the crowded dance floor in the midst of a foam party. A few hours later, they were headed back in cabs to Caesars, the girls in tow, to continue the party.

And then Jim volunteered to host it in their suite.

By the time Rory protested, it was too late. He was simply outvoted by his colleagues, and then Everett Major cajoled Rory, saying that since he and Jim had gotten the biggest room with the best view—and Mrs. Major had flown in that day to join him, so he couldn't use his own luxury suite, of course—Rory's suite was the perfect location. Plus, Rory had been told early on in his career at AdExecs not to deny the boss unless he had a life-or-death reason.

So they finally persuaded Rory to not only host the party with Jim but to join in the festivities. "Harmless fun," they said. "We're all married too, the wives will never find out," they said. And of course, they added, "What happens in Vegas stays in Vegas."

This is all their fault, Rory fumed as he stood in the middle of the mess left from last night's party.

He wandered into the bathroom and averted his eyes from the stopped up toilet and instead looked into the mirror. Staring back at him was the reflection of a thirty-five-year-old, discontent, white advertising account executive. Usually clean cut and clean shaven, Rory sported a five o'clock shadow and dark gray circles under his bloodshot eyes. *Unremarkable* was what he usually thought when he saw his mirror image: medium build, not thin or fat, not muscular or flaccid, with average looks, a head of dark brown hair, plain features, and dull, gray-green eyes. But now a second observation consumed him, holding his thoughts hostage: *guilty.*

It's your own fault, you know, his self-conscience silently told the guy looking back at him.

And then self-righteousness joined the debate in his embattled head. *No, actually it's not the guys' fault, nor mine. Haley is really to blame. If she had showed me any attention over the past few years, I wouldn't have had to seek it here. Besides, it was only a one night stand. She'll never find out.*

But you know, the tiny voice of reason chimed.

Suddenly all of it—the voices, his anger, worry, remorse—were instantly forgotten as he heard a whimpering sound coming from one of the bedrooms.

It wasn't Jim, who was still snoring. No, this sound came from the other bedroom, he was sure of it.

And it became clearer as he listened. Rory knew with a growing fear that what he was hearing was the muffled cry of a woman.

His trancelike state broken, Rory rushed toward the sound. He stopped still in the bedroom doorway. Lying barely covered with a gold-colored silk sheet on the king-sized bed was a gaunt woman of Asian descent. Her wrists were bound to the headboard with scarves, and her mouth was covered with a piece of duct tape.

Once she saw him, she became silent. Her black eyes gleamed with hatred, following Rory as he approached her. He first threw the bedspread over her, but she fought to kick it off, thrashing her legs like weapons, striking out at him like a wild animal. Rory untied her left wrist and she swung at him with her free hand. He darted out of her reach just in time and stood for a moment debating whether to free her other arm, but when she ripped the duct tape off her mouth, hurled loud screams and obscenities at him in a language he didn't understand, and then spit at him, Rory suddenly recognized she was going to come at him full force if he freed her. He walked backward toward the bedroom door, averting his eyes from her half-naked body.

"I'm sorry," he stammered, not knowing if she understood. As she frantically worked to free herself from her last binding, he rushed out of the room, shut the door, and ran to the anonymity of the crowded casino, leaving a still sleeping Jim behind.

CHAPTER ONE

Now, ten years later, a divorced and single Rory still remembered his trip to Las Vegas as if it were yesterday. While most of his fellow employees had slept during the four-hour flight from Las Vegas back to Columbus, Rory had sat and smoldered, making a promise to himself that he would never go back to Vegas again, even if it meant getting fired.

Rory had also vowed to look for a new job, but as the years passed, he realized with increasing despair that it was out of the question. No one left a good job in the middle of an economic downturn, he had told himself, comforting himself with the knowledge that at least with the latest recession, the company cut out the trips to Vegas. Still, Rory felt like he was stuck in quicksand. Hopeless days turned into miserable years as he stuffed his feelings down like he stuffed his starched shirt into his dress pants, drove his Ford economy car to work, put in his time, and drove back again each night to his meager apartment.

Then the call came, and everything changed.

It was Rory's mother, Donna Justice. She got right to the point.

"Your father has taken a turn for the worse, Rory. He may not make it this time. He wants to see you."

Rory's father, Howard, had pulmonary fibrosis. He was diagnosed with the disease several years ago at the age of sixty-eight and was eventually forced to retire from his position as a special agent in the FBI. His health had deteriorated over the past few years, and he couldn't leave the house without taking his oxygen machine with him, and only then for short periods. Then to make matters worse, while he was hospitalized a few months ago he developed a bacterial infection known as Clostridium difficile, or "C-diff." His doctors had tried to battle it without much success, and the drugs for the infection ended up compromising the blood thinner he was taking, causing a stroke.

And just recently, Rory's mother told him that his father was suffering mild dementia.

"What about Daniel?" Rory asked his mom. Daniel Justice, Rory's older brother and only sibling, was a sergeant in the US Army who was stationed in Afghanistan in one of the last American divisions tasked with helping the post-war government retain its tenuous stronghold before the Americans departed the war-torn country to fend for itself. His mother told him she had called Daniel to tell him about his father's condition, and he was scheduled to depart within the next twenty-four hours.

Rory usually travelled to his parents' home in Bethesda, Maryland, a commuter town for many Washington DC employees, a half dozen times or more a year. Sometimes he felt resentment that his brother didn't have to take on the obligation of attending family gatherings such as holidays, birthdays, weddings, and funerals.

"I hope he makes it in time," Donna Justice said, as if reading her son's thoughts.

"He will, Mom. Don't worry." *He better*, Rory thought, feeling a little selfish, but justified.

They had been born and raised in the quaint little town of Rising Sun, Maryland, where Rory had lived until the age of thirteen when the family moved to Bethesda after his father was offered the job with the FBI.

Rory had a more vivid memory of Rising Sun than he did of the posh suburbs of Bethesda, even though he had lived there only during his early formative years. He remembered his family's house in the rural countryside where they had cows for neighbors. He recalled taking the yellow school bus to the local elementary school and coming home to his mom usually baking pies or cookies while his dad worked late most nights as a state police trooper.

He remembered winters sledding with his brother and their friends down the big hill that sloped from the neighboring farmhouse, and summers spent swimming at the local public pool. He recalled Fourth of July fireworks, the county farm fair with its 4-H displays, carnival rides and rodeo shows, and the town's annual summer Sun Fest with its parade of fire trucks and lots of good things to eat.

It was an idyllic childhood, or so it seemed through the fine gauze of a child's memory shrouding it all.

But looking back, Rory realized it was far from idyllic or even typical, if there was such a thing. He didn't recall ever seeing one minority in his neighborhood—no blacks, Asians, Hispanics—and only a few in most parts of the surrounding town and county. There were no minorities in his school or in any of the Rising Sun schools, and none in his Little League or the Peewee football program. Rising Sun had always been almost one hundred percent white, even into the early nineties—and it seemed the town was proud of it.

Rory remembered hearing rumors that the Ku Klux Klan was founded in Rising Sun, and he had often overheard racial remarks made by classmates and sometimes adults. He recalled one incident in which one of his classmates came into school threatening to injure the next black person he saw. It turned out that the boy's dad had lost his job to a young African American man.

One day Rory mustered the courage to ask Daniel what he thought about the town's racial disparity as he sat on his twin bed in the room they shared, watching his older brother's serious face as he concentrated on his latest model plane project spread out on the desk. "Hey, Danny, why aren't there more black people in Rising Sun?"

His brother rolled his eyes. "Geez, Rory, I don't know, go ask Dad."

Disgruntled at being brushed aside by his older brother, Rory stood up in a hurry and his elbow accidentally swiped against the newly glued wing of Daniel's plane, knocking it off the desk and onto the floor.

Daniel glared at him angrily. "Rory, you're gonna get it!"

Rory knew he was in trouble if his brother caught him, so he ran from the room as fast as he could, down the stairs, into the kitchen and the safety of his mother's arms.

He never did think again to ask his parents about their thoughts on the situation and came to believe that people of other races or social backgrounds weren't to be trusted.

Rory's reflections on his flight from Columbus to Baltimore-Washington International Airport were interrupted when the pilot announced the plane was beginning its descent and everyone needed to buckle up, turn off all electronic devices, and prepare for landing. It was sixty-five degrees under partially cloudy skies in DC, and the flight was arriving on schedule.

His mother greeted him at the door to his boyhood home in Bethesda, and together they entered the living room.

Howard Justice lay sleeping in his day bed, which had been set up on the main floor since he could no longer climb the steps of the two-story brick colonial where he lived with his wife.

Rory was surprised to see a strange man of about sixty sitting in the corner of the room at the far side of his dad's bed. He then noticed the man must be a minister since he wore a collar and held an open Bible on his lap.

"Rory, this is Pastor Dave Graybeal from our church, Bethesda United Methodist," Donna said, as the man laid down the Bible and stood to shake hands. "I asked Pastor Graybeal to come over and be with us."

"Nice to meet you, Rory, I've heard a lot of good things about y'all," Pastor Dave said with a beatific smile. He was a short, stout man who exuded cheerfulness. He was new to the church, having moved there from Alabama, and spoke with a southern accent.

"Thank you for being here, Pastor," Rory said with a stiff smile. "I didn't mean to interrupt."

"You're not interrupting, Rory, I've already prayed with your mom and dad and read some passages from the Bible. Would you like me to pray with you?" The minister asked kindly.

How do I answer that without offending him? Rory thought. "Uh, no, that's okay; I'd just like to pray quietly until my dad wakes up, if that's all right with you."

Pastor Dave smiled. "Of course, Rory, I'm just here to offer any comfort I can."

Rory stopped going to church when he got married. He considered himself non-denominational or independent when it came to religion and politics. Non-committed would have been a better description, and that was just fine with him.

He felt like he had gone to church enough as a kid, attending service every Sunday with his parents. It seemed to him enough to last a lifetime.

In his rebellious teenage years, Rory stopped listening and simply went through the motions, going to church only because it was expected of him—and he was told he would face serious consequences if he refused.

One Sunday, when he was seventeen, Rory had sleepily refused to get up and go to church, deciding to suffer the consequences.

He had expected a big argument, but his parents and brother simply walked out of the house without him. Hours went by, and fear set in as the sun rose high in the sky then descended to the horizon, and still his family hadn't returned.

Finally, they came home to a clean house. Instead of sleeping and watching TV all day, Rory, in his growing anxiety, fear, and guilt, had washed the dishes, vacuumed, dusted, and done laundry.

"Where were you all day?" he practically yelled as they walked through the front door.

"Oh, honey, maybe you forgot, it was the church fair and pot luck dinner today," his mother replied nonchalantly.

"Yeah, you missed it," Daniel said with a superior grin. "It was actually a lot of fun."

"That's because your brother here met a girl." His dad reached out and tousled Daniel's mop of curls.

Rory was crestfallen. "You could have reminded me."

"I was going to tell you no car for a week for missing the church service," his father said. "But seeing the look on your face, it seems like you've been punished already."

Being strict Methodists also meant that no smoking, drinking or cursing was allowed in their household, much less gambling or drugs. Instead, the boys got involved in youth activities—Daniel in sports, and Rory, being less athletically inclined, in the Boy Scouts. He earned the high honor of Eagle Scout, which kept him busy and out of trouble.

Rory enjoyed his scouting days, basking in the pride his parents showed him when he received each merit badge and award. But it became increasingly difficult as he neared the age of eighteen to remain a model citizen when the other boys who played pranks and got in trouble tempted him to "loosen up and have some fun," and taunted him when he resisted.

They sneaked beer and *Playboy* magazines around the campfire, or pulled them out of their sleeping bags at scout camp when the adult leaders went to sleep. Rory tried his best to ignore them, feigning headaches or saying he was too tired from the day's activities. It was hard to be good.

— — — — — —

Rory felt fear growing inside him as he sat with his mom and the pastor, anxiously listening to the ticking of the grandfather clock in the foyer. He was filled with apprehension that his father might not make it, and the deepening sense of dread that he had not done enough, said enough, gone to church enough, or prayed enough, nearly consumed him. *Not to mention mom and dad still don't know about the affair I had in Vegas,* he thought.

He was shocked at the vast change in his dad's appearance since the last time he had visited his parents for his dad's seventy-fifth birthday in February. His father was much thinner and frailer now, and his skin looked pale and paper thin, like he had aged fifteen years in the past several months. His glasses looked too big for his sunken cheeks, and his white hair seemed to have receded a little more from his forehead.

Howard Justice lay sleeping now, his breath coming out in rattling gurgles.

"Mom, shouldn't Dad be back in the hospital?" Rory asked, trying to sound calm instead of panicked.

"The last time the hospital released him, they suggested hospice care," his mom said. "So I've had a visiting nurse come every day to help with keeping him hydrated, feeding him what little soft foods he can eat, giving him sponge baths and medicines and so on. Rory, your dad has refused to go back to the hospital or to be kept alive on any machines. He just wants to spend his last days peacefully here at home. It's in his living will, and of course I'm in charge of carrying that out."

Rory took a deep breath and inched closer to the bed.

"Will he recognize me?" Rory asked his mother tentatively.

"It's hard to say, honey. I hope so. He goes in and out of knowing where he is, what day it is, or who we are. Last time he was coherent, he specifically asked to see you."

As if he heard them, Howard's eyes fluttered open, and he said coarsely but distinctly, "Rory?"

Rory came close to the edge of the bed, took his father's hand in his, and bent over so his dad could hear him.

"I'm right here, Dad."

"I'm not going to be around much longer . . ."

"C'mon, Dad, don't say that . . ." Howard cut him off, squeezing his hand, which for him took a lot of effort.

"Don't argue . . . don't have much time . . ." Howard Justice struggled to form the words, gasping for breath, occasionally emitting a hoarse wheeze.

This isn't good, Rory thought, trying not to cry in front of his parents, even though he wanted to.

"I have a big favor to ask." His father's words came out in a whisper, and Rory strained to hear.

"Go ahead, Dad, ask me anything."

"This letter . . . it needs to go to a friend of mine. FBI business . . . very important. It could save a lot of people . . . " Howard Justice's hand shook as he reached for an envelope on the table next to his bed. "I need you to deliver it."

Rory was stunned. *Why me? Is he kidding?* "Dad, are you sure you want me to deliver it? What about someone in the FBI?"

"Don't . . . trust . . . them." His dad was struggling now to breathe and to talk.

"What about Daniel? Certainly he would be more qualified." Rory felt guilty arguing, but he was sure his father must be delusional asking him to take on this kind of responsibility.

"He . . . can't. Has to be . . . you." His dad's breathing came out in rasps in between.

"Who do I give it to? Where do I go? Should I read it? What about . . . ?" Rory had so many questions, but they would have to go unanswered, because Howard Justice was coughing spasmodically, his face turning a deep purplish red.

Donna Justice rushed to his bedside. "Shhh, darling, please calm down." She shot Rory a stern look. "Don't argue with your father, Rory, just take the letter, and do as he asks." Her glare warned what she couldn't bring herself to say: *Can't you see he's dying? Say you'll do this for him even if it doesn't make any sense.*

Was this just nonsense brought on by his dementia? Rory reached out and hesitantly took the envelope from his father's grasp.

"I . . . love you . . . tell Dan too." Howard Justice's eyes fluttered and closed, and he laid his head back on the pillow.

Suddenly there was no time for any more questions, and none of it mattered. His father was slipping away.

"Dad!" Rory wasn't ready to lose him. "I love you, Dad. Please don't leave us."

Donna sat weeping, holding her husband's hand.

Pastor Dave read softly from Psalm 23:

"The Lord is my Shepherd, I shall not want.
He makes me lie down in green pastures,
He leads me beside quiet waters. He restores my soul.
He guides me in paths of righteousness for His name's sake.

Even though I walk through the valley of the shadow of death,
I will fear no evil, for You are with me;
Your rod and Your staff, they comfort me.
You prepare a table before me in the presence of my enemies.
You anoint my head with oil; my cup overflows.
Surely goodness and love will follow me all the days of my life,
And I will dwell in the house of the Lord forever."

Howard Justice took a few more shallow breaths as Pastor Dave read. When the minister closed the Bible, Rory's father exhaled one last ragged time and then stilled. His face lost its last vestige of warmth and color.

Rory laid his head down on his father's quilted legs and sobbed.

CHAPTER TWO

Daniel arrived at the Justice home a little over an hour after their father passed. Donna Justice insisted her husband's body stay where it was until her eldest son got home to see him.

Rory had called his brother to tell him that their dad hadn't made it. Daniel was angry in his anguish.

"Why couldn't he at least wait until I got there?" he wailed into the phone as he drove in the rental car straight from BWI airport.

"I'm sorry, Dan," Rory said. He could feel his brother's pain. "He said he loved you. Those were his last words. We're keeping him right where he is until you get here. Be careful."

Daniel Justice arrived in civilian clothes, immediately brushed past his mother and brother, ignored Pastor Dave, knelt down beside his father's bed, and broke down weeping.

"Dad, this is so unfair. I didn't even get to say goodbye," Daniel said between choked sobs. "Why didn't you wait?"

After a few moments, Pastor Dave broke the grief-strained silence. "Daniel?"

Rory's brother looked up, his tear-streaked face not registering his own name at first.

"I'm Dave Graybeal, pastor at your parents' church." The minister rose and firmly shook Daniel's hand, speaking evenly. "I know you're upset your father passed before you got here. I am really sorry that happened. It doesn't seem fair that God would take him like that. But your father knew you loved him—just like God knows the love in our hearts without us even needing to tell Him—and your name was the last word on his lips. It's hard to say why God chooses the timing He does, but rest assured your father is definitely in a better place, free from pain and suffering, smiling down on you at this very minute."

Those last words registered, and Daniel seemed to give up his anger. He nodded his thanks for the reassurance and smiled through his tears.

This minister is really good, Rory thought. *He knows just what to say, and he seems sincere. I wonder if I should ask him about the letter.* Rory's musings were interrupted when a driver from the funeral home showed up, ready to transport Howard Justice's body to the morgue.

Pastor Dave and the family held hands in a circle around the deceased and said the Lord's Prayer before they bid a final, tearful farewell.

Donna and her two sons went to the kitchen to have some coffee and to make plans for the funeral.

The funeral service was held following a family wake at Bethesda United Methodist Church. Pastor Dave officiated and talked about

Howard in glowing terms, calling him a man of deep convictions who served his country, his community, and his family.

The church was packed full with six hundred people as past and present FBI employees, members of the congregation and a host of friends and family came to pay their respects. A former FBI agent who had worked closely with Howard read a letter from Kathleen Tower, the President of the United States, and Daniel, looking especially sharp in his military dress uniform, delivered the eulogy.

Daniel sat next to his wife and their two sons who were both among the pallbearers in addition to three young men from the church and Rory's son Rick.

Rory sat alone, wedged between his mother and Daniel. He had noticed at one point during the service that Rick was sitting in the back of the church with his mother and sister. Rory had found out from his mom the day before that Rick had accepted her request to be a pallbearer, and that his ex-wife and daughter would also be attending.

Even though Rory knew that Haley would be there, the knowledge didn't lessen the stab of resentment he felt toward his ex-wife as he walked with his mom on his arm behind the casket into the vestibule and saw her standing at the back of the church.

Haley was gorgeous as usual, dressed in a simple navy sheath with a single strand of pearls, her long brunette hair loose on her shoulders.

The look she gave him with her cool gray-blue eyes betrayed the animosity she still felt for Rory, and he quickly diverted his gaze straight ahead, concentrating on supporting his mom and holding it together.

His twenty-year-old daughter Riley had grown to look as beautiful as her mother. She didn't even glance at him but instead looked down and away when he passed by. Rory hadn't seen her or Rick for the past two years, ever since Riley had turned eighteen and decided she no longer wished to see her father again.

It wasn't for my lack of trying. After all these years, Rory still felt the sting of bitterness from his divorce and the estrangement from his kids.

Rory had met Haley in a creative writing class at Ohio State. He liked her the minute he set eyes on her, and when he found out she was struggling with her assignments, he offered to tutor her since creative writing came easily to him. Homework sessions turned into dating, and soon they were a couple.

Haley had planned to stay on at Ohio State's Moritz College of Law to get her Juris Doctor degree, while Rory took the job at the *Dispatch* after graduation. They moved into a tiny apartment off campus, and Haley's first semester was underway when she got pregnant with Rick.

Her ultra conservative, well-to-do parents from northern New Jersey virtually disowned her, telling her she could pay for her own education or drop out now that she was pregnant.

Despite some misgivings from a few friends who thought Haley was too "high maintenance," Rory decided to do the right thing, and one cold November morning, he married Haley at the local courthouse.

Haley stayed in school while Rick worked sixty hours a week at the *Dispatch* and as a waiter on the weekends at a local restaurant. Rick was born just after Haley finished her finals that May.

Soon the young couple sank into debt, simply because Rory didn't make enough to cover all the bills and pay for formula, baby food, diapers and all of the things an infant required. Once Rick was a year old, they agreed that Haley would take a break from law school and work as a legal secretary until they had saved enough for her to finish her degree.

When she got pregnant with Riley a few months later, everything seemed to change. It was a difficult pregnancy and delivery, and the post-partum blues Haley experienced never completely dissipated, turning into full-blown depression.

Haley decided she could never go back to school now that she had two toddlers to raise. She was miserable and filled with resentment over her family's rejection, her lost law career, her stifled daily existence with two kids in the small ranch house they had managed to purchase, and living what she considered a poor lifestyle.

She returned to work as a legal secretary for several years but when she found out Rory had interviewed for the higher paying job at AdExecs, she told him she wanted to take a leave of absence from her job to stay home with the kids, that they needed her to run them to sports practices and the like. Rory later found out Haley had lied to him, that she had actually been fired because her depression had caused her to miss too much time at work. A few more part-time jobs came and went, and then Haley stopped working altogether, claiming she had developed back pain in addition to her clinical depression.

Meanwhile, Rory worked two jobs on top of managing the household duties and running the kids to after-school activities as well as dentist and doctor appointments.

Rory eventually gave up pleading and complaining and harassing his wife to get a job, meanwhile watching his paychecks, his pension and his 401K dwindle away to nothing as their debt climbed. Heated arguments gave way to a stone wall of silence over time and they hadn't been intimate in over a year before Rory took off for his trip to Vegas.

When Rory returned home, his pent up guilt only made him more on edge and what little tolerance he had for his wife's laziness and lack of motivation crumbled. He moved his clothes into the basement and the two slept in separate rooms.

One day Haley called Rory at work to tell him she needed him to take Rick to soccer practice and Chad Weeks answered. Rory was in a meeting and Chad happened to be in Rory's office looking for a file.

Once past the introductions, Haley innocently asked Chad how Las Vegas was.

"It was great, but that's all I can say," Chad said slyly, baiting his colleague's wife. For several years, even before Vegas, Chad had held a secret resentment that the boss favored Rory. While he had a cubicle, Rory had an office. While Rory had an expense account, Chad had none. And Chad just couldn't figure out why, since he felt he was clearly more ambitious and more in tune with the AdExecs' cutthroat culture and loose morals than Rory would ever be.

"Did my husband behave out there?" Haley was now curious.

"I wouldn't know, he left the party, uh, early to, um, borrow my room."

"Was he alone?"

"You'll have to ask him yourself Mrs. Justice. As they say, 'what happens in Vegas'…"

"I know," Haley snapped. "Please just tell him to call me."

Haley was waiting for Rory when he got home with Rick that night after soccer practice, arms crossed and ready for a confrontation.

Rory, tired, off-guard and defenseless, wearily told her the truth.

They didn't speak for a week, although Rory tried repeatedly to apologize. He finally talked Haley into going with him to see a marriage counselor. But time and again, they sat through sessions where Haley ended up arguing that the therapist was simply taking Rory's side.

Rory also took his wife to see the family doctor for her increasing back pain. But after numerous tests and scans, nothing was found, and she seemed to only get worse. Rory saw the prescription bottles in their bathroom multiply and empty and felt helpless to do anything about it. He knew his wife was abusing pain pills but when he asked her, she would turn on him, blaming him for causing her stress that added to her back pain.

Still feeling guilty about the affair, Rory eventually stopped asking.

Haley also started chain smoking and drinking several glasses of wine each day.

One doctor refused to write another prescription for pain meds, and Haley threatened to sue him. The physician pulled Rory aside after the visit to speak to him privately while Haley used the restroom. "Your wife doesn't need to see me for pain pills, Rory," he said. "She needs to see a psychiatrist."

It got to the point where almost every day when Rory returned home from work, he found Haley sleeping, the house a mess and nothing prepared for dinner. The kids would tell him they were starving, and he would have to drop his briefcase, pull off his tie and whip up something in a pan or heat up something he had cooked the night before. They frequently had breakfast for dinner because it was easy.

Then one night Rory came home from a particularly long workday and exploded.

Haley happened to be awake and was sitting outside on the porch drinking coffee and smoking a cigarette.

"What's for dinner?" Rory asked, knowing the answer.

"I don't know; what did you bring us?" Haley replied flippantly.

"Mom, Dad, Ricky's pulling my hair," they heard Riley scream from her room.

Haley evasively took another drag from her cigarette while Rory stood before her, dressed in his suit and tie, clutching his briefcase in anger.

"Aren't you going to go see what's wrong?" he asked, struggling to keep his voice level.

"Why don't you?" his wife challenged, peering up at him without blinking, her eyes glazed with disinterest and defiance.

"Because I've been working hard for the past nine hours to pay for the little bit of food we have in this house, which, need I remind you, I shopped and paid for, then I sat in traffic to get home, knowing that my worthless no-good wife hasn't made any dinner even though she's been home all day with nothing better to do than drink coffee and smoke cigarettes and watch television and sleep."

"You're just a big bully and a nag," Haley retorted, grinding out her cigarette, crossing her legs, and sitting back in the patio chair.

"Mom!" Riley shrieked, and then their daughter was standing before them, her face red and tear-streaked. She threw herself into her mother's arms. Rick ran up next carrying a few torn loose-leaf papers in his hands.

"That little brat ripped my homework on purpose!" Rick was on the verge of tears. "Dad, can you help me redo it tonight? And punish her?"

"Maybe your mother can help you while I'm cooking dinner," he offered.

"I'm no good at math," Haley countered. "Besides, why don't we just order a pizza?"

"Yay!" the kids chimed in unison, forgetting their battle for a moment.

Rory clenched his teeth, resisting the urge to hit his wife in the head with his briefcase. "We don't have the money for that," he snarled.

"Dad, we never eat out or get takeout," Rick said.

"Maybe if your lazy mother got a job, we would be able to!" he hollered.

Haley sat holding Riley in her lap. "How dare you speak to me that way?" she said icily.

"Dad, that wasn't nice," Rick said, sidling up to his mother.

"Yeah, dad, that was mean," Riley chimed in her girlish voice.

Rory stood helplessly, fighting tears of anger and hatred, feeling betrayed and defeated. He took a deep breath and counted to five, his insides on fire.

"You're right." He exhaled. "I will call for a pizza."

When the pizza delivery boy arrived twenty minutes later, Rory was gone. He had left a twenty-dollar bill for the pizza and a note to Haley telling her he was done.

Haley had apparently squirreled away part of their savings over time and used the money to hire a crackerjack attorney. As a result, she ended up not only with full custody of the children but the house and half of his paycheck each month for child support, plus half of what little was left of his pension and retirement fund.

Rory had to move into a tiny, one-bedroom apartment he could barely afford with what was left of his pay.

His son was fourteen, his daughter eleven when everything was finalized. According to the divorce decree, he got visitation with his kids every other weekend and one night each week. At first, the visits went well. He and Rick and Riley took walks in the local park, ate out at their favorite fast-food restaurants, and watched movies together.

But over time, Rory's relationship with his kids became strained. Both of his children seemed less talkative and more despondent, and on several occasions, they said they weren't feeling well and wanted to stay home with their mom.

Rory tried to chalk up their behavior to teenage moodiness, but he knew deep down it was more.

Haley had poisoned them against him with her exaggerations and lies, he was sure of it. He asked how the house was, how the dog was doing, if their mom was feeling okay, were they eating and sleeping all right, doing their homework, but they simply said everything was fine. If he found out about something involving

Haley (he still received her medical bills), they told him their mom had asked them not to talk about it.

When Rick went off to Saint Mary's College in Maryland, he rarely saw his father, and when he did, their interaction felt forced. Riley also seemed to pull away from her dad so much that Rory finally gave in to her request that she not be required to visit him anymore.

Seeing his daughter averting her eyes from him in the back of the church, Rory felt his heart hurt all over again. He had missed so much of their lives—driving lessons, school proms, first dates, first jobs—and probably much more that he didn't even know about, the kinds of small but meaningful moments that can only take place when parents live in the same house with their children.

They still hate me, he realized, blinking back tears, remembering the time he had browsed around on Facebook and noticed that his daughter had actually referred to him as her "sperm donor."

When his blurred vision cleared, he looked up and saw Rick outside, helping to load the coffin into the hearse to be transported to the cemetery.

This time, it was Rory who averted his gaze, striking up a perfunctory conversation with one of his aunts in the lobby.

One thing Rory felt like he hadn't missed, or was glad he had avoided, was his son's social life as a young adult.

Because Rory had also found out through Facebook that Rick was gay.

His son was a striking combination of both his parents, with his mom's wavy dark brown hair and Rory's green eyes. Growing up, people often commented on how cute little Ricky Justice was, even strangers in the grocery store.

Those good looks had only matured, and Rick Justice could have easily been a male model had he not chosen recently to transfer to Wesley Theological Seminary in Washington DC to study to become a Methodist minister.

Since Rory had missed his son's late teenage years and early twenties, he hadn't seen first-hand how Rick's mannerisms increasingly became somewhat effeminate with time. He was shocked and outraged when he saw online that some kid was calling his son gay. And then he was blown away when Rick answered on his Facebook wall, "So what if I am?"

It's all Haley's fault, Rory thought. She had always coddled their son, even as a teenager. Looking back Rory could see Haley had been codependent on Rick, a word he had learned when reading a book about addiction and recovery.

Rory had a lot to be angry about where Haley was concerned, but turning Rick gay was the worst crime she had committed in his opinion. Above all else, he was maddest about that.

As Rory listened to Pastor Dave read from the Bible during the burial ceremony, he felt a tear slide down his face, even though he thought he had cried them all out in the past seven days.

No one will know that I'm crying over my kids, he thought, sniffing back his tears. Rory felt like he had let his father down somehow between the divorce, the alienation from his children and his lackluster career. *I'm not half the man my father was*, he thought dejectedly, mourning his life along with his father's death.

It had taken considerable effort for Rory to lift one heavy foot after another just to walk up the grassy hill to Howard Justice's final resting place at Parklawn Memorial Park. Following a three-volley salute by members of the US Army including his brother, Pastor Dave said a final prayer, and each of the family members took a red rose from a nearby arrangement and placed it on the bronze casket, paying final respects.

A celebration-of-life lunch followed at the church reception hall, where volunteers had prepared a huge spread of food. Rory noticed the absence of his ex-wife and children and felt a mixture of relief and desolation.

Still, it's easier now that they're gone, he thought bitterly, hating his ex-wife for turning his children against him. All Rory wanted to do at this point, ironically, was get back to work and his solitary but normal life in Columbus.

And then he remembered the letter.

CHAPTER THREE

L ater that evening, after the immediate family said their final goodbyes, Rory sat alone with his mother at the kitchen table and took the letter out of his inside jacket pocket, holding it in his hands. "Rory Only" was written on it in cursive written by a shaky hand.

"Well, I am exhausted, honey, and best I should be getting to bed," Donna Justice said, sensing that Rory wanted to open the letter and might possibly want to discuss it with her.

"Mom, really, I think Dad would be fine with me reading this in front of you."

"I don't know about that, son," she said. "Your father was always a man of few words, but the words he did use were to the point. It says 'Rory only.' You haven't told anyone else about it, have you?"

"No. I thought about telling Pastor Dave or even Daniel, but then with everything going on, to be honest, I forgot all about it until just now."

"Good. I think your father wanted you to read it alone, so I'm going upstairs now. Make yourself comfortable."

Rory had decided to stay a few nights with his mom before he returned home to Ohio. Daniel only had a few days' leave, and of course he wanted to spend as much time with his family as possible before returning to duty in Afghanistan, so Rory had agreed to watch over their mother. Donna was a strong lady for seventy-four, and assured them she'd be fine living by herself, but Rory had insisted he stay if only for a while.

"Thanks, Mom. Goodnight . . . I love you." Rory hugged his mom tight.

"I love you, Rory. Don't worry so much. You're too young for that. We'll talk in the morning."

Rory poured himself a glass of milk, got some Oreo cookies out of the pantry, took a deep breath, and sat down to read his dad's letter.

Dear Rory,

First of all, I hope you haven't shared any of this with anyone yet—but if you have mentioned it, I ask that you please read this letter alone and then keep it to yourself.

I know I am asking a lot of you, but you were the only person I could trust besides your mother (who, of course, couldn't carry it out) and Daniel, who has a family and is still on active duty. Please don't tell either of them anything—your mom because she'll worry, your brother because he may put himself at risk in his position if anyone finds out he knows anything.

I hope I'm not putting you in danger, either, but someone has to take this message in person to the right authorities. Here's the thing: I learned a while back (I can't say who told me—suffice it to say I still have connections in the Bureau) that Islamic State terrorists from the Middle East have been infiltrating the casinos in Las Vegas for years, and one by one they are slowly taking them over and running the city into the ground.

They have formed a new mafia, which has become known as ISM for Islamic State Mafia. Of course, mafias are nothing new to Las Vegas. The casinos were run by various mafia factions from New York to Chicago from the 1940s to the 1980s when some rich Mormons, politicians, and Wall Street tycoons got in the mix and took over for the most part. But this new breed of Islamic mafia infiltrating the city is fueled by wealthy oil magnates from the Middle East who not only want to get richer, but who want to punish America and eventually bring our country under Islamic State rule.

I realize you, like most other Americans, believe what our administration and government has led you to believe; that the extremist Jihad terrorist regime from the Middle East, the Islamic State, has been reduced in size and their power has virtually been eliminated. That may have seemed true at one point, but I have inside information that leads me to believe that the Islamic State terrorists have regrouped and are operating undercover inside America. I'm sure our government, including the FBI, is either covering this up at some level or, at the very least, doesn't want to admit it's true. But history has shown that terrorism always transforms or reforms and rebuilds again, since evil can never be totally eradicated.

My sources say these terrorists now see Vegas as their gateway to take over the United States and eventually the world. The really bad news is that this new ISM is even more dangerous, powerful, and criminal than the Italian or Jewish mafias ever were. They treat people like they're dogs, especially women, whom they use as sex slaves. They even mistreat the circus animals in their care. They rake in more money illegally and do more drug dealing than anyone ever has before, but they don't put anything back into upkeep. They slaughter people for the slightest disobedience, they underpay their employees, and they have one mission in mind: to destroy anyone who doesn't believe in their "religion" and way of life.

I have come across their most recent plans to do this. During the past year, the ISM has been storing nuclear materials in the casinos, using them as a front, which is why they don't care if they run them into the ground. It's the perfect cover—it affords them the opportunity to take advantage of tourists and Las Vegas citizens while hatching their ultimate plan—to destroy our country from the inside out. As you read this, they are finishing building the nuclear bomb that will blow up Las Vegas and possibly a good part of the western United States.

Enclosed you will find a letter from my source detailing the suspected nuclear plans. Take these documents to the authorities in Vegas. There's a sheriff by the name of John Dade who I want you to personally see on my behalf. He will know what to do.

I know this all sounds a little crazy, and you're probably wondering by now if these are just the ravings of an old man *with dementia. Rory, I assure you I was of sound mind when I wrote this letter, and this is a matter of life and death for the city of Las Vegas and possibly for the country as a whole. I know this won't be easy for you. But I have complete faith that you will carry this out and do the right thing.*

Please give Sheriff Dade my best regards. I love you, Rory. Godspeed,
Dad

p.s. Rory, I encourage you to let go of all of the resentments you hold on to. They're only hurting you, and life is too short. Trust me on that.

p.p.s. You'll see I've attached a check made out to you for travel expenses and spending money. You'll need it. Please don't waste any time. And thank you, Rory.

Behind the letter in the envelope was another sealed envelope marked John Dade as well as a check made out to Rory for five thousand dollars. Rory laid it all on the kitchen table and rubbed his eyes with his fingers. *You've got to be kidding, Dad*, he said silently, looking at the ceiling. *Las Vegas? Come on! You have no idea what you're asking, no clue as to the depths of my hatred for that worthless dung heap of a city that isn't even worth saving.*

Doubt along with bad memories flooded Rory's mind. He knew deep down that beneath his hatred for Vegas was the remorse that he felt for cheating with the call girl there and the fear that he might be tempted again to do who only knew what.

I've lost enough thanks to that no good city. Nothing good can possibly come from going back there again. He wanted badly to consult with someone, anyone, but knew he couldn't. Once again, as he had at the funeral, Rory felt like the loneliest man on earth.

Then Pastor Dave's words came back to him. "It's hard to say why God chooses the timing He does, but rest assured, your father is definitely in a better place, free from pain and suffering, smiling down on you at this very minute." *Indeed, Dad is looking at me this very minute*, Rory thought uneasily. *To not carry this out would be to betray him. Still . . .what if . . . ?* Rory couldn't help think he should question the validity of all of this with someone.

I'll sleep on it, he decided, and climbed the stairs to his old bedroom.

But sleep eluded him.

Rory finally drifted off only to wake up an hour later to the sunrise streaming in the window.

I'll have to cut my stay here short if I'm going to do this. His mind raced with new worries. AdExecs had only given him a total of four days of bereavement leave and with two already spent, he wouldn't have enough time to get to Vegas and back. He would just have to think of a plausible excuse and ask for a few more days off. He had to keep this trip to himself.

Rory shaved, showered, dressed, and met his mom downstairs. She was also up early and had made a full breakfast of eggs, sausage, toast, and hash browns. Rory wasn't hungry in the least but managed to eat a few bites to please her.

But mothers always noticed something was wrong if you weren't eating.

"So the letter was pretty bad, huh?" Donna asked her son sitting across from him at the kitchen table, her face frowning with worry.

She took his hand in her frail, knotted one. "Rory, maybe your dad was starting to slip when he wrote it. I told you he had dementia. I couldn't sleep myself last night thinking about the whole thing. Wherever he is asking you to go, whatever he is asking you to do—doesn't mean you have to go there and do it. In fact, I changed my mind. Maybe we should open the letter and read it together and then decide if...."

"No, Mom, I think Dad was probably coherent when he wrote it." Rory cut her short. "It's just . . . it's just that I hate the thought of going where he asked me to go and doing what he needs me to do. I'm not a confrontational sort of person."

"Rory, I don't want you to put yourself in any danger. I don't like the sound of this. If you'd like, I can ask Daniel, or maybe one of dad's FBI buddies, to talk to you about it."

"No, you were right last night; Dad asked me not to share any of this with anyone, even you, because he doesn't want you to worry. I promise once I'm done carrying out his wishes I'll let you know all about it."

"Can you tell me where you're headed?"

"I'm afraid not."

"It's not overseas is it?"

"No mom, it's in America."

"Well, at least that's a relief. Can you call me when you get there and let me know if you're okay?"

"Of course." *If I can*, Rory thought, fear rising within him along with the little bit of breakfast he had just consumed. "I'm afraid I'll have to leave today so I can go back to work afterward without missing too much time."

"No worries, dear. I'll call Daniel and ask him to come over with the kids for a little while, or maybe for dinner. I'll be all right."

Daniel gets the easy job again, Rory sulked.

Bags packed for a week's "vacation" after telling the AdExecs human resources director that he needed more time to mourn his father's death, Rory boarded Flight 1207 bound from Dulles Airport to Las Vegas, Nevada, with a one-hour stop in Houston.

The flight from Washington DC to Houston was uneventful. Rory fortunately received an aisle seat and kept to himself, passing the time by reading copies of the *Wall Street Journal* and *AdWeek* magazine he had purchased at the airport gift shop.

He ruminated on how he could possibly start making more commission in such a depressed economy. He knew the first thing businesses usually cut was advertising. You had to make them think they couldn't survive without it. You had to tell them about new ideas, opportunities, and bargains.

But sooner or later, they cut back anyway. Then you had to find fresh meat: new clients, entrepreneurs who had lost their jobs and started their own businesses and who needed to get the word out. It took twice as much work to get a handful of these new small companies as it used to take to land one major client in the old days.

More work for less money. *I hate my job*, Rory thought, looking past the two passengers next to him to gaze out of the plane's tiny oval window into the gray, cloud-streaked sky. Problem was, he wasn't sure what else he was qualified to do, or wanted to do for that matter.

Oh well, a subject for another day, he thought, and pushed the problem to the back of his mind, concentrating instead on the crossword puzzle in the *Journal* until the plane descended for its landing.

Once the plane was on the runway and grinding to a stop, the co-pilot's voice came over the speaker system. "Ladies and gentlemen, we would like to apologize in advance to those who will be taking the connecting flight to Las Vegas, Nevada. That flight has been delayed by an hour due to unexpected repairs being made on the intended plane. Please check at the gate for more information, and thank you for flying with us today."

I guess I'll have to get another magazine. Rory sighed, lugging his carry-on bag into the terminal.

He sat in the boarding area of the George Bush Intercontinental Airport reading a copy of *Gentlemen's Quarterly* and waiting for Flight 2406 to be called. After forty minutes passed, a female attendant took the microphone and announced that the flight would be delayed another three hours due to additional repairs.

Great, Rory thought sarcastically. *Now I might as well take a stroll and get something to eat. This trip is already going badly.*

Or maybe it's not meant to happen. That thought crept unexpected and unwelcome into Rory's psyche. But once it lodged in his brain, it didn't leave him.

Maybe this is a sign that I'm not supposed to be going at all. The more Rory dwelled on this notion, the more he believed it to be probable instead of just possible.

He sat eating a burger in the airport pub, thinking. As he ambled along the concourse, gazing aimlessly in the various shop windows, a poster caught his eye.

Take a break from your worries . . . relax and find relief from everyday stress . . . you just might find that life has a whole new meaning.

The poster depicted a gorgeous sea of clear, turquoise water lapping at a white sand beach. At the bottom was the logo for the Royal Caribbean cruise ship *Voyager of the Seas* with a message that the cruise line had ships departing twice daily for various, exotic Caribbean destinations from the port of Galveston, Texas, only an hour's drive away.

Rory had never ventured on a cruise before, but had always dreamed of doing so. He had never had the money or the time.

Now he had both.

He returned to the gate where Las Vegas Flight 2406 was supposed to board. A big sign behind the attendants' station said it had been cancelled, and to inquire at the airline's main desk about getting a refund or scheduling a new flight.

After standing in line for over an hour with the other disgruntled passengers trying to get a new airline ticket to Las Vegas, Rory, extremely anxious, started pondering a way out. His doubts about whether to go on this trip had multiplied with each roadblock. *Maybe it wasn't meant to be.*

Rory looked around in exasperation and then he saw it. A US mailbox was several yards away. They were stationed at several gates throughout the airport, but none had ever caught Rory's eye before now.

His dad's letter, tucked safely in his carry-on bag, now seemed to weigh a hundred pounds. *Maybe I could just mail it?* Beads of perspiration formed on Rory's forehead and he removed his jacket, sweating now sandwiched between the other frustrated people in line. *But your father asked you to hand deliver it,* he reminded himself.

Still, who knows if it even contains the truth? Rory considered the fact that his mother told him his father had dementia toward the end. *Knowing my luck, I'll get all the way to Vegas only to be a laughingstock when they read this letter.*

Rory knew the potential humiliation would be too much for him to bear.

Suddenly the answer crystalized and he made a decision. He would get out of line, hail a cab and actually go to the nearest US Post Office to mail the letter to Sheriff John Dade via certified, insured overnight mail and follow up with a phone call to make sure it was received.

And since he had the next several days off from work and most of the five thousand dollars left that his father had given him, perhaps he could take that seven-day cruise aboard the *Voyager of the Seas*.

Luckily, he had brought his passport with him just in case of emergency. *Be prepared.* The boy scout motto was ingrained in his being.

And yet, this crazy idea of jumping aboard a cruise ship made his heart jump. *I saw that poster for a reason*, he smiled, for once trusting fate.

Besides, I deserve a vacation. Dad told me to let go of my resentments. What better way than to take a cruise to forget about everything and to find new meaning for my life? Maybe this is what was meant to happen all along. "Next." Rory was close enough to hear the grouchy attendant behind the airline counter calling gruffly although there were still two dozen people in front of him.

Rory quietly slipped out of the line and walked away to hail a cab to the nearest post office and then to Galveston.

CHAPTER FOUR

- - - - - - - -

Aﬅer a quick taxi ride down to Galveston and a relatively short wait to get his ticket and boarding pass, Rory was standing on the top deck of the *Voyager*, giddily waving along with several other passengers at nobody in particular. He was grinning like a fool as conga party music blared from the ship's loudspeaker.

He had purchased a few summer outfits and a swimsuit in one of the gift shops at the airport along with some sunscreen, a hat, sunglasses, and a pair of flip-flops. *I'm on vacation!* Rory marveled, feeling more alive and free than he had in a long, long time.

It had all been so easy, it must have been meant to be, he had reasoned along the way, going from airport to taxi to cruise ship embarkation to setting sail. A twinge of guilt pestered him for a few moments as the Galveston skyline disappeared from view, but then he walked it off along the length of the ship. He approached the ship's bow and joined a large cluster of passengers peering out at the horizon where a glorious sunset lit up the sky.

Moments later, it was time to get dressed for his six o'clock dinner seating in the main dining room.

Rory was seated at a table with seven strangers: two were sisters from Alabama, one widowed and one divorced, both vivacious, giggly blondes in their forties. There was a single man in his sixties—a stoic and well-spoken professor from Texas A&M University on fall break, a married couple around his age celebrating their twenty-fifth wedding anniversary, and another young couple on their honeymoon.

Dinner that night consisted of lobster bisque, hearts of palm, a choice of braised duckling, veal chops or lobster tail, and an assortment of breads and desserts.

Rory had a glass of wine with dinner, noticing that the blonde sisters drank down an aperitif, three glasses of wine, and an after-dinner Irish coffee, their voices and laughter becoming louder with each drink.

At least the professor was an intelligent and interesting dinner companion, although Rory felt like he had to work at keeping the conversation going, which was a bit of a strain despite his career background. The anniversary couple was friendly, although a little too pompous, and the honeymooners seemed to be madly in love with each other and ignored the rest of them for the most part.

Rory was glad when dinner was over and he could retire to his room. He had splurged on a suite with a balcony and enjoyed the warm breeze riffling through his hair. It was exhilarating to see the indigo blue water rushing by the ship's hull as a full moon rose over the Gulf of Mexico. There was a fuzzy, orange-red glow around the moon, and Rory recalled one of his father's old adages: "Ring around the moon, rain around noon." Clouds were forming across the sky and Rory noticed the sea seemed a little choppy and rough.

Maybe a storm is coming, he thought, and he withdrew inside, lying on his bed and flipping on the television.

"Although it's just a small storm right now, Hurricane Lola looks like it could pick up force over the Caribbean Sea just south of the coast of the Bahamas if it continues on its path…" the weather reporter said.

Guess the little airport travel agency that sold me the cruise ticket wasn't about to give me the weather forecast, Rory thought sarcastically. To take his mind off of the rough seas and impending bad weather, he shut off the TV and picked up a copy of the trip's itinerary that had been laid out on his bed. Tomorrow would be a "fun day at sea." Activities were scheduled every half hour: ping-pong and shuffleboard games, trivia contests, dance, yoga and aerobics classes, cooking and mixology sessions, pool parties, shopping seminars and "so much more!" And that was just the daytime schedule. At night, Rory could choose to go to dinner and a show, listen to a variety of bands, go dancing or sing karaoke, drink at one of several bars, or, of course, do some gambling in the ship's casino.

During the next few days, the ship would stop at various ports of call: Cozumel, Mexico, Grand Cayman in the Cayman Islands and Montego Bay, Jamaica. Rory had signed up for a few adventures including snorkeling in Cozumel and a hike to Dunns River Falls in Jamaica.

After that, he would have another two "fun days at sea" before returning to Galveston then Columbus and his job at AdExecs. *May as well make the most of my time away from work and responsibility,* he thought, turning out the light.

- - - - - -

Suddenly the cruise ship was tilting sideways, and water rushed over the side, gushing into the restaurant, the casino, the auditorium. The big boat was capsizing, sinking.

Rory startled awake and saw his father sitting at the foot of his bed, speaking to him.

"You weren't supposed to be on this cruise ship, Rory. I hope you know that. You let your fear take over. I'm very disappointed in you."

Rory gawked as water seeped under his cabin door and rose up along the sides of the bed where he huddled under the covers, afraid to move.

"This storm wouldn't be happening if you hadn't gotten on board," Howard Justice, or apparently his ghost, continued in a steady, chastising voice, the water around the bed rising slowly. His father appeared lifelike, although about ten years younger and healthy, the way he looked before his lung disease destroyed him. He was still dressed in the suit in which he was buried, but he didn't seem to feel the water as it pooled around his ankles, covering his shiny black shoes and soaking the hems of his pants.

"You're saying this is my fault?" Rory's voice was shrill in his own ears. His shocked brain didn't register that he was talking to a man who had just died days ago. It was truly as if his father was actually *present*.

"Yes, Rory. God is angry that you didn't go do what I sent you to do, so he sent this storm to let you know."

"But why would he endanger all of these other people?" Rory was getting hysterical, and yet he still felt a semblance of rationality, and surprised himself by his own statement and his feeling of concern for the other passengers.

"God works in mysterious ways, son."

"Dad, what am I supposed to do? It's too late now." The water had been rising as they spoke, and its surface was now just a foot from the top of the bed, just below his dad's knees.

"It's never too late, Rory. I think you know what you need to do." And with that, his father disappeared, and the water sloshed over the bed, soaking him.

Rory woke with a start, seemingly in a cold sweat. He looked up and saw water dripping from the ceiling of his cabin onto his bed.

He had mistakenly left the air conditioning set at too cold a temperature, and beads of cool water had condensed on the ceiling and were now dripping down on him.

It was only a dream, Rory realized, gulping in a big breath of air. *Dad wasn't here. The ship isn't sinking.*

He got up to turn off the A/C, take a shower, and try to forget that the nightmare ever occurred.

Nearly everything planned for the "fun day at sea" was cancelled the next day as the impending storm escalated, sending slashing rain and wind across the decks of the ship, forcing everyone indoors. The captain had announced earlier in the morning that reports showed there was nothing to worry about at this point. Lola was predicted to veer off course and lose strength in the next few days, and they were traveling ahead of the hurricane.

But that afternoon proved those predictions wrong as the sea swelled with gale-force winds, rocking the huge cruise ship and sending everyone below deck to the bars and casino.

Rory decided to have a drink and even try his hand at roulette to keep his anxiety and seasickness at bay, as well as the dream from the night before, which still haunted him.

He had to admit that when the little ball rolled around the big wheel and hit his number, it was a thrill. Then it hit again two spins later, and Rory felt ecstatic. He ordered another scotch and soda from one of the passing waitresses to celebrate.

He didn't have too much time to gloat or even finish his second drink. Minutes after he raked in his chips for a fourth time, a tall, broad-shouldered man wearing a black suit stepped up behind him flashing a security guard badge.

"Rory Justice? I need you to come with me. The captain has asked to see you."

Oh no, they think I cheated. Rory felt perspiration dampen his forehead. *I knew this was too good to be true.*

As he got up off his stool, Rory suddenly felt the floor heave up beneath him, and he stumbled into the huge security officer, who caught him and set him back on his feet. The ship sounded almost like it was creaking or groaning, and a few cries of panic erupted from the casino crowd.

Suddenly more officers filled the casino, and the captain's voice boomed over the public address system warning everyone to return to their rooms and await further instruction.

The guard firmly wrapped his beefy hand around Rory's upper arm and guided him down a long corridor, then up four flights of narrow steps.

Rory found himself standing in the foyer of the captain's quarters.

— — — — — —

"Did you contact the FBI and ask what the captain of the *Voyager* has done so far?" Las Vegas Sheriff Ned Thomas spit a mouthful of tobacco juice into a coffee cup, stood, and wiped his mouth with his uniform sleeve, glaring down at the scrawny young deputy seated before him.

"Yes, sir, they just called and said they've got Rory Justice in the captain's quarters for questioning." The deputy sat stick straight in his chair, staring ahead.

"Good. Let me know when they contact you again after questioning him. I know they're taking it from here, but we need to stay on top of this."

"What's the FBI going to do with him?" The deputy asked in a high-pitched nasal voice pushing a lock of hair out of his wide, brown doe eyes.

"That's none of your business, son." Ned Thomas stood looking out of the small, dingy window of his office with his back to the deputy. He couldn't see the color rising in the young man's face as he continued. "I do happen to know that they plan to take him off that ship and bring him back here, whatever it takes."

Sheriff Thomas turned around and held his chin up with pride, looking down his nose at his intimidated underling. The fact that the deputy's face was beet red from shame and embarrassment only made him feel prouder, more superior. This was how Ned liked it. He knew he wasn't supposed to be releasing any information to his staff just yet, but he wanted to let his deputies know that he was a man to be reckoned with—and that he needed to be kept in the know on important matters, despite being new in the position. He still couldn't believe his luck when the letter from Rory Justice, addressed to John Dade, arrived at the Las Vegas Metropolitan Police Department's headquarters the very day after he had become the new sheriff.

"We obviously did our job informing the FBI," the burly new sheriff said, hands on his hips. "But I'd like to stay in the loop, since I assume we will be called in to help when Mr. Justice gets here."

He strode around his beat-up desk and across the room where he towered over the slim deputy who stood staring straight ahead. "I do not want you to breathe a word of this to anyone once you walk out that door, is that understood?"

It was all the deputy could do to nod and stammer out, "Yuh . . . yes, sir."

"That will be all."

Once the deputy left his office, Sheriff Thomas sat back down in his worn leather chair and ruminated on how he could parlay his part in the Rory Justice affair into a promotion or even a raise.

He could kick himself that he had even called the FBI in the first place, even though he knew he had little choice since the ship was in international waters.

At least he had gotten the opportunity to read the letter and get involved. The timing of his promotion yesterday couldn't have been any better.

It had been announced at the Mayor's press conference.

"Ladies and gentlemen, I would like to announce that John Dade has chosen to take an early retirement from his position as sheriff," Las Vegas Mayor Stanley Isaac Cooper had announced matter-of-factly into the microphone before the thirty or so members of the press gathered before him.

The mayor was perched behind the podium in the seventh-floor press room of the behemoth, glass-ensconced City Hall, dressed impeccably in a custom-made Italian dark gray suit, his white cuffs bearing his stitched initials, SIC, his thick, silver-blonde hair perfectly coiffed.

"I'm sorry Mr. Dade could not be here today," the Mayor continued, looking down somberly at his notes. "He has come down with some type of cold or flu. But we would absolutely like to extend our sincerest gratitude for his many years of service to our fair city." The tall, handsome mayor looked seriously into the cameras pointing his way. He was a consummate politician who thrived in the media spotlight, and like an actor, could portray a wide range of emotions at will. "John was always a man of humility and integrity, and he will be missed." Stanley Cooper smiled and flashed his brilliant white teeth, which were a stark contrast in the midst of his suntanned face. "Of course, with all that hard work serving a city like Las Vegas, who can blame the man for wanting to retire a year early? I only hope he feels better soon so he can start enjoying it."

Mayor Cooper's expression became earnest again, but the smile remained. "Now it is my pleasure to introduce you to our new sheriff, former Assistant Deputy Ned Thomas."

Not so comfortable in the harsh media glare and much less polished in his appearance and manners than the mayor, Ned Thomas brusquely sidled up to his new boss behind the podium and forced a smile for the reporters as flashes popped. Mayor Cooper shook his hand and motioned for him to speak into the microphone. Ned had already been warned by the mayor to be very brief.

"Thank you, Mayor Cooper. On behalf of the Las Vegas Police Department, I would also like to thank John Dade for his leadership and service, and say that I am honored to take the position as your next sheriff. Thank you."

Ned waved a hand at the media and was beginning to turn away from the microphone when a female television news reporter shouted a question to him. "Was Sheriff Dade forced to take an early retirement?"

Ned looked helplessly at Mayor Cooper, who practically pushed him aside to reclaim the microphone before the new sheriff could botch his press conference.

"Absolutely not," the mayor said, successfully hiding his disdain for the young woman who asked such a bold question. He explained, offering typical verbose platitudes. "It was strictly his choice. Within the ramifications of budgetary discussions, the city council discussed with Sheriff Dade various strategies to reshape a variety of expenditures within the department, viewing all possible remediation, and an early retirement package was proffered in conjunction with those conversations."

"So this has nothing to do with the fact that there has been a sharp increase in crime lately and that there are rumors circling about a new mafia in town?" barked a sharply dressed young man in the back of the crowd. "There have been reports that Sheriff Dade was working on uncovering a radical Islamic organization possibly running some of the casinos, and that he was coerced into early retirement for snooping into these affairs?"

Mayor Cooper cleared his throat but remained stern and unflustered. "Young man, I wish to quell once and for all any rumor of an alleged new mafia," he rebuked. "And we are not opposed to any new business entities no matter what their race or religion. Our goal is to provide more jobs and opportunities in this city. Need I remind you that the city is an equal opportunity employer?"

"Can we hear from our new sheriff on this subject?" the young man bravely countered.

Stanley Cooper shot a quick look of warning at Ned, who stiffly took the microphone, standing tall despite his five-foot-six frame. "I would like to reiterate what the mayor just said," Ned commented, and then his pride took over and he puffed out his chest, not seeing Stanley Cooper glaring at him. "I have no knowledge that Sheriff Dade was working on any such operation. All I know was that he was simply getting older and ready for retirement, and the city decided I was the man for the job. I believe all of this hype about a new mafia is strictly rumor, but let me just state for the record that if any such crime organization were to form, I would be the first to put them in their place and squash them. Thank you." Ned forced another smile before walking away from the podium.

More questions were hurled, but Mayor Cooper simply said, "That will be all for today. Thank you again for your time."

Ned Thomas knew his job would be anything but easy. With several recessions over the years, tourism had dropped significantly and Las Vegas had suffered, having the highest unemployment and foreclosure rates in the nation.

Although he was aware of the ISM reports, he refused to believe the rumors that some of the highest-ranking government leaders, mostly incumbent politicians, had been so desperate for support in the midst of the city's impending financial ruin that they had given in to their requests. Some rumors circulating hinted that when the crime bosses came knocking at the beleaguered leaders' doors promising to invest millions to restore the city and, in turn, their reputations, they bargained with them even though they knew their new partners were possibly Islamic terrorists. Some rumormongers on social media claimed a few of the more corrupt politicians had even struck deals with the ISM to get kickbacks.

On its face, the city hadn't changed much: the Bellagio fountains and strippers still danced, the lights on the Strip and big name stars still dazzled, and liquor and money still flowed through the nightclubs and casinos.

For frequent tourists, the city may have appeared to grow a little seedier lately. But local business owners and residents blamed the latest recession, and figured that as soon as the economy improved, Vegas would reconstruct itself yet again like a gaudy glamour girl getting a fresh makeup job.

Ned Thomas was up for the challenge to move the city forward. He figured if there was such a thing as a secret Islamic mafia running the casinos, he was just the man to turn things around. Not only was he several years younger than the former sheriff; he considered himself to be smarter and more powerful. He had confidence he could handle anything or anyone that crossed his doorstep.

So the new sheriff didn't even question his sudden promotion.

Ned had opened the mail that morning as he did any other day. When he read the letter from Howard Justice, his mouth had dropped open. Since it was signed by an FBI agent, albeit a retired one, he had little choice but to follow protocol and place a call into the Bureau office in Las Vegas, even though he thought the claims in the letter seemed outrageous.

That had set off an immediate chain reaction that had left him out in the cold.

He scowled, regretting his decision to call the FBI.

He decided not to wait for his deputy and to call the *Voyager* captain himself to find out what was going on.

"Mr. Justice is not in custody; he is merely being questioned by the captain. It has not been decided yet whether he will remain on the ship, but at this point, we do not have reason to call in the Coast Guard to have him removed. We know the FBI has been notified, and we will report to them in due time. Yes, that's all we can report so far." Staff Captain Jeremy Styles grimaced as he hung up the phone and turned around in the captain's quarters to face his commander. "That was the sheriff in Vegas," the red-haired young deputy said in his typical Australian accent. "A real piece of work. Acts like he's got some kind of authority over us. We're out at sea for God's sake."

"Just ignore it," Captain Lyle Whittaker addressed his second-in-command. "We've got bigger fish to fry I'm afraid."

The captain gazed out of his window at the rolling gray clouds that grew darker with the dusk. Lightning flashed in the distance.

"The storm, Captain?"

"Yes, Jeremy." The fifty-seven-year-old captain spoke gruffly with a slight trace of a German accent. He had migrated as a teenager to America with his family from Berlin and had been on the seas ever since, working his way up the ladder of cruise ship jobs. Thus, he hadn't had much of an opportunity, or inclination really, to Americanize himself or his dialect. "And our passenger, Rory Justice, whoever he is—the FBI is claiming he may be a terrorist, or at the very least seems to know something about some nuclear bomb being built in the United States, possibly in Las Vegas. They are saying we need to interrogate him, and if he confesses to anything, get him off the ship. They even said they have a submarine already deployed from the naval port in Corpus Christi should we find any of this to be true. It will be on standby in the Gulf awaiting my command to get Mr. Justice off our ship should he pose any threat. They said they need to ensure he arrives back on shore without any danger coming to anyone else or to him, for that matter, just in case he is being watched by other terrorists. The sub apparently will keep him covert. Can you believe that? They don't even trust this guy to go with the Coast Guard!"

"Where is he now?"

"I had two of our best security guards bring him up for questioning. Right now he's on the other side of that door." Captain Whittaker pointed to his private cabin entry. Rory was seated on the other side in a mini-foyer, flanked by the guards. "They say he's playing nice, even seems a little shook up—not at all the terrorist type. So let's see for ourselves."

He motioned toward the door, and Jeremy Styles walked over and opened it.

Rory was brought to his feet and firmly shown into the captain's chambers.

Captain Whittaker was seated in a stuffed leather chair, a tumbler of bourbon and ice sitting on the coffee table in front of him. Jeremy closed the cabin door once Rory was inside and sat in a couch opposite his boss, then motioned for Rory to be seated on the other end.

Rory obeyed, nervously fidgeting and tapping his foot.

"Why do you think you were called here to speak with me tonight?" the captain asked coolly.

Rory could feel the eyes of Staff Captain Styles boring into the side of his head and dared not look sideways. He realized he was at a strategic disadvantage: if he looked at one man he couldn't see the other, yet both of them could simultaneously stare directly at him.

"I have no idea, sir. I was gambling like the other passengers to wait out the storm. I think it's only the second—no, the third time I've ever gambled in my life. I'm definitely not a gambler. I was having dumb luck I guess."

Shut up, you moron, he told himself. *Don't dig your grave deeper.*

"Well, this has nothing to do with that." The captain spoke slowly, deliberately.

As if he's toying with me, Rory thought. "Well, honestly then, I have no idea."

"Why are you on this ship, Mr. Justice?"

"The same reason as anyone else, I guess." Rory was confused. He couldn't imagine what the captain was getting at now. "For a little vacation."

The captain grew agitated, his stern features becoming even harsher as he frowned in frustration. He sat forward in his chair, poured himself another drink, and reclined back to sip it. Finally, he took a deep breath then let it out slowly.

"Why don't you tell me a little bit about yourself? Where are you from, where do you work, and where are you headed after this?"

Rory looked down at the coffee table and saw a copy of his passport. *Surely, he knows all of this already*, he thought. *But better answer him straight. This man doesn't look like someone I should mess with.*

"I am originally from a little town in Maryland, and now live in Columbus, Ohio. I work at AdExecs, an advertising agency, as an account executive. *Uh oh. Maybe my boss somehow contacted the ship in an effort to find me,* Rory thought, his heart beating fast. "I'm headed back to work as soon as the trip is over. Why, am I in trouble with work?"

"No." The captain stood and paced before resuming the interrogation. He stopped and bent down, his face just inches away, his steel gray eyes boring into Rory's.

"Did you recently mail a letter to someone in Las Vegas?" The captain's voice was just above a whisper.

Rory was silent for a moment. *How did they find that out? It had been less than forty-eight hours!* He could picture his dad shaking his head in shame and frustration, and he instantly knew he had made a huge mistake mailing the letter and getting on the cruise ship instead of going to the sheriff in person as his father had instructed.

"Mr. Justice? I suggest you answer the captain's questions," Staff Captain Styles warned.

Rory snuck a glance over at the captain's second in command. Although he was in his thirties, Jeremy Styles didn't look a day over eighteen and reminded Rory of Richie in the seventies show *Happy Days* played by a very young Ron Howard. With his Australian accent and such a youthful voice, his sharp tone seemed a bit ludicrous. Rory stifled an urge to laugh at the absurdity of it all, and bit the inside of his mouth to keep from smiling.

"Yes, I did."

The captain stood up, a look of barely concealed surprise that Rory had told the truth registering in his features. He paused for a moment, his eyes narrowed in disbelief, and then he recovered his controlled composure and sat back down. "Please tell us what that letter entailed."

"I'm afraid I can't sir. It was a letter from my father, who is . . . was retired from the FBI." Rory sighed. "He just passed away last week. He asked me to deliver it to a Sheriff John Dade in Las Vegas. It was sealed, for his eyes only." Rory paused, hanging his head in shame. "I mailed it instead, deciding I wanted to take this cruise to get away for a little while."

"Do you know what the letter says?"

"I have an idea. But I haven't read it. I only read the letter my father wrote to me telling me to meet with Sheriff Dade."

"And that was your only job—to deliver it to Sheriff Dade?"

"Yes, and I guess I failed at that."

A sharp rap on the door to the captain's quarters interrupted the conversation. Jeremy Styles stood and opened it, motioning the uniformed guard to come in.

The captain stood waiting. "Did you find anything?"

"Nothing, sir."

"And you did a thorough check of Mr. Justice's compartment?"

"Yes, sir."

Rory felt his mouth hang open in astonishment. *They were searching his room!*

"Thank you. That will be all."

Jeremy opened the door again, and the guard left as quickly and unceremoniously as he had entered.

Rory stood indignantly, facing the captain. "Do you think I'm a terrorist or something?"

The captain smirked. "Well, Mr. Justice, you tell me. Are you?"

"Of course not! I'm a Christian!"

"Prove it."

Rory slumped back down onto the couch, dejected. He couldn't fathom a way to do that.

CHAPTER FIVE

'm telling you, he's innocent!" Lyle Whittaker roared into the phone. "I've been working these cruise lines for twenty years, and I've seen tens of thousands of people from all over the world of every shape, size, age, and color. I've sat at dinner with most of them, and I can tell the fakes, the cheats, and the liars in a heartbeat. I sat with Mr. Justice for over an hour grilling him. He's no more a terrorist than my dead mum, bless her soul."

Jeremy sat, coffee cup in hand, watching the captain pace. His boss's breakfast lay uneaten on the table, which was a sign he was clearly agitated, since it was his favorite meal of the day.

"What did they say?" Jeremy asked after the captain hung up.

"They said they still have to proceed as if he's lying until they have proof otherwise. The crew of the USS *Alaska* is on their way to get Rory Justice now and arrest him for alleged terrorist threats or some other such nonsense."

The captain paced, his brows drawn together in frustration. He stopped suddenly and looked at his second in command. "Well, I'm going to call them back and tell them I'm the captain of this ship, and as such, they have no jurisdiction over me or my passengers."

"But, Captain . . . ." Jeremy was silenced by his superior's glare.

A minute later, the captain was talking to an FBI official once more. Jeremy excused himself to get more coffee for them both. When he returned, the captain was shouting again. "Just try to block our way! I'll show you who's in charge!" And with that, he slammed down the phone receiver.

Jeremy almost dropped the two cups and saucers, which rattled as he shakily set them on the coffee table. He looked questioningly at the captain, not daring to ask anything out loud.

"Would you believe that these guys are threatening to block us from coming into port in Cozumel?" the captain boomed, pacing again.

"Wow." Jeremy shook his head in disbelief. "This guy is causing quite a stir."

"Well, I for one am not going to sacrifice Mr. Justice's rights and throw him off the ship just because I'm afraid of a little conflict with the American government, not to mention ruin the vacation plans of four thousand passengers under my watch."

"So what are you, um, proposing we do?" the boyish second in command asked hesitantly.

"I suggest we go the opposite direction to the port in Grand Cayman so that these folks on board can do what they paid good money to do—have some fun." The captain looked at Jeremy squarely. "Do you concur, Mr. Styles?"

"Yes sir, Captain."

"Good, because I'll need your support as well as that of the rest of the crew. We'll just announce throughout the day starting at lunch that the ship had to change direction due to the storm and we'll be reversing the itinerary but still keeping to the agenda so they can enjoy all of the port excursions they're counting on doing. We'll use the storm as an excuse."

"Sounds like a plan. What do we do with Mr. Justice?"

"Where is he now?"

"Still in the brig, sir, where he spent the night per your orders. The night watch reported he apparently slept through the night, awoke at 0800 hours, ate his breakfast, and is now reading a magazine. I believe it's called *Ad Week*. He seems to be in fairly good spirits, all things considered."

"Good. Go tell the guard to release him."

Jeremy looked at his captain, baffled. "But sir, don't you want to question him again and…"

"No." The captain emphatically cut him off. "There's no need. I know all I need to know. It's bad enough we locked him up for one night. Tell him we have no reason to detain him further. He is free to go about his normal activities."

Rory had just finished breakfast and was sitting on his bed in the brig, the ship's holding cell in the lowest level for those who allegedly committed crimes onboard or otherwise needed to be detained, when the news came that he was being freed.

The room, if you wanted to call it that, was a far cry from his cabin in first class. This one had no window, a steel toilet and sink, and a small cot with a vinyl-covered mattress and pillow. There was no lock on the inside of the door, and he could not get out on his own since the door was kept locked from the outside.

Although he hadn't been arrested or handcuffed, Rory had been led here the night before by two security guards after Jeremy Styles had informed him, following his interrogation, that the FBI had ordered that the captain detain him at least overnight until they had a chance to investigate the matter further.

Rory realized it would have been folly to resist; he was no match for the two big, strong security guards who had each firmly held one of his upper arms as they brusquely walked him from the captain's quarters to the brig.

But once he was left alone, he had started to feel angry. *I can't believe I'm being held against my will despite the fact I've done nothing wrong,* he'd ruminated, sitting on the sparse cot. *I paid good money to escape work for a week and enjoy a little rest and relaxation, and here I am sitting in what amounts to a jail cell.*

I'm definitely going to get a refund, he thought before falling into a fitful sleep. *When I get home, someone at the head of this cruise line is going to be hearing from me, and it isn't going to be pretty.*

His anger didn't have much of a chance to resurface that morning. Soon after he awoke, he was given a tray with a fairly decent breakfast—scrambled eggs, bacon and toast with coffee—and only minutes after he finished eating, one of the guards unlocked his room and told him the staff captain had given him orders to release him.

Rory stood up from his cot, waiting for some type of apology, but when it didn't come, he decided it was best to move on and deal with all of this after the trip was over.

And in the back of his mind, he felt a small measure of unease, the kind of emotional hangover that comes from a mix of regret and remorse for making a bad choice, or failing to make a good one. It had hung like a fog in his head since his father had visited him in his dream. *I guess what happened last night wasn't too awful, since I probably wasn't supposed to be on the ship in the first place,* he thought, his resentment dissipating.

As Rory walked back up the stairwell to the ship's main floor to take the elevator to the seventh deck where his room was located, he felt the floor shift beneath his feet, and he stumbled sideways like a drunk.

When he heard a distant scream, he hurried up the steps to the main lobby and quickly walked onto the main deck to look out to sea. Despite the hard slashing rain, a handful of passengers were huddled together in raincoats holding onto the rail, gazing at the horizon. The sky was slate gray and filled with dark storm clouds. The waves slapped against the sides of the massive cruise ship, which churned through the choppy sea, dipping and rising against wave after wave.

Rory hustled back into the lobby, took the elevator, and went to his room. *Nice to be back,* he thought. He was thankful to lie once again on his larger, much more comfortable bed and read a few pages of the paperback he had bought in the ship's gift shop, but found it hard to concentrate and started to feel nauseous.

Rory put the book down and flipped on the news to the Weather Channel. He watched with surprise as the meteorologist forecast that Hurricane Lola was predicted to decrease from a Category 2 to a Category 1 storm by nightfall as it made its way east from its position between the Bahamas and Cuba. *You certainly couldn't tell that aboard this ship,* he thought.

The weather report was interrupted by a message from the captain:

"Greetings, Royal Caribbean cruise passengers! We wish to inform you that the *Voyager of the Seas* has changed its course due to the path of Hurricane Lola. We will be reversing our order of ports of call and docking tonight in Grand Cayman instead of Cozumel, Mexico. We will still honor all paid excursions, weather permitting. The ship will arrive at port at eighteen hundred hours. Meanwhile, have a fun day at sea—and check with the front desk for changes in itinerary aboard the ship due to inclement weather."

Inclement weather! That's an understatement. They'll say anything to keep us happy, Rory thought dismally, turning off the television.

He was afraid to go to the casino again, but felt claustrophobic all of a sudden, even though his stateroom seemed roomy now compared to the holding cell. Although he wasn't hungry, he decided to go for an early lunch in the main dining room.

As he stood in the buffet line waiting to fix a salad, he spotted the blonde sisters from dinner the evening before at a window table. He quickly returned his gaze back to the buffet and filled his plate with whatever was in front of him, hoping they would ignore him. But one of them was suddenly standing next to him.

"Hey, Rory, you must be hungry!"

He looked up to see the one sister cheerfully beaming a pink-lipstick smile at him.

"Uh . . . yeah, I guess I am." Rory looked down at his plate. He hadn't even realized how much food he had plopped there in his attempt not to be noticed. It was filled with fried chicken, mashed potatoes, salad, macaroni and cheese, baked beans, and a scoop of red Jell-O and banana mold. Rory sighed, feeling sick again.

"Why don't you come sit with Linda and me?"

Rory stared at her blankly. He had forgotten their names.

"You do remember my sister and me from last night's dinner, right? I know I had a lot to drink, but at least I remember you!" The blonde laughed in her high-pitched way. He did remember that. "C'mon, sit with us!" And before he had a chance to object, she was pulling him by his shirt sleeve toward their table.

"Hey, Rory!" Linda stood and gave him a hug, nearly toppling his plate of food to the ground. "What happened to you last night? Mindy and I were all over the ship and didn't see you anywhere!"

I bet you were, Rory said silently in his mind. "I, um, ran into the captain, and we chatted for a while." *Not a lie*, he thought, reluctantly sitting at the table and digging in to his massive plate of food. He noticed the women only had two large Bloody Marys sitting in front of them and concluded they were probably nursing a hangover.

"The captain! He's such a hunk!" Linda vivaciously cooed.

"He is quite fascinating . . . ." Rory was interrupted by an equally excited Mindy.

"Wow, no fair! We've been trying to run into him ever since we came on board, right sis? So what did you talk about?"

Rory realized if he did all of the talking, he would never finish his plate and get away from these two, so he turned the conversation around. "Not much, it was brief. So what did you two do last night?" Rory smiled and winked, and his trick worked. The two sisters talked rapidly, nearly in unison, about their adventures in the pool, in the disco, at the casino . . . . Meanwhile, he wolfed down his food nodding and smiling.

"Well, ladies, sorry I have to go, but I sort of have a headache and want to get some rest for our big day tomorrow in Grand Cayman." *Also not a lie.* His head did hurt after hearing these two women prattle on. He stood, gave each a hug, and said his goodbyes, fighting down his indigestion.

By the time he got back to his room, his head was throbbing. Rory took some aspirin and lay down to rest his eyes. Not realizing how exhausted he was from the night before, he was soon fast asleep.

But his nap was haunted once again by his father.

This time, Howard Justice was standing at the foot of his bed in cruise wear. He had on a blue Hawaiian shirt, Bermuda shorts, and white socks with boat shoes, making Rory smile. He remembered that outfit from his childhood.

"Son, I decided to come get you."

"Great, Dad. I'll be ready in a minute." In his dream, Rory stood in his cabin in front of the bathroom mirror, shaving.

"You don't need to get ready for where we're going."

Rory stopped, set his razor on the vanity, and turned around to face his dad. "What do you mean? I thought you were joining me for dinner. It's casual night; you'll fit right in. Wait until you meet Linda and Mindy. They're crazy, but you might find them entertaining. Don't worry. Mom will have no reason to be jealous. Actually, I find them a bit annoying."

"Be quiet, Rory. We're not going to dinner." He noticed the stern look on his father's face and felt a cold chill of dread. Suddenly, in his dream, Rory realized his father wasn't alive—he was reappearing from the dead, or rather, from his resurrected place in heaven. Rory tried to ignore the fact that Howard Justice's skin shone a translucent white.

"Why not? Aren't you hungry? What's wrong? Where do you want to go?"

"I need to take you off this ship, son. It's for your own sake, and for the safety of all of the people on board."

Rory shivered as fear seized him. "I want to stay on this cruise. I paid good money . . . ."

"The money I gave you to go to Las Vegas."

"But, Dad, you know how much I hate that place and all of the people there . . . ."

"They are the people who need your help, Rory. You need to go there. That's why you need to get off the ship. You need to follow through with what I asked you to do—in person."

"And what if I don't?" Rory knew he sounded defiant, childish, like when he used to talk back to his parents when he was seven years old, but he couldn't help it. He was afraid.

He watched as his father walked to the window of his room and drew back the heavy curtain, which Rory had pulled shut to darken the room.

"Come here," Howard Justice commanded.

Rory walked over to look out. He stared in awe at the most amazing sky and ocean he had ever seen. The clouds had united to create a monster vortex of grays that ranged from the darkest black to the brightest white, swirling and undulating. It was both terrifying and beautiful. Under the cloud mass, the ocean was a shiny sheet of silver glass. But in the distance Rory could see a monster wave forming, rolling, growing. It looked like it was still many miles away, but it was headed straight toward them.

Rory knew he was witnessing Hurricane Lola. He turned to ask his dad "what if?" and "how long?" but his father was gone.

— — — — — —

"This is crazy." Captain Whittaker hunched over the control panels, leaning on his hands, his head bent with worry. He dreaded looking out of the windows again and stared instead at the dozens of monitors that surrounded him in the engine control room. He had already watched long enough in astonishment as Lola, originally predicted to continue east and fizzle out along the way, menacingly approached the *Voyager*. Instead of heading out and away to sea as predicted, the storm had suddenly reversed its course and propelled south, picking up velocity, churning its way over the past few hours from a Category 1 to a Category 3 hurricane. Now it was predicted to possibly increase all the way to a Category 5 and make landfall off the coast of Grand Cayman Island, right where they were headed.

Captain Whittaker realized he couldn't very well steer the ship east toward Jamaica into the hurricane, but the opposite direction was now blocked by the US Navy unless he surrendered Rory Justice. He knew that even if he chose to do the latter and navigated the *Voyager* in the other direction, it might be too late to avoid Lola's path of destruction.

He knew he had to warn the passengers, but right now, even he, the brave and mighty captain, was at a loss for words.

Jeremy Styles could also find no words of wisdom or comfort to reassure his captain. He too was dazed with shock.

Lyle Whittaker finally straightened and turned to face his staff captain, his face ashen. "I don't know what to do."

Jeremy had never heard his boss utter that statement before. "We could try praying, Captain." The words had come out involuntarily. He knew the captain wasn't a religious man, had never heard him speak of God or anything spiritual before. Jeremy believed in the concept of a Higher Being, but he wasn't particularly religious or spiritual either. He hadn't been raised in any faith nor talked of God with anyone before.

If anything, he considered himself an agnostic. But this . . . this larger than life monstrosity that loomed in sight suddenly convinced him that there had to be a Power, a God who wasn't manmade or of this earth, but was greater than all of it to create such a magnificent force of nature.

"Go ahead, Mr. Styles. It certainly can't hurt."

Jeremy closed his eyes and bowed his head, and did his best to pray. "Dear, uh, God . . . please have mercy on us and help us find our way through this storm, and save the passengers on board the *Voyager*. Please. And thank you. Amen."

He slowly opened his eyes, hoping for a miracle. But Lola was still raging out the window, presenting herself in all of her horrifying splendor.

Both Jeremy and the captain had witnessed their share of hurricanes before, but none as terrifying as this.

Suddenly they heard a rap on the door to the control room. Jeremy opened it, and standing there in jeans and a T-shirt was Rory Justice. His face was white, and he looked like he had seen a ghost.

"Mr. Justice." It was more of a statement than a greeting from the captain. "You shouldn't be here. Obviously, you've seen the storm out there so you need to go back to your cabin. I am just about to make an announcement to all of the passengers to begin preparations for a possible rescue."

"That won't be necessary, Captain." Rory spoke with conviction. "I'm ready for you to turn me over to the authorities. I believe that once you do that, you and the rest of the people aboard the ship will be out of danger since at least they will unblock one of your directions."

"And what . . . who caused you to think that? Never mind. We don't have time for these games, Mr. Justice. If you'll just follow my orders and . . . ."

"God, Captain—in answer to your question. And right now His orders supersede yours."

Jeremy backed into the control panels, astonished that his prayer had perhaps worked after all. He spoke with conviction. "Captain, I think we should listen to Mr. Justice. Should I call the FBI while you make your announcement?"

The three men looked at each other warily for a moment, and then all three sprang into action.

CHAPTER SIX

T he USS *Alaska* floated only a hundred nautical miles away, awaiting instruction. It was a brand new attack sub that had launched a month prior for drills.

The sea hurled against the sides of the cruise ship as Hurricane Lola blew closer. Fortunately, the experienced captain and crew of the *Voyager* were able to draw within twenty yards of the sub as it surfaced, surprising the most jaded cruise ship customers with a sight none had ever witnessed, although only a few dozen passengers had braved the pelting rain and wind that thrashed on the deck to see it.

The big metal sub bobbled on the uneven surf, a half dozen US Navy submariners waving from the top of the tower, waiting for the transfer of the prisoner.

The *Voyager* angled itself parallel to the *Alaska*, and four crewmembers lowered Rory Justice, who had been fitted into a wetsuit and harness, into a rescue lifeboat where three other crewmen were waiting to row him to the sub.

Rory feared the rescue boat might capsize and he might drown as he was lowered into it in a kneeling position, the waves were so rough.

Once the lifeboat was within ten feet of the submarine, Rory was fastened into another harness that had been lowered from the tower by members of the *Alaska* crew and was hoisted up, swaying precariously in the wind, and then landed safely onto the submarine's surface. The cruise ship passengers who had stayed to watch were clapping and cheering. Rory wondered if it was because they were glad he was off of their boat or because he had made it safely onto the submarine. He chose to believe the latter, since it was already humiliating enough to be lying face down, petrified, on the cold, hard metal surface of the submarine tower deck, a prisoner.

The *Alaska*'s crew didn't waste any time with theatrics. Rory Justice was now a threat. The FBI had told them he was an alleged terrorist and ordered them to transport him back to Corpus Christi. Two submariners roughly pulled Rory to his feet, yanked his arms behind his back, and handcuffed his wrists as a naval officer read him his rights.

Flanked on his front and rear by naval guards, he was sent scrambling down the tiny metal ladder in the narrow tower. Rory stumbled and nearly fell since he couldn't use his hands on the rails.

As he descended into the bowels of the submarine, he noticed the air was stuffy, warm and dank and smelled like a combination of ammonia, body odor, and some other industrial smells permeating the interior.

He had to twist as he passed through narrow corridors to avoid obstructions, step over door hatches and duck through low-ceilinged doorways until he ultimately was tossed into a small, solitary berth reserved for prisoners.

Since the USS *Alaska* had a full crew on board who weren't expecting to take on another man, a makeshift bunk had been set up in the torpedo room as the prisoner quarters. A plastic mat was placed on a storage rack, where torpedoes and missiles were usually kept, as his bedding. Rory did have the luxury of having a door instead of the customary curtain that gave most of the crew privacy in the berthing area. He assumed it wasn't for his benefit, like the cabins with doors were for the captain and executive officers, but rather for his protection, and more importantly, for theirs.

Rory still had a hard time believing that he was suspected of being a hardcore terrorist. *It's surreal*, he thought as he rubbed his sore wrists where the steel rings had chafed his skin. *At least they removed the cuffs*, he thought sardonically. But he knew he was still imprisoned.

Even though he was exhausted, Rory couldn't sleep at all that night. He felt nauseous; the submarine had submerged again to four hundred feet below sea level, but on the way down to the ocean's depths, had experienced some turbulence from the proximity of the hurricane. Rory lay there on his tiny cot staring at the rack above him, willing himself not to be sick. He felt sticky with the damp sweat of humidity, close quarters, and fear. The eerie silence was deafening.

Rory had never realized he was claustrophobic to some degree. But just knowing that he was stuck in this big metal tube hundreds of feet below the sea's surface with no escape made it feel as real as a vise clamped around his lungs. He willed himself to breathe, concentrating on sucking air in and out, in and out, calming his racing mind, and slowing his thumping heartbeat. The exertion of his will only exacerbated his anxiety when he remembered a scene from the movie *The Shawshank Redemption* in which prisoner Andy Dufresne, played by actor Tim Robbins, was thrown into solitary confinement in a tiny box in the yard for two months. It was literally a box not big enough to stand in with no light, no windows, and no fresh air. Rory had always wondered how a man could survive such an ordeal. Next to drowning, being suffocated was one of his biggest fears.

Now he was finding out firsthand, and again wondered if he would survive. *It's as if I'm trapped inside something . . . a machine . . . or a being.*

No one had told him where the sub was headed, how long it would take to get there, how long he would have to endure his captivity.

Breathe, he kept telling himself. *Try to sleep.*

Finally, when he could take no more of his inner voice screaming "Breathe!" or his heart feeling like it would burst, he decided to try something different: he would accept that he couldn't sleep and take his mind off the present by escaping into something, anything.

He hadn't been given the luxury of any books or magazines to read, much less any electronics. His phone had been confiscated, and he had no laptop or music. There was nothing in his tiny berth except his bunk, a metal toilet and sink, and a shelf to put his belongings. *What a joke, I don't even have any.* He laughed to himself, suddenly wondering if this was a first sign that he was already beginning to lose his mind.

Rory wasn't sure what made him think of it; he certainly didn't exercise at home, but he decided to do sit-ups, push-ups, jumping jacks, and jogging in place until he fell back onto his bunk exhausted. He finally fell asleep at three in the morning.

Since there was no daylight, Rory didn't know he had only slept three hours until someone told him; the submariner on morning watch knocked on his door, barking out that it was 0600 hours, time to wake up and eat his breakfast.

The submariner, who was accompanied by another crewman for security, handed him a tray with a plate of lukewarm eggs, toast and a cup of coffee. *Not exactly like cruise ship food, but it could be worse.* He had half expected to get bread and water since he was a prisoner. Rory suddenly realized he hadn't had anything to eat since lunch the day before, and he wolfed the food down. He was told that when he was finished eating, he would be escorted to the galley, or ship's kitchen, where he would be put to work under strict supervision, of course.

The submarine's supply officer and head cook, a beefy Italian man in his fifties who introduced himself only as "Tony," gruffly instructed Rory to help the mess cook, a young blonde crewmember in his twenties who was peeling potatoes. Tony introduced Rory to Ralph, one of three crewmembers who constituted the supply department, the group on board who prepared that day's meals.

Ralph eagerly shook Rory's hand then sheepishly blushed under the stern gaze of the head cook. He turned back to his work in the narrow kitchen. But once Tony left the room, saying he had to go to the head, and there better not be any funny business while he was gone, Ralph started talking non-stop.

"Hey, did you hear that the hurricane died out once we dove back down here?" Ralph peeled and talked at the same time. Apparently, he had mastered the art.

"How would you be able to tell, being this deep?" Rory hoped he didn't sound sarcastic. He truly didn't know and was curious.

Ralph wasn't easily offended. "Sonar. This new sub has all kinds of fancy gadgetry to see and hear things miles away, including hurricanes. The head operations officer said it was the strangest thing. I was talking to him at breakfast this morning. He said he had never seen anything like it, and he's been working his station on a number of subs for over twenty years. Said he's never felt a hurricane rise up so fast before, and never seen one die down so quickly."

Rory was silent, pondering the news, remembering what his dad had said in his dream, the puzzle pieces in his mind clicking into place. *I need to take you off this ship, son. It's for your own sake and the safety of all of the people on board.*

The thought crossed Rory's mind that perhaps the storm had calmed down because God wanted him to get off the cruise ship and go do what his dad had called him to do. In fact, maybe the hurricane had picked up force the longer he stayed on board. *No, that couldn't be possible. I'm letting my claustrophobic imagination get the best of me.*

Still, he couldn't help but ask, "Do you know what happened to the *Voyager*?"

"Yeah, apparently right after you got off and boarded the sub and the hurricane died down, the coast was clear for them to go to Cozumel later that night. They're all probably playing on the beach right now, basking in the sun while we're slaving away here in the dark bowels of this blessed submarine."

Rory let his mind wander for a moment to the tranquil blue waters and sun-drenched white sand beach. *That's where I should be*, he thought, but then he willed himself to stop his self-torment. What good would that do anyway? So he tried to steer his mind back to questioning Ralph. "Why do you work on a submarine if you hate it so much?"

"To get away from my old man." Ralph peeled potatoes now with renewed vigor. "I didn't want to end up like him, so I went into the military. He was a good-for-nothin' alcoholic. They said sub work pays well since nobody wants to do it, so I signed up. I hope to save up enough money so one day I can sail around on those cruise ships. Doesn't look like either one of us will be seeing the sun for a good long time, though, huh? But one day . . . ."

"One day what?" Tony yelled the words as he stepped back into the galley, surprising the young mess cook. Ralph jerked in a startled reaction, and his right arm bumped into a plastic jug of heavy-duty bleach on the counter, knocking it onto its side. The cap on it was loose, and the contents spilled out—onto the head and shoulders of Rory, who had bent down to pick up some potato peels from the floor.

The bleach was an industrial-strength type used for hard-to-clean iron skillets and other metal surfaces on the sub. The submariners didn't use it unless they wore latex gloves to protect their skin from its corrosive power.

Before Rory knew what was happening, toxic bleach was pouring down his head, neck and shoulders, which were exposed because he was wearing only a tank top.

"Aghhh!" It took a moment for the burning sensation to begin, but when it did, a stunned Rory cried out in pain.

Tony barked orders to everyone while Ralph just stood there, his mouth gaping.

"Someone call the Doc, stat! Benjie, get lots of water and rinse him off as best you can. Keep him calm! Don't let him touch his eyes! Joe, go get Captain Brown. Ralph, don't just stand there! Put on gloves and help clean this up before someone else gets hurt!"

After Rory was stripped and doused with water, he was taken to the sick bay where he was treated by the hospital corpsman, known only as Doc, who administered pain medication and wrapped dry cloth bandages around his upper torso, neck and left hand.

Rory was shaking uncontrollably from shock while he was being bandaged, so the medical specialist gave him an injection of morphine to calm him. Then Doc helped Rory lie down in one of the infirmary cots, covered him with light blankets, and dimmed the lights. Rory mercifully fell asleep after a half hour with the aid of the painkillers.

Rory awoke with a start, drenched in sweat, feeling itchy all over. He had only slept for a few hours and woke up in the middle of the night, although he didn't know if it was night or day.

Doc had stayed in the infirmary with Rory, keeping watch over him while he slept. The hospital corpsman removed the blankets, gave Rory some water, some liquid nutrition, and some acetaminophen with codeine, and then gently removed the bandages and rewrapped him with new ones.

Rory couldn't sleep for a while, having dozed for so long already. His mind was on rewind and kept playing back all of the events leading up to his recent downfall: his father giving him the letter and then passing away, deciding to take the cruise, being tossed about in the storm, being trapped inside a submarine submerged four hundred feet below water; and now lying on a tiny infirmary cot, his body covered in bleach burns. Then, worse still, his mind went forward, fearing what might happen next. *What will I look like once these bandages come off? Where are they taking me? Will I end up in prison? Oh, God, I don't know if I can take anymore.*

Rory suddenly felt a fresh wave of fear and gloom wash over him. He needed something, anything to help him focus on the present.

"Doc, can I have a book to read, or something to write on? I feel like I'm going to go crazy if I stay in my head right now. I need to take my mind off everything. Please . . . ."

"Sure. Here." The kind medical specialist handed Rory a legal notepad and pencil he kept handy for his own lags in time; a man could go crazy if he thought too much in the underwater confines of a submarine, and there were only so many books and movies in the sub's small library.

Rory decided to try to write a letter to his dad. Since he was left-handed and now would be forced to use his right hand, it wasn't going to be easy, but Rory welcomed the challenge. He decided to write a poem—he thought it might focus his mind even more to try to rhyme. *Thank God he gave me a pencil*, Rory thought, writing, erasing, creating. He worked and reworked his poem until he was satisfied. He titled it "Dear Dad":

The harder I try, Dad, to hide from you,
The deeper I sink into desperation.

The farther I run from what I need to do,
The further I fall into desolation.
I've never been one to rely on others,
I thought I was better than the rest.
But I've only been running away from life,
And now I'm being put to the test.
Still I know that you are always there,
As I see the error of my ways,
Just like I know God has always been,
All these minutes, hours, and days.
All these years, all of the times I've failed,
I don't think I've ever sunk this low,
Or strayed this far, or seen such dark.
I have such a long way to go.
I seem to be filled with shame and dread.
Time moves too slow or too fast.
I have to keep learning many times over,
I can't change the future or the past.
If I didn't have faith that you instilled
I know I'd be completely lost.
As hard as it is, I'll try to stay grateful
And believe this is all worth the cost.
All I can do now is pray you'll help,
And ask God to hear my plea.
I swear if I get out of here alive
I'll do all you asked of me.

Exhausted from his effort but content with the results, Rory finally drifted off into a deep slumber.

CHAPTER SEVEN

Rory was napping the next day, his third day aboard the USS *Alaska,* when he heard the knock on the door. He had been placed in the executive officer's berth since he needed better sleep to rest and heal, something he couldn't get in his former quarters according to Doc. The XO's room still afforded Rory privacy, but since the door could only be locked from the inside, a guard stood watch round the clock. After all, Rory was still an alleged terrorist and prisoner.

His skin had already begun to mend, and he was weaning himself off of the pain medications.

Still, he did not expect to hear the news from the guard, who stood accompanied by a second submariner at his doorway.

"We're going to be surfacing and heading ashore at the naval base in Corpus Christi, Texas, at nineteen-hundred hours," the guard said, not revealing any emotion in his voice nor looking Rory in the eye. "You will want to be ready to disembark in thirty minutes."

And with that, he unceremoniously closed the door behind him.

A dozen questions crowded into Rory's head: *Where will I go from here? What will the FBI do with me? What happens if they question me and don't believe me? What am I supposed to do if I am eventually freed? How do I follow through on what Dad wanted me to do?*

Rory felt woefully clueless. He sat on his bed staring at his bandaged left hand. Then he remembered the small mirror over the sink in the XO's quarters. He walked over and gazed at his reflection. He looked pallid and tired, with dark circles under his eyes, but the bleach hadn't damaged his face.

It could have been a lot worse. Still, Rory hung his head, unable to look at himself. *How ironic*, he thought dismally. *I went on a cruise, a trip that was supposed to be a high point in my life, and ended up a prisoner on a submarine, experiencing the lowest point I have ever reached. . . all in a matter of days . . . all because I failed to obey my father's request.*

He listened as the crew worked in sync to surface the ship, shouting orders, doing their assigned jobs, pushing buttons, pulling levers, cranking gears.

Soon Rory could feel a smooth pull and shift as the sub surfaced, but this time, it was slow and subtle instead of jolting because they were in the Gulf of Mexico, there wasn't a hurricane, and the water was peacefully calm.

He was dressed and ready when the next knock came. This time, the XO himself faced Rory along with the same two guards who had come a half hour earlier. Upon the officer's instruction, they placed Rory in handcuffs and led him down the narrow hall of the submarine to await disembarkation with the rest of the crew.

Rory was escorted to the metal steps leading up the tower and, flanked by guards, led up into the daylight. He was then guided off the submarine onto shore, the paved grounds of the US naval port in Corpus Christi.

Still shackled, Rory knew he probably still had a lot of hardship to face, but he was at least glad to climb out of the bowels of the *Alaska* and onto dry land.

Several FBI special agents waited on deck to relieve the submarine guards of Rory's custody. One of the FBI agents, a tall, young, brutish man, marched behind Rory holding a gun at his back.

This is insane, Rory thought, walking as if in a parade, two agents ahead of him, and two agents behind, his bandaged torso and shoulders chafing from his wrists manacled behind him. He felt angry but remembered the promise he had made in his prayer, and decided to keep his mouth shut.

Once inside the port building, the agents seated Rory, still handcuffed, in a chair at a desk in a nondescript office, and stood to await further orders from the man seated behind the desk, apparently an officer in charge, who stood speaking with someone on the phone.

"Yes, we have him. Correct. The vehicles are ready. We should arrive by oh-eight-hundred hours Monday. Yes, tell them to meet us at nine a.m."

Monday? Rory hadn't worn a watch or had a cell phone or an alarm clock to keep track of time on the submarine, but he had counted the days and was pretty sure it was Saturday. *This whole thing just keeps getting better*, he thought ruefully.

The official snapped his cell phone shut. He was a stocky, menacing looking black man.

"Uh, excuse me, Sergeant?" Rory made eye contact then glanced away after looking into a pair of the darkest, meanest eyes he had ever seen.

When the big black man didn't answer but kept glaring at him, Rory swallowed then continued. "Um, can you tell me where I'm going next?"

After a full minute of eery silence, the official spoke. "It's not Sergeant; it's FBI Special Agent in Charge," he replied with an undercurrent of disdain, his voice deep but silky smooth. "And not that it's any of your business, Mr. Justice, but you are going to Las Vegas, where you will answer to the FBI and the local authorities who have jurisdiction over this matter."

"We're not flying?" Rory tried to keep his tone even so as not to make this hulking special agent any angrier than he obviously already was.

"No, we're not flying." The note of sarcasm was undeniable. And with that, the agent waved his hand in a dismissive motion to the other agents and stormed out of the room leaving Rory with a dozen unanswered questions in his befuddled mind.

Minutes later, Rory, who was wearing the same outfit he had worn the entire three days on the sub—literally the shirt on his back plus the one pair of pants and shoes that he had worn onboard—was sitting in the back seat of a plain, navy blue Chevy Malibu with tinted windows, with two FBI agents seated in the front. They would be following another midsized sedan of some sort, this one silver in color.

They could dump me out in the desert and no one would know, Rory thought a few hours later, feeling punchy as the cars raced along Interstate 10.

The two drivers pulled over at midnight into a Super 8 Motel. *Nothing but the best*, Rory thought sarcastically. Sitting by himself in the back seat behind a metal grate that divided him from the driver and other FBI agent in the front of the sedan, he had tried to follow the road signs along the way to keep track of where they were going but had fallen asleep, the remnants of his pain medication taking effect. When he awoke, he overheard them talking. They were in Fort Stockton, Texas, about halfway between San Antonio and El Paso. *Texas is so big, we'll be lucky to get to Vegas in three days*, Rory thought dismally. He was hot, tired, hungry, and sore, and above all else, he needed a hot shower.

He had overheard the agents talking at one point, and discovered why he was being driven by car to Las Vegas instead of flying: the FBI wanted to keep Rory's whereabouts and identity top secret. They also didn't want to jeopardize the lives of any civilians in a plane or airport if Rory was, in fact, a nuclear terrorist.

This was also the reasoning, he figured, behind travelling in low-key cars and staying in a Super 8 Motel.

Rory was told he would be staying in a double-room suite with the two agents who had accompanied him on the long ride thus far. Their names—although he assumed these were aliases—were Special Agent Smith and Special Agent Jones. They would be in the larger of the two rooms, and he would be in an adjoining room that could only be unlocked from their side. That way he couldn't sneak out and try to escape.

Like I would even try, Rory thought. He wasn't crazy or brave enough to run from the FBI; besides, they were in the middle of nowhere surrounded by rugged desert terrain.

Rory didn't get to see much of Fort Stockton. Agent Jones woke him up out of a deep sleep at 7 a.m., bringing him a cup of coffee and a Danish, telling him he had twenty minutes to eat, shave, and shower before it was time to hit the road.

Standing unclothed on the bathroom's cold, hard floor, Rory slowly peeled the bandages from his neck and saw that his skin was mottled where the bleach had hit. He had been fully weaned off of the pain medication for his burns and believed it was now time to finally remove his wraps; he unceremoniously started to strip them away, throwing them into the wastebasket along with the last clean set Doc had given him.

After Rory removed the last of the bandanges from his shoulders, he stared long and hard at himself in the mirror, twisting and turning to see as much of his upper body as possible. He suddenly felt a wave of compassion for the legendary pop star Michael Jackson, who had suffered much of his life with the skin depigmentation disease of Vitiligo.

Rory noticed chalky white splotches across the back of his neck, shoulders, and upper arms, and wanted to cry. He vowed to never go to the beach or pool again without wearing at least a T-shirt.

Soon they were driving west again on I-10, the fourth longest interstate highway in the United States, and Rory was living through another seemingly unending day—ten and a half hours to be exact—in the backseat of the Malibu. Except for pit stops at gas stations just outside the cities of El Paso, Texas, Las Cruces, New Mexico, and Tucson, Arizona to hit the restroom and grab drinks and snacks, the ride had been excruciatingly monotonous through hundreds of miles of parched brownish red landscape and little or no scenery.

I hate the west, Rory decided somewhere along the way. *I thought the Midwest was plain and ugly, but it's not half as bad as this desert wasteland. At least there are trees, lakes and shade in Ohio.*

Each time they exited the car to go to the bathroom and get something to eat and drink, the heat was oppressive, hitting Rory like a blast from a furnace, like nothing he had ever felt before. At his first encounter with the weather at their first pit stop, the dry, hundred-degree air sucked the breath out of his lungs. He had doubled over, feeling nauseous and light-headed, which had sent the FBI agents into fits of laughter at his expense.

Rory fought a headache along with feelings of humiliation and self-pity for the rest of the trip, but was too proud to ask either of the officers for any pain relievers, so he suffered in silence.

When the hot desert sun went down and the temperature dropped thirty degrees, Rory shivered from the cold, but again, he was too proud to ask to borrow one of their extra jackets or blankets, which he had spotted in the trunk.

They spent the next night at another Super 8 in Wickenburg, Arizona. Rory slept fitfully, tossing and turning that night, knowing Las Vegas was only a four or five hour drive away.

"Sin City" suddenly loomed ahead, but Rory was completely unprepared for this version of the city he had visited before. It was a ghost town. Once tall, glamorous, architecturally astounding casino buildings that together formed a microcosm of the world—buildings that reflected landmarks in Paris, Greece, Italy, Egypt, America—all had been reduced to a shambles of crumbled concrete and marble, and charred, twisted steel.

Flakes of white ash fell from the sky like snow, and there was a notable absence of color. What once before was a full spectrum of every hue was now a landscape of grays and browns.

A stench stung Rory's nostrils, and he had to cover his nose and mouth with his arm. He could only think of one word to describe the smell: death.

His brain slowly comprehended what his eyes already perceived: Las Vegas had been blown up by a nuclear bomb.

There were about a dozen survivors that Rory could see, a few stumbling along the streets like zombies, heads down, dragging their feet, their skin and hair burned and bloodied from intense radiation. Rory guessed that everyone else had been reduced to bones and ashes and were now part of the rubble of the buildings. He could hear cries, wails, and moans in the distance.

As he walked in a daze behind the two FBI agents, he felt a tug on his pants leg and looked down. A man wearing a hooded sweatshirt, his face nearly unrecognizable and half mangled into a substance like bloody hamburger meat, was sitting slumped on the sidewalk. Two burned, trembling bloody fingers clutched him, all that remained of the man's hand. Rory instinctively pulled away in disgust and he was paralyzed by fear, not sure what to do next.

Suddenly, the old man reached up his two fingers and removed the hood from his head. He was mostly bald, with only a few strands of gray hair, but Rory instantly recognized him when he looked into his eyes.

"Hello, son." Howard Justice gave him a crooked grin, exposing a few broken, blackened teeth.

Rory nearly fell backward in horror.

"Dad?"

"Yes, Rory, it's me—Dad."

In a panic, Rory searched for his two guards, but they had vanished. He looked down at his father.

"But . . . y-you're . . . ."

"Dead, I know, son. We've been through this before. I only look this bad down here to fit in. Don't worry about that. You need to listen to me. We don't have much time. All that you see happening here will take place if you don't do something to stop it."

Rory listened somberly as his father quickly gave him a glimpse into the future.

"The nuclear bomb I told you about is planted somewhere underground in one of the casinos," Howard Justice explained, wheezing every few words, his breath ragged. "It's set to go off on July sixth, when the city will be packed with people who have travelled here to see the biggest boxing match of all time—a fight between heavyweights Jay-Jay Moss, the black Hispanic powerhouse out of New York, and Carmen Gallo, the new "Italian Stallion" out of Chicago."

His father stretched out his thin, scarred arm, pointing to the nuclear holocaust around him. "This is what will happen if you don't follow through on what I asked you to do. It's why you're here."

Rory's gaze followed his dad's outstretched arm, wondering what he, one man, could do to prevent such a large-scale tragedy.

When he looked down to ask how and why, his dad was gone, and once again, Rory awoke, covered in sweat in his hotel bed. It had been another terrible but very real dream.

After four more nauseating hours of riding in the backseat of the Malibu behind Smith and Jones, Rory could finally see the skyscrapers on the horizon, rising up out of nowhere from the flat, parched desert like the city of Oz.

I guess I'm not in Ohio anymore, he thought miserably.

And with a sense of dread, he realized his life as he knew it back in Columbus was most likely over, and his future lay ahead in this godforsaken city. He was sure he'd be fired from AdExecs for his long absence from work.

As they turned onto the famous Strip, Rory reluctantly looked out of his car window at the buildings, all familiar again and nothing like his dream; it was the same Las Vegas, and Rory felt weirdly disappointed.

A little seedier perhaps, Rory acknowledged, surveying the slightly worn exteriors of the shops and restaurants. Of course, it had been ten years since he had last visited.

The casino hotel resorts seemed inexplicably less shiny, less colorful. Perhaps it was the cloudy sky, which cast a gray pall on everything.

But Rory couldn't shake the uneasy feeling that it was something more, and with dread for the future, he desperately wished he could return to the past, could go back in time and return to his tedious job, his lonely apartment, his boring hometown, his "normal" albeit lackluster life.

He saw a dirty, scrawny man holding a brown cardboard sign. They were stopped at a traffic light, so Rory decided to read the sign. He could just make out the words scrawled in black: "The end is near—be a sheep, not a goat. Matthew 25."

Rory wondered what the sign meant. He vaguely remembered some New Testament story about Jesus separating the sheep from the goats, something about the goats asking Jesus, "Lord, when did we see you hungry or thirsty or a stranger or needing clothes or sick or in prison, and did not help you?"

The light turned green, and Rory glanced up from the sign and felt a sharp pain in his chest as he found himself staring into the rheumy gray eyes of the old beggar. Just as quickly, he lost sight of the man when the car turned a corner and pulled up in front of the Las Vegas Police Department.

CHAPTER EIGHT

R ory sat in the ten-foot-square interrogation room, which was bare except for a small table and two metal folding chairs. He was waiting for . . . what? He wasn't quite sure. At least they had removed the handcuffs. Rory rubbed his sore wrists.

His bleach burns had healed, although his skin would be forever scarred with white patches.

Now he sat, still a prisoner held captive for an alleged crime he wasn't even sure how to define.

A burly white man with a black mustache and heavy black eyebrows lumbered in. He was wearing jeans, a black T-shirt, and an FBI baseball cap. He sported tattooed "sleeves" on both of his arms. *He looks like some Wrestlemania fighter*, Rory thought. *Well, if they're planning to intimidate me, they chose the right guy.* The hulk flipped open his wallet-sized credential case, flashed his FBI identification and badge, then sat across the table from Rory, who made quick eye contact and then looked down. *This is absolutely crazy*, was all Rory could run through his mind as the agent stared at him with his black beady eyes.

"Mr. Justice." It came out as a statement in a gravelly voice that completely matched its owner. "I'm FBI Special Agent Mark Glover. I'd like to ask you a few questions."

Agent Glover fired questions at Rory for nearly two hours, his voice starting softly and slowly, then rising in a rapid, rough staccato while he paced, circling Rory like a tiger eyeing its prey.

Rory answered each question, recounting his story.

"So what do you know about the nuclear event your dad was warning Sheriff Dade about?" Agent Glover sat down at the hard, metal table directly across from Rory.

"Nothing, really, just that it's going to happen."

Mark Glover leaned across the table, his huge bicep muscles taut, his intense face just inches away from Rory's. He squinted his eyes warily. His voice was barely above a whisper. "C'mon, Rory, you have to know something. Or do you think your dad was just bluffing . . . that all of this is just . . . well, the ravings of a man who was getting older and maybe losing his mind?"

Rory bristled at the comment. But then he took a deep breath. *I thought the same thing at first. And then came the dreams . . . the nightmares.*

He sat up straight, remembering. "What day is it?"

"May twenty-seventh. Why?"

"Can you get me a calendar?"

Agent Glover stood hesitantly then exited the interrogation room and returned with a day planner.

Rory quickly thumbed through the thin book until he landed on a particular page. He shook his head.

"What is it?" Agitated, Mark Glover impatiently removed his cap, revealing a shiny, bald head.

"I know this sounds crazy, but my dad visited me in a dream." Rory continued quickly before he lost his nerve. "It was so real. Las Vegas had already been nuked. It was like that movie *The Day After*, where the whole city has been blown up. It was like a nuclear wasteland. I saw my dad in the dream. Actually, he has visited me a few times now. He said this would happen if we didn't stop them. And he told me when it would happen."

"When?" The FBI agent seemed mesmerized, at least for the moment.

"During the big fight between Jay-Jay Moss and Carmen Gallo on July sixth—in forty days."

"Them being the terrorists?"

"Yes, the ISM, the Islamic State Mafia." Rory noticed the weathered FBI agent's face twitch almost imperceptibly. *I've probably just confessed too much.* Rory was so overtired and anxious he was starting to feel paranoid. *Of course, I'm sure this guy has already read the letter and knows more than I do. Still....*

"Thank you, Mr. Justice, that will be all." Agent Glover promptly ended the interrogation and walked out of the room.

"Just like the reports from the captains of the *Voyager* and the USS *Alaska* and the statements from the FBI agents who made the road trip here, my report will also state that Rory Justice is not in the least bit exhibiting any personality traits or behavioral aspects of a suspected terrorist," Special Agent Mark Glover concluded. "He doesn't seem to be hiding anything and I concur he is telling the truth."

Agent Glover delivered his conclusion to Sheriff Ned Thomas and FBI Special Agent in Charge Rodney Steele in the hallway outside the room following the interrogation. They could see Rory through the one-way glass. He was slumped forward, rubbing his eyes.

"How can you possibly know that after one session?" Sheriff Thomas asked skeptically.

"He knows," said Steele, practically scowling at Ned Thomas, silencing him.

Known as Chief by his colleagues, Rodney Steele was a wiry man of about sixty who had paid his dues rising up through the ranks from a tough rookie street cop in New York City to detective, then NARC agent, SWAT team member, FBI agent, and finally, Las Vegas Special Agent in Charge of the FBI Bureau in Las Vegas. He had lost an arm in addition to his innocence in service when a stray bullet had hit him in a narcotics sting operation. He was no-nonsense, knew his stuff, and believed in his agents.

The sheriff sulked but remained quiet.

The three men turned away from the window and proceeded into a nearby conference room.

"So now what, we just turn him loose?" Sheriff Thomas was flustered, his face turning from pink to crimson.

"Not yet." Chief Steele sat drumming his fingers on the table. He stood abruptly. "Although we have no evidence to detain Rory Justice further, we still need to handle this matter as a national security threat. We need to remove any doubt whatsoever Mr. Justice and John Dade are somehow involved in this alleged ISM scheme. The only way to do that is to make sure neither of them have read the letter. Mark's questioning contends that Rory hasn't read it, but we can further confirm it if we monitor their reactions by reading it aloud. We'll be able to pick up on whether any of its contents come as less than a surprise to either. We will also be able to deduce whether they're telling the truth about not knowing each other. It's time Rory met the man his father wanted him to meet all along. Go get Dade."

Rory sat fidgeting in his chair in the interrogation room. The clock on the wall ticked loudly reminding him of the slowly passing minutes. *All to wear a suspect down*, he thought. He had been sitting alone for at least twenty minutes.

He nearly jumped out of his chair when the door opened and Agent Glover walked in followed by a man Rory hadn't seen yet—a man whose appearance shouted tough ex-Marine: he was stocky with ruddy skin and a gray flat-top, and wore a suit jacket with a name badge. It read "Dade."

Agent Glover made a cursory introduction between them, although none was needed at that point.

"You don't look much like yer dad." The former sheriff took Rory's hand in a firm handshake, squeezing his fingers. His western drawl was engaging, and Rory felt himself relax in his presence. *Dad's friend and confidante*, Rory reminded himself. *He may be the only one on my side.*

"No, I look like my mom, uh, Mister Dade."

"Call me John."

"John. It's nice to finally meet you. My fault it hasn't happened until now." Rory felt his cheeks flush with guilt.

"No worries, son. You're here now's all that matters. And of course, the problem we have on our hands . . . ."

He was interrupted as if on cue by the arrival of Chief Steele and Sheriff Thomas, who walked into the room and introduced themselves to Rory.

The five men stood awkwardly around the table in the cramped room.

"Shall we make ourselves more comfortable in the conference room?" Sheriff Thomas spoke up, exuding the exaggerated air of a gracious host. "That may be more accommodating."

"Sure, why not," Chief Steele said. "We may be here a while."

Once seated in the larger conference room, which was much less confined with its pastel walls and windows looking out over a grassy yard, the five men seemed to relax a little, although the air still felt tense in Rory's opinion.

Sheriff Thomas motioned for his predecessor and Rory to sit on one side of the long oak table, while he took a seat across from them together with Agent Glover and Chief Steele.

Rory immediately didn't like Ned Thomas, sensing a stiff defensiveness in the man who had been introduced as Las Vegas Sheriff, a title that had formerly belonged to John Dade, who was introduced merely as Mr. Dade.

He feels threatened, Rory guessed, suddenly feeling a little insecure himself.

Chief Steele began the meeting in his gruff tone, looking around the conference table at each man with his iron gray eyes. He was wearing a long-sleeved, pressed collared shirt, and one sleeve that otherwise would have dangled limply due to his missing arm was tucked neatly into his pants pocket. "First things first: I prefer that we not discuss this 'problem,' as Mr. Dade put it, outside of this room, gentlemen."

Rory and John Dade nodded in agreement.

"As you can see by now, you are no longer wearing handcuffs," Steele said to Rory, motioning to his wrists. "That's because Agent Glover here, who interrogated you, believes your story. You are now a free man."

Rory felt all of their eyes bearing on him like laser beams, and he looked down for a moment at his hands. *They're probably expecting me to jump up and run for the door*, he thought. *But I'm here now; may as well see what this is all about.*

"Thank you." Rory said, not knowing what else to say.

Sheriff Thomas sneered, unconcerned that Rory noticed it.

"What do we do now?" Rory felt compelled to speak in the uncomfortable silence. He was the only man in the room who wasn't a cop, an FBI agent, or military man. He was just an advertising account executive probably soon to lose even that meager title.

"Now we will read the letter your father wanted you to hand deliver. But before we do, Mr. Justice, let me extend the sincere apology of the FBI for holding you captive on the *Alaska*. I'm sure you understand you were a suspected terrorist and had to be treated as such."

"Understood."

"And while you are free to go, and not compelled to help us further, the FBI would like to ask your help to see this matter through, if you so choose. After I read the letter, I'll order in some lunch, and you and Mr. Dade can speak privately and let us know your intentions. Would you like to stay for now?"

A picture of his dad squatting on the sidewalk of a nuked Vegas flashed into Rory's memory. "Of course." *I can always change my mind*, he mused uneasily, knowing he was probably fooling himself.

"Sheriff Thomas, please read the letter." Rory could see the sheriff's chest literally puff with pride at the Chief's request. Steele handed him the envelope, sealed within an evidence bag.

Ned Thomas removed it, stood, and cleared his throat.

"*Dear John,*" he began, looking over his bifocals at John Dade.

"I know I haven't seen you for years, and I do apologize for that. I have not done well physically of late with my lung disease, and if you are reading this letter, well, that means I am most likely up in heaven—at least let's hope so.

Rory sighed, and fought to hold back tears.

"I am writing to you about a matter of grave danger. I chose you because you are one of my closest friends and the only person in the world with whom I trust the nation's security, since I would trust you with my life.

They all noticed John sniff with emotion and rub an unexpected tear from his face.

"Toward the end of my career, before I had to step down as Executive Director of the National Security Branch a few years ago due to my failing health, I was informed of a terrorist

threat in Las Vegas that I had the Counterterrorism Division investigate.

I couldn't bring it to your attention at the time because it was an internal FBI matter, and as you know, policy calls for us to notify as few people as possible until absolutely necessary to do otherwise.

I was told by my source that several years ago, a sect of the Islamic State terrorist regime called ISM, which stands for Islamic State Mafia, started infiltrating the casinos in Las Vegas and setting up shop in some of them, taking over the most insidious trades including sex and drug trafficking. Reports from undercover field agents have revealed that this new mafia has grown in power, and an increasing number of US citizens have become victims of violent crimes in Vegas. Some have even been murdered. Meanwhile, some police officers, perhaps even a few higher up government officials, both locally in Las Vegas and in our nation's capital, have become suspect of possibly working with the ISM. I believe there is obviously a cover-up at hand.

Ned Thomas paused and cleared his throat, looking over the rim of his glasses at John Dade. The sheriff then looked around the room, his face a deep red. "Gentlemen, I assure you all that I am not aware of any such cover-up, nor have I been part of one."

"We know, or else you wouldn't be here," Chief Steele addressed the sheriff tersely. "Please finish the letter."

Bravo, Rory silently cheered the FBI boss, glad the pompous sheriff's ego was deflated a bit.

Ned Thomas's face turned an even darker shade of red, and he cleared his throat again, attempting to regain his composure before continuing to read.

"Upon investigation, we have discovered that key government officials in Las Vegas have been looking the other way, probably as their pockets are being lined, to allow this Mafia sect to do their thing. And more digging turned up the very real suspicion that these same terrorists are building a nuclear bomb.

One of our agents, who unfortunately was killed by ISM members on the streets of Las Vegas, informed us that their plan is to plant the bomb in one of the casinos. He also uncovered inside information revealing the schematics—the bomb is being built so that it cannot be detected by drones, dogs, x-rays, lasers, acoustics or even any of our latest sophisticated espionage technology. I'm not sure when or exactly where the bomb will go off, although I strongly suspect it may be detonated at a place and time to kill as many Americans as possible and to send a message to the United States that the whole country is in jeopardy.

Once my health deteriorated and I was forced to take an early retirement, I had to sit back and watch as this information got stalled somewhere and then was literally shelved. When I tried to find out more information, I was told it was no longer a priority of the director, who said that the investigation revealed no such plans for a nuclear bomb, and the case was closed.

I believe that either the ISM has paid off or seriously threatened someone in the Bureau, or our country's administration doesn't want to admit the Islamic State jihad has revived itself and regrouped here in our own country—or maybe both.

But I am convinced beyond a doubt that the original allegations are real and being carried out as I write this. I have enclosed the schematic of the nuclear weapon based on what my source witnessed before he was murdered. You must not show this to anyone until you do your own investigation or they—the FBI, the CIA, etc.—may bring you in for questioning and stall everything long enough that it might be too late to do anything to stop it. Or worse yet, they may suspect we—me, you, Rory—are part of this scheme somehow. If there really is a cover-up going on, I wouldn't put it past them to frame us.

Rory saw Ned Thomas look at John Dade then quickly return his attention to the letter lest he get called out by Chief Steele again. *Dad was addressing John, not knowing that someone may have been paid to run him out of office,* Rory realized. *Oh well, at least he's here now.* Except for his initial display of emotion, John had sat stone-faced and silent.

Sheriff Thomas continued reading:

"I know this is a lot to ask of you to undertake, and I'm sorry, but if there's even a remote possibility that it is true, you owe it to your city and we owe it to our country to find the truth, to bring these terrorists to justice and most importantly, to protect innocent people. Of course I can't trust any mail or dispatch service so I am entrusting my son Rory to bring you this letter under strict confidence.

John gazed quizzically over at Rory for the first time during the reading. Rory felt his face turn hot with shame and averted his eyes, staring down at his hands.

"Please don't hesitate to ask him to help you. I'm not sure if he will be able to, but I believe he could be an asset to you. While he doesn't see it, Rory is a man with a big heart. I believe you will be able to convince him that he needs to look beyond himself to serve others. I hope whatever faith in God I have instilled in him will take hold, and he will agree to be part of your team.

Ned looked up from the letter at Rory, who avoided eye contact. If it was possible, Rory felt his own face grow redder and hotter. He felt desire throb through every fiber of his being to run like a rat out of the room and fly to a remote island, never to be seen again. But he sat frozen, staring at his hands clenched together in his lap for fear the officers might see him trembling with embarrassment.

Mercifully, Sheriff Thomas was almost to the end.

"I believe in both of you. Thank you and Godspeed in your efforts.
Your friend,
Howard Justice."

After an hour break for lunch, which consisted of cold cut sandwiches and chips called in from a local deli, the group reconvened in the conference room.

Rory and John Dade ate together in a small empty deputy's office down the hall. Ned Thomas had offered it to them, excusing himself, saying he had a few work matters to handle.

Meanwhile, the Sheriff, Agent Glover and Chief Steele skipped lunch and convened separately behind closed doors. Together they discussed Rory's and Dade's reactions to the reading of the letter and determined there was no way they were part of any covert terrorist plan.

Fortunately, the deputy's office also had a door, which Rory had surreptitiously closed once Sheriff Thomas walked away.

While John hungrily chomped on his second sandwich, having wolfed down the first, Rory ate a few bites slowly, too nervous to eat much of anything.

They sat next to each other in front of the missing deputy's desk, which they cleared and used as a lunch table.

Rory broke the silence, pushing the uneaten portion of his sandwich away.

"John, I just want to say again that I'm sorry."

"'Shokay." John cut him off between a mouthful of food, which he subsequently finished chewing and swallowing. "Rory, please don't apologize anymore. It won't change anything. Besides, I think you've already been through enough punishment."

"Thanks." Rory took a swig of his soda, washing down his food along with the remnants of his lingering remorse. He liked John and felt an immediate kinship to his father's long-time compatriot and friend. "So are you going to help the FBI investigate this? I wouldn't blame you if you didn't. It sounds like someone gave you the shaft anyway. I just don't trust that

Ned Thomas. I think they should look into his background a little further."

"Ned's okay." John polished off his last bite and chugged some soda. "He may be a little full of himself and not the sharpest tool in the shed. And it was slightly annoying that he was a little too eager to replace me after all I did for him. He's probably too arrogant to realize that I helped him get where he is today. But I don't believe he's a part of this Mafia gang. He was just a convenient replacement to push me out of the way—a guy who was itching to climb to the top, but too dumb and egotistical to look beyond his nose into what they're doing."

"Wow, you're pretty forgiving."

"I was ready to call it quits soon anyway. But now this . . . ." John shook his head.

"So you're going to stay involved?"

"If they'll have me. How 'bout you? Your father has a lot of faith in you. Frankly, even though I just met you, and even though you skipped out of bringing me the letter, so do I." John smacked Rory on the back good-naturedly.

"Well, you have more faith in me than I do in myself. So did my dad. Neither of you realize how much I hate this place."

"Las Vegas? Why?"

"Why not? It's full of sleaze. Why should I care what happens to Vegas?"

"Well, then, why are you still sitting here with me?" John leaned back in his chair and crossed one leg over the other. Rory noticed for the first time he was wearing faded leather cowboy boots under his jeans. *It figures,* he thought.

"I honestly don't know."

"Yes, I think you do. You're here because you do care somewhere deep down about what your father thinks . . . and maybe even what God thinks."

Rory tried not to roll his eyes at the mention of God, but he did recall, albeit unwillingly, the promise he had made to his dad in his poem on the submarine.

"I'd like to work with you if I stay," he said. Already Rory had developed a sense of confidence in this old-fashioned cowboy sheriff, surprising himself, since he rarely trusted anyone.

"That's a deal," John said with a grin, standing and offering his beefy hand. The two men shook on it just as they heard a knock on the door, summoning them.

The five men met back in the conference room at one o'clock.

Chief Steele led the discussion, outlining his plan to find the ISM and rid the city of them. He went around the room and asked each man, one by one, if he wanted to be part of this new project, and if so, why.

"It's my job," Agent Glover said.

John Dade piped in next. "Sounds like I'm already committed in the letter." He chuckled. "Matter of fact, this project has my name all over it."

Ned Thomas sat up straighter and cleared his throat. "No offense, but I believe my department and I will obviously be needed on this mission," he said, and Rory had to fight not to laugh out loud.

Finally, everyone turned expectantly to Rory, who hesitated for a moment then spoke. "I guess I owe it to my dad." He noticed John unsuccessfully try to suppress a smile.

"This, of course, will be highly confidential, and only a select handful of the most trusted officers, both in the FBI and the Las Vegas Sheriff's Department, will be recruited," Chief Steele admonished the group. "Let me thank you gentlemen ahead of time. This won't be easy, and it may very well be dangerous. But it sounds like you're all committed. So let's get started."

CHAPTER NINE

R ory had to call AdExecs immediately to resign from his job. Unable to tell them the real reason since the Vegas project was top secret, he simply told Mr. Majors he had found other employment and apologized for not being able to give two weeks' notice, adding grudgingly that he appreciated all that the company had done for him over the years.

Although he wouldn't miss any of his co-workers, Rory still had mixed feelings about quitting. He knew he was now in uncharted seas and wondered if he had made a mistake in not going back to the comfort of his familiar pond. *Too late*, he told himself. *You've already cut the line and raised the anchor.*

Fortunately, he didn't have too much time to mull it over. They were told the team would start work immediately.

Chief Steele told Rory he would receive a salary for his work as well as a small stipend to rent an apartment nearby. He would also be given a company car during his stay. "Nothing glamorous," Steele emphasized. "Just enough to get you around town."

The new FBI/police team quickly set up its new headquarters in a vacant, stand-alone warehouse building off of Schuster Street just blocks from the Strip. It would be dedicated solely for use by Operation No Dice, the name Agent Glover had given the special task force whose mission was two-fold: to rid the city of the ISM terrorists and to find and deactivate the nuclear bomb that was lying somewhere under one of the casino resorts.

Glover named the new headquarters building the Condo, an acronym for Covert Operation No Dice Offices. From the outside, the building looked like nothing more than an obscure, box-like structure with a few small windows.

Within a matter of days, the inside of the Condo was transformed from an abandoned warehouse into office cubicles. The team consisted of Rory and twelve others: Chief Steele and five of his people, Sheriff Thomas and his posse of four, and John Dade.

Technology experts had helped turn half of the large Condo interior into a state-of-the-art satellite station set up with the latest surveillance technology, an entire wall filled with large digital screens, smart boards, and electronic maps.

Chief Steele and Sheriff Thomas were the only men allotted separate office rooms with doors that were bulletproof and soundproof.

Rory was assigned to a cubicle with John, their desks pushed together so they faced each other.

The chief ordered Rory to undergo firearms and tactical training. He endured two weeks of grueling combat training at the dusty, sprawling Spring Valley training complex outside the city with a grizzly weather-beaten ex-Marine as his chief instructor.

He learned combative handgun skills, low-light shooting and fighting at night, tactical trauma care, vehicular assault and counter ambush tactics, close quarter battle, tactical rescues, reconnaissance and mission planning and more maneuvers than he figured he would probably ever remember, much less need.

At the end of his training, Rory was physically and mentally exhausted but felt at least he could handle a gun, and that he was ready to be part of the team.

Unfortunately, he heard rumblings that some team members didn't feel the same way about him.

Rory had stayed home the day after training to rest since he was sick with a stomach virus. The rest of the team members gathered in the Condo for their morning briefing.

Ned Thomas spoke up immediately. "Before we get started, I'd like to say something," he said, drawing a vexed glare from Chief Steele. "I just don't think Rory Justice has what it takes to be part of this team. He can't even handle the training, he doesn't have our level of experience, and frankly, I'm still not sure he can be trusted."

Chief Steele stood up at the end of the long conference table. "Sheriff Thomas, I appreciate your concerns, but might I remind you that if it weren't for Rory and his father, none of us would be on this project. Furthermore, I trust Mr. Justice, and since I'm the head of the team, I need you all to trust me on this. If you don't want to be part of it, now's your chance to speak up."

"Of course I do," Ned Thomas interjected. "I just thought I should be honest about my doubts."

"Noted."

"And I don't think I am the only one with concerns." The sheriff looked around the table, and two of his men nodded, glancing at the chief but remaining silent.

Chief Steele rubbed his chin, choosing his words. "Since we gave Rory Justice the choice to join the team, and he has followed through on all of his training, I think it would be unfair to take this opportunity from him. But feelings aside, I believe we need him. Most of us have some level of notoriety or recognition here in Vegas, whereas Mr. Justice is anonymous. That's why I'm putting him on the streets."

Ned Thomas drew in a sharp breath of surprise.

Rory, to his chagrin, was assigned to a team they were calling the "front line." They would be working the streets to find out whatever they could about the Mafia within the circles in which it operated. *In other words, I'm to mingle with the hookers, pimps, thugs, and drug addicts,* Rory realized. *The very people I despise the most.*

His team members were two undercover police officers: Susan McAfree, a forty-something, wiry, pretty but tough and feisty redhead from the Las Vegas Special Victims Unit, and Sergeant Carlos Fuentes, a short, stocky Latino in his thirties from the NARC Unit.

They would be one of several teams assigned to investigate certain crime pockets in the city. Their mission was to try to expose Mafia members in an effort to arrest them and bring them in for interrogation in hopes of putting them behind bars and ultimately finding out if there actually was a nuclear weapon as Howard Justice had predicted.

— — — — — —

Rory puffed on a cigar outside the glitzy strip joint. He had never liked smoking cigarettes and couldn't muster enough willpower to even fake it, but he did tolerate smoking cigars, and once in a while, he even enjoyed it. Steele said he had to smoke something if he wanted to fit in.

He and his new partners had been assigned to hang out at a strip club named Wildcats just off the north end of the Strip on Highland Drive where many of the topless bars and clubs were located. The name flashed in large neon pink letters next to the lit sign of three women scantily clad in various cat outfits—a leopard, tiger, and lion—each wearing cat ears, a tail and little else.

Rory, who gave himself the alias of Ronny, and Carlos, who changed his name to Luis, entered the two-story whitewashed building after standing in a short line of men for about twenty minutes. Rory wore a lightweight black leather jacket, a black T-shirt, and jeans, and Carlos sported army fatigue pants and an olive green T-shirt.

Once inside, they each handed the doorman a fifty-dollar bill for the cover charge. They had been told ahead of time by someone who tipped off their team that Wildcats was one of the more expensive strip clubs, one of the raciest, and if a guy brought enough cash, it would be "worth his while," all of which indicated the ISM was probably running it.

Rory had no basis of comparison as he had never been to such a club in his life and didn't know quite what to expect.

But he was soon to find out.

Hip-hop music blared loudly as they made their way into a crowded strobe-lit room where women in lingerie circulated among the customers and two topless women pole-danced on a stage.

Carlos had also informed Rory that in order for them to discover anything about who was running the place and what was actually going on behind the scenes, they would have to fit in, which meant paying for the services of the women and prying the information out of them or eavesdropping in the back rooms.

Cell phones were strictly prohibited and were confiscated by a bouncer at the front door, to be given back to the customers when they left. Knowing this ahead of time, Rory and Carlos hadn't bothered to even bring them, which would make communication difficult. They knew they would probably have to split up, so they agreed to meet again at the front entrance in exactly one hour.

Rory had no idea what he would possibly do for all that time, but he followed Carlos's lead when a pair of young women, who looked to be in their early twenties, sidled up to them and started making small talk.

"How you doing, sugar?" The light-skinned black girl spoke in a husky voice to "Luis," introducing herself as Candy.

Carlos smiled, leaning in close to her. "I'm doing better now, Candy."

He knows how to play the part, Rory thought nervously. *Or maybe he's not playing. I am so far out of my league.*

"This is Tiffany," Candy said, introducing her friend to Rory. The blonde girl smiled, almost shyly. *This doesn't come naturally for her either,* he guessed.

She had long, straight, honey blonde hair with bangs and was petite and pretty with pale skin, heavily made-up blue-green eyes, and bright red lips that parted to reveal a nice smile.

Rory kept his eyes on her face, not wanting to look down, although he couldn't help but notice she wore only a leopard print teddy with stockings, high heels, and the trademark cat ears and tail. Candy was dressed in similar attire.

"Hi," Rory said, drawing a glare from Carlos. *Ok, that was lame. C'mon, think of something more.* "I'm Ron from the Midwest."

"Hmmm, probably one of those urban cowboys," Candy said, nudging Tiffany.

"You ready for a wild ride, Ron?" Tiffany picked up her cue, opening the door to . . . *who knows what*, Rory thought, trying not to panic.

"I sure am," he answered in a fake Midwestern drawl.

He watched Carlos roll his eyes in his peripheral vision.

"C'mon, you two, we'll take you where the action really is." Candy took Carlos by the hand, and Tiffany followed suit with Rory.

Soon they were stepping out of the warehouse-sized dance hall with its overwhelming light and sound into a more dimly lit hallway.

On either side of the hallway were private rooms with doors. They walked its length and turned down another hallway with more doors on each side.

A few guttural sounds emitted from behind the closed doors—an occasional moan, grunt, slap or scream—but they were muffled by the music, its base thumping beats still playing loud enough to disguise voices.

They stopped in front of the last two doors at the end of the second hallway, which veered into yet another dark hallway to the left.

Candy opened the door to the first room and led Carlos inside. Before he disappeared from view, he looked back at Rory and winked with a smile that didn't reach his eyes, which were serious and seemed to say, *be careful.* Tiffany led Rory to the next room, the last one in the corridor.

The room was sparsely furnished, painted entirely in red. There was a queen-sized bed with a red spread and pillows, a partition in the corner for undressing or changing costume, a floor lamp in the other corner, and a flat-screened television on the wall showing an adult video. There was also a floor-to-ceiling pole in another corner, and hanging on the wall was a variety of whips and other paraphernalia that Rory wasn't even sure how to identify.

Suddenly he felt sick to his stomach, and thought that he might pass out, so he sat on the edge of the bed. The air was warm and thick, and he started to perspire.

"Why don't you take off your jacket?" Tiffany approached him, and he let her remove it since he felt too sweaty and weak to do it himself.

When she went to remove his shirt, he stopped her, taking both her hands in his and looking her in the eyes.

"Tiffany, I—"

"Oh I get it. You're gay, right?"

Rory almost laughed out loud at the ludicrousness of her statement, but figured a small fib wouldn't hurt at this point. "Right. But my friend doesn't know. So can we just talk?" He watched a look of relief visibly cross her features, and she smiled.

"Sure, but you don't get your money back." They had quickly agreed on one hundred and fifty dollars before entering the room, which Rory had handed her in cash.

"I know, that's okay. But can we turn that darned television off?" The sounds emitting from the screen were adding to Rory's nausea.

Tiffany crossed the room, picked up a remote control, and turned off the TV. She went behind the partition then reappeared with a cheap black satin robe wrapped around her, and sat on the bed a few feet away.

"So, talk." She took off her five-inch heels and rubbed her feet, apparently disinterested in what he had to say.

"Actually, I need you to talk. I am still paying you, and since the sign said satisfaction guaranteed, that's not too much to ask, I wouldn't think." Rory referred to a sign above the doorway to the first hall they had entered.

"What do you want to know?"

"For starters, how old are you really?"

"Twenty-four."

"That's a lie." Rory wasn't sure, but he figured he'd try to fish out the truth.

"Okay, eighteen." Rory suddenly realized this girl who was offering her body for him to take advantage of, use, and possibly abuse was no older than his daughter Riley, who was hopefully safe and sound in her room back home a few thousand miles away. He felt nauseous again but swallowed it down, fighting the recollection of the night he spent in Caesars Palace with the blonde call girl ten years ago. She had seemed to be about his age, but who knew? *Put it out of your mind, you have a job to do,* he silently reprimanded himself, focusing all of his attention on Tiffany, concentrating on extracting information from her as coolly as he could.

"And why do you do this?"

"Do what?"

"Strip and, um, all the rest."

"Uh, because I have to." Her sarcastic tone reflected her disdain, as if to say, "What, are you an idiot?"

"No, you don't."

"You don't know that. You don't know me. I need the money. It's . . . ."

A sharp, crashing sound interrupted her. It came from the side of the room closest to the end of the hallway.

"You're a no good—!" They heard a girl's high-pitched scream following the harshly uttered epithet and then a loud crack, the sound of a hand loudly smacking someone's skin.

"How dare you not charge for your services?" Even though the voice was muted and distant, Rory could distinguish it was a man who spoke English with an Arabic accent.

They heard another smack and then a thud, like the sound of someone kicking a body. Then they heard the sound of a whimper, and begging. "Please, don't . . . ." a young female voice pleaded. But the smacks and thuds and banging continued, one after another, interspersed with more cries and screams that slowly faded.

Tiffany jumped up from the bed, her face ashen. "Oh, my God." She stood frozen, panicked. "That's my friend Danielle. She's only sixteen. He's going to kill her!"

"Who is?" Rory stood.

"His name is Jameel. He works for the Master. We've got to save her."

Tiffany headed toward the door, but Rory grabbed her by the arm, stopping her.

"Wait a minute. He'll kill you too. Hush." Rory put his hand up to Tiffany's mouth to silence her. "Listen." The room was quiet. The sounds had stopped. "He must have quit beating her. Let's give him a minute to leave, and then I'll help you go find her."

Tiffany was weeping quietly, mascara running down her cheeks.

Rory opened his arms and enveloped her in them, thinking of Riley.

After holding her shaking body for a few minutes, calming her, Rory took Tiffany by the hand and slowly opened the door, peered both ways, and then stepped out into the hallway, pulling her behind him.

Rory led Tiffany around the corner to the left into the third hallway. It was dark, more ominous and seemed eerily quiet except for the now distant staccato of hip-hop music.

They stood long enough to hear a far-off sound of crying coming from the other end of the hallway. Feeling their way through the dark, they turned the corner to the right, and halfway down the next corridor, their eyes adjusting to the blackness, they saw Danielle lying on the floor of a cage like a ragdoll, unconscious.

Tiffany let go of Rory's hand, ran to the cage, and shook the barred door. "Danielle," she cried in a loud whisper, but her friend didn't move.

The cries had come from another girl in the next cage, an Asian girl, also a teenager, who sat huddled on the floor, her back to the wall of the cage, hugging her knees.

"I think he killed her," the young Asian girl said.

"Kimi, how long have you been locked up back here?" Tiffany walked over to the other girl's cage and rattled the door, hoping to wrench it open.

"I don't know, a few days. He brings me bread and water and makes me eat and drink it like an animal." Rory noticed the girl didn't have any clothes on, and wore only underwear and a dog collar around her neck. She was so thin she looked almost like a skeleton, her backbone protruding through her pallid skin. There was a stained plastic pad, about an inch thick and five feet long, covering the floor of the cage where he guessed she must sleep. When she finally turned to face them, they saw that she was covered in bruises and had dark gray circles under her eyes.

Suddenly all three of them heard moaning coming from Danielle's cage, and the young brunette teenager stirred, rolling to one side.

"Thank God!" Tiffany said, going to her friend's cage door.

Rory tried to think fast. *How can we get these girls out of here before this lunatic comes back and finds us all?*

As if his thoughts became reality, they heard heavy footsteps approaching.

"There's a door at the end of this hallway," Kimi whispered urgently. "Quick, you two better get out of here." She turned and sat back down on the floor, slumping forward, feigning sleep. "Go!"

"But we can't leave you!" Tiffany desperately looked from Kimi to Danielle to Rory, searching his eyes for help.

"We need to go," Rory said. "If we stay, she's right, he'll kill us all." Rory's mind seemed to work on autopilot. There was no time to think. The footsteps were louder and closer. "I promise, we'll come back for both of you," he told Kimi, then grabbed Tiffany's hand and yanked her with him, fumbling through the dark, running for the door, running for their lives.

— — — — —

CHAPTER TEN

R ory and Tiffany escaped out the back door of the strip club and were standing in an asphalt lot full of trash bins.

After throwing his jacket over her shoulders to cover her, Rory led Tiffany around the building to the front, sneaking along the concrete façade to stay out of the glaring lights of the parking lot. Rory peeked around the corner of the front of the club and saw Carlos standing alone next to his car, smoking a cigarette.

Motioning for Tiffany to stay put, Rory walked up to Carlos, trying to keep his nerves at bay.

Carlos turned when he felt his partner's hand tap him on the shoulder. "Where have you been? I've been waiting for twenty minutes!"

"Shhh. Keep your voice down. There's no time to talk. I'll explain later. Just start the car and give me your jacket, hat, and sunglasses. I'll meet you back here in two minutes. We need to get out of here fast."

Not giving him a chance to ask questions, Rory snuck back to where Tiffany stood, shaking with fear, handed her the jacket to wrap around her waist and the hat and sunglasses to wear, and with his arm around her like she was his girlfriend, he walked with her out into the open, saying a quick foxhole prayer.

They both strolled as casually as they could to the waiting car. Carlos gave them a wide-eyed look of shock from behind the wheel but was smart enough not to ask any questions until they were on their way back to the station.

Lieutenant McAfree had worked with female victims of domestic abuse and sexual assault for almost twenty years after joining the force following graduation from college and the police academy. She was skilled at showing victims compassion yet knowledgeable enough to be firm when she needed to be, and was rarely sucked in by manipulation, drama, or emotion.

Tiffany had been hesitant at first to talk to anyone including Susan, afraid to divulge any information that might be used against her.

But Chief Steele had convinced her that she would be given full immunity and witness protection by the FBI and Sheriff's department and would be put in a safe house with round-the-clock guards. More importantly, he promised her the police and FBI would do what it took to rescue the other girls and bring them to safety if she cooperated.

Rory, Carlos, Chief Steele, and Agent Glover watched and listened to the interrogation through the two-way mirror.

"So tell me what went on back there," Lieutenant McAfree said in a quiet voice.

Tiffany sat up stiffly in the hard metal chair, looking uncomfortable in the khaki pants and long-sleeved blouse Susan had given her to replace her skimpy outfit.

She seemed even younger and more vulnerable under the bright fluorescent light, which made her skin appear translucent against the collar of the white shirt.

Receiving no answer, the lieutenant leaned in and reached for Tiffany's hand, but the young girl wrenched it back, turning her face defiantly, refusing to make eye contact.

"Tiffany, I know it's hard to talk about all of this, but I know you want to help those girls—your friends who are still stuck back there."

Tiffany turned to look at Susan, and Rory noticed through the glass that she was tapping her foot anxiously as Susan lay out on the table several photos of Jameel and the Master.

A tear strayed down Tiffany's cheek, which grew a hot red—with anger and shame, Rory imagined.

"Danielle and Kimi aren't the only ones who were beaten and starved," she finally said, her voice cracking. She wiped away tears, and seemingly out of nowhere, Susan produced a box of tissues and handed her one, waiting for the teenage girl to collect herself.

"It's okay, Tiffany," Susan said, her voice soothing. "Whatever you tell me will be confidential. And telling it will help you get through this and hopefully help us catch these dirt bags."

"Sometimes the guys who worked there would . . . use us for their own pleasure too."

"You mean, they would rape you?" Lieutenant McAfree asked gently.

"Yes. You'd be lucky if that's all they did."

"What do you mean?"

"They'd rough up some of the girls while they'd have their way with them. Or they'd sub them out to their Muslim gang friends. Since we aren't Muslims, they treat us as less than human. Sometimes, I'd wake up to three or four of them in the room . . . ." Tiffany cried into her tissue, dabbing away the vestiges of mascara that streaked down her cheeks. The air apparently grew warm in the small interrogation room, and Rory noticed Tiffany roll up her sleeves without thinking, revealing thin track lines along the undersides of her arms.

"Did they drug you?" McAfree also saw the tracks on Tiffany's forearms.

"Yes. I had never done drugs before I came into Wildcats. But one night after I started working there, Jameel came into my room and said I had a long night ahead of me, and since I was new, he would help me out by giving me a little pick-me-up. I tried to tell him no, I didn't need it, figuring he meant some type of drugs. But before I could resist, he grabbed my arm and stuck a needle in it. It was heroin. I think I blacked out. When I came to, this guy was on top of me, hitting me and hurting me."

Tiffany started to weep—big heaving sobs that she had held back for a long time. She had seen what they did to girls who cried and she had stopped showing any emotion a long time ago.

After a few minutes, she wiped her tears again, took a deep breath, and continued. "After that I was hooked. I'd take anything to numb me. I gave most of the money I made from stripping and prostitution over to Jameel or his men for more drugs. They had me right where they wanted me. It was one big vicious cycle. And the one time I hinted that I might want to get out of the business, one of them told me that if I ever tried to leave, I'd be as good as dead—that I may as well plan to spend the rest of my days there until I was too old and unattractive to be of use to them anymore. I swore to myself I'd somehow find a way to get out."

Susan took Tiffany's hand in her own and glanced up for a moment in their direction as if to say, "It's okay."

Looking on, Rory felt a combination of admiration and respect for Susan McAfree wash over him.

The lieutenant didn't even have to ask how it all got started. Tiffany seemed to want to unload her guilt and shame, not needing to be asked.

"All I wanted to do was make some quick money dancing in a strip club so I could put myself through college. My parents had divorced when I turned fifteen, and my dad left. I lived with my alcoholic mom, who couldn't take care of me. She and her boyfriend kicked me out and I had nowhere to go. When I was promised room and board at Wildcats in addition to a lot of money, I thought I would just stay for the summer. They said all I had to do was dance topless and that would be it." She sighed heavily. "They are all liars."

Tiffany finished her story and eventually gave Susan the names of all the people and places she knew in the business, finally trusting the redheaded cop and wanting to help out of gratitude for being brought out alive.

"Jameel Tahan. Age forty-two. Birthplace is Cairo. Gained entry to the US three years ago to work here in Vegas for Amad Safar, aka the Master. We know Safar has been in Vegas for about five years now, and we're trying to find out more info on him as we speak. We're not sure if he's in charge of the whole ISM outfit or, like Tahan, just another player." Mark Glover outlined what had been gleaned from the investigative profiling his FBI team had assembled once Rory and Carlos had reported what they had discovered and Tiffany had been questioned.

When the rundown of both ISM members was finished, Chief Steele turned to Rory, Carlos, John, and Susan. "Okay, here's the plan."

Steele outlined to them that the FBI, in conjunction with some of Sheriff Thomas's forces, would conduct a simultaneous surprise raid on Wildcats and five other notorious strip clubs suspected of being run by the Mafia.

The Operation's goal wasn't only to root out the Mafia members in hopes of eventually finding their leader and the nuclear bomb; it was to close down the strip joints that were operating as sex-slave warehouses.

Chief Steele had ordered the police to offer the girls who worked in these places a special arrangement. In exchange for their testimony of what they had seen, heard, and experienced while employed there, the young women would be given immunity. If they were arrested and convicted of any related charges in their line of work, such as drug use or prostitution, the US Attorney's office would automatically grant them probation with mandatory community service and counseling as well as drug rehabilitation.

If they weren't arrested or charged, they would be offered free job counseling, a stipend to get them started in new lines of work, and witness protection as needed.

— — — — — —

The raid was set for the following week.

SWAT team members would be stationed at each of the five major Mafia-run nightclubs: Wildcats, Cobra, Brandy's, the Black Panther, and Hot Pink.

When given the signal, the armed agents would "descend" or break down the doors and storm in, taking as many prisoners as possible.

Ambulances would be parked on standby for girls who needed them or any victims of gunfire if it broke out.

The signal would be initiated by Lieutenant Susan McAfree, who was going undercover as a decoy stripper looking for a job at Brandy's, where the Master purportedly held court.

Prior to the sting going down, Susan would plant bugging devices throughout the building, and once the team retrieved enough information about the Mafia suspects and she gave them the green light, the SWAT team would converge on the five nightclubs after she escaped to safety.

Her goal was to get in, get to know the girls who worked there, then find out what they knew about Jameel, the Master, and whoever else was of Arab or Middle Eastern descent and thus most likely part of the ISM.

She also was instructed to find out if any of the strippers were being abused like Danielle and Kimi were at Wildcats.

She wouldn't be alone; shortly after she was to apply and get the job, a different wired FBI agent posing as a john, like Rory and Carlos had done at Wildcats, would go in every few hours to keep tabs on her.

— — — — — —

Rory nearly fell out of his chair when Susan sashayed into the Condo wearing black stilettos. Her shoulder-length wavy red hair, which she usually wore in a tight bun, had been teased out around her face in soft curls. She normally wore little to no makeup, but for the sting operation, her face had been transformed into that of a supermodel with crimson lipstick and plum-colored eye shadow and eyeliner accentuating her big brown eyes.

He tried not to stare when she briefly, playfully opened the front of her oversized raincoat to reveal a red halter-top that hugged her curves and showed her midriff and a very short black skirt that showcased her long legs enmeshed in fishnet stockings. He was used to seeing her every day in her police uniform, and his voice caught in his throat and he coughed, nearly choking until he took a gulp of water.

The rest of the guys whistled appreciatively.

"Knock it off before I punch one of ya," she reprimanded them, closing her raincoat.

If she doesn't I will, Rory thought, a sudden feeling of protectiveness toward her grabbing him by surprise.

"Show's over guys, go back to work," Agent Glover barked at them from his desk.

Rory, Carlos, John Dade, and most of the rest of the Operation No Dice team were stationed at the Condo as the sting went down.

Reports were called in by the minute from the field agents. Chief Steele had taken two men with him and was in the field with the SWAT commanders outside of Brandy's.

Rory sat with John and Carlos in the Condo's small kitchen area drinking coffee and eating sandwiches that had been ordered in. They were halfway through dinner when Mark Glover poked his head in the kitchen doorway. He stood, his bulky body filling the frame, looking at each of them silently. He was clearly at a loss for words.

"What is it, Mark?" Carlos prodded him.

"I have bad news. Steele just told me Susan's missing. When the SWAT team went in to Brandy's, we thought she'd already been safely removed by the FBI agent inside. We just got word she's still in there. It sounds like halfway through the back passageway she and her "john" partner were discovered as they tried to escape, and they somehow became separated from each other . . . ." Mark's two-way radio beeped and he picked it up. Static muffled the voice on the other end. "What? All right, keep looking! You've got to get her out of there!"

Rory felt his stomach lurch, dropped his half-eaten sandwich, stood and grabbed his coat from his desk chair, and headed for the front door.

Mark grabbed him by his arm. "Where do you think you're going?"

"I'm going to try to save her. I've seen what happens in there . . . ."

"We've got a whole SWAT team in there, Rory. She'll be fine."

Rory turned, anger making his heart race. "What if she isn't?"

"We'll send John in, or I'll go. You and Carlos are marked targets already. You can't go in there."

"I don't really care. Carlos has a family; I understand why he can't go. I've got no one. I'm going, and you better not stop me."

John had already put his coat on and headed out behind Rory. "Let him go, Mark, I'll go with him. You need to stay here."

- - - - - -

Rory had never seen a SWAT team in operation. When he and John arrived, a swarm of masked men stood like a barricade in full black gear wearing boots and helmets and bearing machine guns, blocking their way.

"We're with the FBI, on your side," Rory said, trying to push his way past two burly SWAT guys towering over him. Up close, they almost looked like aliens. But Rory was not afraid. He was on a mission.

John obviously knew better than to think they could somehow persuade them, and grabbed his partner, wrapping a beefy arm around his chest, holding him back. "They've got orders, Rory. Let's try to find Steele."

Rory thought his heart would burst out of his chest; he could literally feel his blood pressure rising. *I've got to save her.* There was no time to reason why this one thought kept resounding throughout his being like a siren blaring inside him, drowning out all other thoughts and feelings.

He pushed John's arm away and pressed forward until he felt the cold metal of a gun barrel against his face. *I've got to save her . . . .*

And then he saw her.

Two SWAT team members on either side ushered her toward the waiting ambulance just ahead of them. She was wrapped from her head down in a thick gray blanket; she kept her eyes downcast, and just a few red curls revealed her identity. More women wrapped in similar blankets were being escorted behind her into other waiting ambulances and police cars.

"Susan!" Rory shouted her name, the gun barrel still holding him back, but she couldn't hear him with all of the chaos.

"C'mon, Rory, she'll be okay," John said behind him. "At least we came and found that out. But now we're just in the way, and we need to let these guys do their jobs."

Rory reluctantly stepped away and let John lead him back to his waiting squad car.

They arrived back at the Condo to hear more bad news.

"A sixteen-year-old girl died before the SWAT team was able to rescue her at Wildcats," Mark Glover informed them. "They tried to resuscitate her, but she had passed away minutes earlier of internal injuries and a blunt force trauma to her head. Her name was Danielle."

Rory sat and put his head in his arms. Black stars danced before his eyes, and he thought for a moment he'd pass out.

"I'm sorry, you knew her?" Agent Glover asked, seeing Rory's reaction.

"Yes," Rory raised his head once his vision cleared, his voice choked with grief. "She was Tiffany's friend. Carlos and I saw her when we were undercover in there. They beat her to death. I should have gotten her out of there." Suddenly he was seething with guilt and rage. "So did they catch any of these Mafia barbarians?" *I hope they are all tortured and hanged,* he thought angrily.

"Yes, at least a dozen, although a few escaped. Still, we hope we captured enough of them to get to the bottom of all of this."

"What about the other girls?" Rory asked.

"Seven others were rushed by ambulance to Sunrise Hospital with various injuries," Agent Glover said solemnly. "One is in Intensive Care, three are in critical condition, and the others were treated and released back into police custody."

"What happens next?" John Dade wondered aloud.

"Everyone who was caught is being booked in the four Vegas police stations, which were alerted and staffed ahead of time in preparation for the sting. There are more than a hundred and fifty in all including the girls. Of course they'll wait for those in the hospital to get better before they bring them in for questioning."

"How is Susan?" Rory was almost afraid to ask but had to know.

"We just got a call that she's fine. She was treated and released and hopefully is at home resting."

"They didn't . . . ?" Rory left the question unspoken, but everyone knew what he meant.

"No, she was not assaulted, just emotionally battered and a little tired."

"Thank God." Rory exhaled a sigh of relief.

Susan shocked them all when she walked through the door to the Condo a few hours later looking different from her typically confident, policewoman self. Instead of wearing her uniform, she was dressed in civilian clothes—jeans and a lightweight powder blue sweater, her hair down around her shoulders. She looked vulnerable, and sadness clouded her big brown eyes.

Rory sat at his desk across from John, sorting through stacks of papers that had been confiscated in the raid from the various clubs, everything from accounting records to copies of visas, green cards, and naturalization certificates. Rory was grateful for the menial task as he was having trouble focusing; it was already approaching 11 p.m.

He looked up when he felt her presence; he thought she looked beautiful, despite the fact that she looked very tired.

"What are you doing back at work, Lieutenant?" Rodney Steele walked up and pulled out a chair for her to sit in, but she ignored his gallantry.

"I want to help. I can see there's a lot more work to be done." She gestured her hand in a sweeping motion, indicating the massive amounts of paperwork, the phone bank, which was completely manned, and the satellite video screens being viewed by several agents. The Condo's interior, which seemed full when just the OND members were present, was now packed with at least two dozen law enforcement officials, some back from out in the field and some brought in on special assignment.

"Well, you've already done enough, and it's late . . . ."

Susan swayed a little, losing her balance, and grabbed hold of a nearby desk. "Maybe I will take that chair. I do feel a little light-headed."

Rodney Steele put his one arm around Susan's waist. Even though he was strong and she was petite, settling her down into the chair was awkward for the one-armed FBI chief, and they stumbled. Rory jumped to his feet, eager to help.

"You've been through a lot in forty-eight hours, Lieutenant McAfree. How about if I have Mr. Justice take you back to the hospital just to make sure everything's okay?" Chief Steele was all about using proper titles and last names while at work, and encouraged them to do the same.

"That won't be necessary, Chief. I'm fine. It's probably just that I haven't had enough sleep, and I guess I haven't had anything to eat since this morning. The food they feed the girls is pitiful."

"I could take you for a sandwich and coffee," Rory heard himself offer.

Susan looked up, her brown eyes locking with his green ones. He wasn't sure if he saw defiance or gratitude in them, or maybe a strange combination of both. She sighed. "All right. But then I'm coming back to help, and . . . ."

"No, you are going straight home and getting some sleep so you can come back ready to go tomorrow," Chief Steele said sternly. "And that, Lieutenant, is an order."

Rory and Susan sat across from each other in the little diner three blocks down the road. It wasn't fancy, but the locals ate there and the food was decent. Rory was surprised when Susan ordered a bowl of chili, a grilled cheese sandwich, an iced tea, and a piece of homemade cherry pie a la mode and coffee for dessert. He was further amazed when she ate every bite.

He ordered a piece of pie and some milk, and sat while she ate her dinner making small talk, filling her in on everything they had pieced together so far on the Mafia ring they were investigating. He bided his time, waiting until she was almost finished, to ask her questions that had been building up, burning inside him.

"So how was it in there, Lieutenant?"

"You saw for yourself in Wildcats, didn't you Mr. Justice? And call me Susan."

"Deal, if you call me Rory." He saw her smile and felt his heart jump. "I guess it was the same. Pretty bad, huh? I hope you weren't, uh, mishandled or abused?" *Careful,* he warned himself, his heart now thumping.

"Nah, luckily the undercover agents posing as customers found me on the dance floor and we just hung out together in the back room." Susan ate the last bite of pie and ice cream and licked her spoon. "Did you want details?"

Although her tone was playfully sarcastic, and he knew she was just toying with him, Rory felt the sting of her words. He realized he shouldn't have probed her for information, and he knew that his questions had arisen from a feeling of jealousy that other men had seen her in that skimpy costume. But it was more than that. He wanted to make sure she was okay. He realized he felt overprotective . . . like a big brother, or partner . . . or *more*. *Like some macho man*, he derided himself, feeling suddenly mad at himself for even asking or caring.

"I was just concerned, that's all," he said, trying to sound nonchalant. "We were all afraid for you when you didn't come out right away and the SWAT team descended. You didn't know it, but I was there when you came out of the building. I'm glad you made it out okay."

"I'm sorry, I shouldn't have teased you." Susan now looked sincerely contrite as she sipped her coffee. "And thank you for caring. To be honest, I was afraid too, a few times in fact, and I'm a cop. I don't know how those girls survive in there. I've worked with many victims, but these new Mafia guys give the word sadomasochism a whole new meaning."

"Yeah, I used to think those girls all asked for what they got working in places like that, sinking that low," Rory admitted. "Now I see that many of them sign up for something they didn't bargain for and didn't deserve—no human being deserves to be treated that way."

"Hmmm, maybe there's hope for you yet, Mr. Justice . . . Rory." Susan McAfree smiled. "I took you for the ultra-conservative, judgmental type."

Rory felt a little offended, but knew she was right in her assessment. "You're pretty astute. More so than I am. Do you mind if I ask you another question?"

"Shoot."

"Why do you do what you do? Stay in this line of work, all of these years, here in Las Vegas of all places? I have to admit, there have been a few times when I've been ready to call it quits, and I've only been involved in this assignment for a week or so. It's depressing. And you're so smart and . . . ." Rory realized he was venturing onto dangerous ground again. He had wanted to say "attractive," but knew it might sound condescending.

"And what?" her eyes gleamed playfully again.

"And . . . you have so much more to offer."

"Why, thank you, Rory Justice." Susan smiled and blushed, showing a lighter, feminine side he had never seen before. But then her expression turned shadowy, like a cloud was passing overhead. "I guess I do what I do to help people, especially battered and abused women, because I've been where they've been."

Rory sat in silence, his hands wrapped tightly around his coffee mug. He looked down at the black liquid in his cup, not sure what to say, waiting.

"It was a long time ago and I'm over it now," Susan continued matter-of-factly. "Counseling helped. I was eleven when it started. My parents travelled a lot for their jobs, and my uncle babysat my younger brother and me. He played games with me, like hide and seek, after my brother went to bed. I tried to hide really well, but he always found me, and then . . . well, you know, he sexually assaulted me. When it turned ugly, he threatened that if I told anyone, he would hurt my little brother really badly, and I would be sorry. It went on for almost two years, and then he was in a car accident that disfigured him. He had to have his leg amputated . . . and of course, I was old enough to take care of us at that point. I used to think maybe God punished him by making him lose a leg. Anyhow, I always believed that one day I would work in a field that would help victims and punish the bad guys. I grew up in a nice white-collar town in Arizona. I guess I came here because Vegas is full of victims and bad guys."

Rory was dumbstruck for a few minutes, his heart aching for her. "I'm sorry you went through all that, Susan."

She yawned and smiled sleepily. "Sorry, it's not the company. I am still really tired. I don't think I could drink enough coffee to keep me awake at this point. Could you take me home?"

Rory was happy to oblige. Susan lived on the outskirts of the city in a nice little rancher. He pulled up next to the curb and parked in front of the house.

She turned to face him. "I'm embarrassed to ask, but do you think you could see me inside? After the bust on these guys, I just don't feel entirely safe right now, especially since we obviously didn't catch them all." For a moment, Rory thought she looked like a young, vulnerable girl and he wanted to take her in his arms and hold her. *But that's not what she needs right now,* he reminded himself.

"Sure, no problem," he said. Before he could walk around to open the passenger door for her, she was already out of the car and headed up the walkway. He hurried to at least hold the screen porch door while she unlocked the front door. "Do you want me to come in while you make sure everything is all right?"

She grinned. "Hmmm . . . yes, I think I can trust you."

Rory felt his cheeks turn hot. He stood in the foyer while she went through the house flipping on light switches and opening doors. Once she was in the kitchen, she called out, "Would you like anything to drink?"

"I don't drink much," Rory responded, feeling for the first time that he almost wished he did.

"Good, neither do I," she said. "How about a soda?"

"No, that's okay. Can I use your bathroom?"

"Of course, second door down the hall to the right."

Rory noticed that Susan had contemporary taste, with a few pieces of framed, colorful modern art hanging here and there, but she definitely wasn't into knickknacks or a lot of decorations. He liked it. Her place had a clean, comfortable feel that wasn't overly feminine or masculine.

When Rory walked out of the hallway into the living room, he saw Susan lying on the couch fast asleep, her head resting on a throw pillow, her legs curled up. He saw her holstered gun on the coffee table and a blanket nearby, and he covered her, smiling to himself. A sudden rush of a feeling he refused to label tugged at his heart. *Sweet dreams, Lieutenant,* he whispered, and saw himself out, locking the door behind him.

CHAPTER ELEVEN

Tiffany asked Susan and Rory to accompany her to Sunrise Hospital to visit her friends who were still being treated for various injuries, malnutrition, and mistreatment following the sting operation.

Kimi was one of the patients still in critical condition. The ER doctors had hydrated her and given her intravenous nutrition, adding anti-anxiety medication when she had a panic attack and hyperventilated.

Rory and Susan waited in the hallway for Tiffany to finish her visit.

"She looks a lot better than she did back in the club," Tiffany said, smiling. Then her expression turned serious again.

"There's one more person I need to see. Remember Candy, the black girl I was with when you first met me?"

Rory felt himself blushing, self-conscious in front of Lieutenant McAfree. "Yes, I remember."

"Well, she is also here in critical condition. Her room is a few doors down. Kimi said when Jameel found out I was gone, he turned on her. I need to go in and see her. Will you come with me?" Tiffany implored Susan.

"Why don't you go with her while I go visit some of the others?" Rory told Susan.

But Tiffany took his hand. "No, that's okay. I want you both to go with me."

Rory and Susan followed Tiffany cautiously into the hospital room where Candy lay resting, her eyes closed.

Her whole face was swollen and bruised, one eye sealed shut. Her hair had been shaved, and a large white bandage covered her head. One of her arms was in a cast, the other hooked up to various IV lines.

Tiffany and Susan slowly approached her while Rory stood back in a corner of the room.

"Candy?" It came out of Tiffany's mouth in almost a whisper. The young black woman opened her good eye, painfully sat up a fraction in the bed, and glared at her former club mate.

"Go!" The voice from the formerly beautiful stripper was hoarse, choked with pain and fury.

"Are you okay?" Tiffany took a step backward.

Venomous hatred emanated from Candy's face.

"No, I'm not okay, and it's all your fault. Just get out. All of you."

Tiffany's face crumpled. "Oh, Candy, I'm so sorry. You've got to know I wanted you to come with me that night, but I didn't have a choice. Rory here rescued me, and then we were almost killed but managed to escape."

Rory cringed when Tiffany motioned toward him.

"It doesn't matter." Candy spoke in a deadpan voice. "We're all going to die."

"No, the FBI and police are going to protect you," Susan interjected in a soft voice. "You won't have to go back."

"Who is this and why is she here?" Candy nearly spat out the words as she glanced diffidently at Susan then turned her cold gaze back to Tiffany.

"This is Lieutenant McAfree. She also risked her life to save us," Tiffany said.

"You're so dumb." Rory watched Tiffany's face register hurt shock at Candy's mean words to her former club mate. "You think just because Jameel and the Master are behind bars the rest won't come after us? None of us are safe. I wish I had died back there."

Just then a nurse walked in.

"I'm going to have to ask you all to leave now. I think Miss Candy here needs to rest." The nurse shooed them toward the door.

"I'm sorry," Tiffany said as they exited, but her words fell on deaf ears, and she was sobbing as soon as they were out in the hallway.

Rory and Carlos sat in chairs offstage. They had promised Tiffany they would attend when she had asked, but didn't feel comfortable sitting in the audience.

Rory looked out at the nearly two hundred women seated in the College of Southern Nevada auditorium. They ranged in age from fourteen to fifty and were of every color, race, nationality, and social status.

They were gathered to hear Tiffany speak.

At first depressed after all she had been through and then nearly suicidal with despair after visiting Candy, Tiffany was checked into Sunrise Hospital's psychiatric unit with Susan's help. The teen had worked hard each day with a counselor in an intensive inpatient program, and following two weeks of therapy, was released and ready to fulfill her community service time.

Her counselor had strongly recommended that she address some of the other girls who had gone through the same ordeal she had endured to share her story and hopefully save them from being trapped in the sex slave industry like she had been.

It was as if the hospital staff had worked a miracle. Tiffany went in a broken ragdoll; she came out as a whole new woman, ready to carry her message to anybody who would listen.

The FBI team and Sheriff's department had corralled almost all of the women who had come in during the sting operation to attend the presentation. Some had been prosecuted and sentenced to community service, and others were free of charges but wanted to help in return for the support they had been given. They were joined by dozens of college students who had signed up for the seminar after seeing fliers plastered across local campuses. There were even a few victims who had healed enough to be released from the hospital.

Tiffany took the podium onstage with confidence, looking nothing like the stripper Rory had met that night at the club, nor the frightened girl he had accompanied to the hospital. She was dressed in a navy pinstriped skirt and matching blazer with a white blouse, all business. Behind her sat Agent Glover, Lieutenant McAfree, and one of Sheriff Thomas's deputies who had worked on the raid. They had billed the event in promotional and marketing materials as a panel discussion on the local sex trade industry, and had titled the program "It's Just Not Worth It," featuring keynote speaker Tiffany, a former dancer at the now closed Wildcats.

"Hello, my name is Theresa Brindle." Snickers erupted from some of the women who knew her by her stage name.

They're not all here because they want to be, Rory realized. *Some probably want to go right back to the clubs and are just biding their time.*

"Ok, many of you know me as Tiffany, which was my stage name at Wildcats where I danced as a stripper." The audience settled down to listen.

"But that's not all I did, and that's what brings me here to speak to you today. I did far more than dance or strip. If I hadn't, if I had refused to do what I was told to do, no matter how degrading it was, I probably wouldn't be standing here today." Theresa's voice caught in a wave of emotion, and she wiped a tear. ". . . just like my friend Danielle, who didn't make it out alive.

"She was only sixteen with her whole life ahead of her. But when she didn't turn over the money the pimps at Wildcats expected, they kicked and beat her so bad that she died on a cold cement floor in a cage not even fit for a dog.

"Those of you who have been in the industry know what I'm talking about. Those of you who haven't, please trust me: you need to know what happens in these places so you will never walk in the door. Just like Danielle, if you do walk in, you may never walk out again. You see, they sell you on the idea that it's a glamorous job, and more than that, it's a high-paying job, dancing for the patrons. They tell you that all you have to do is look pretty, chat with the customers, take your turn doing a dance—you don't even have to know how to dance, just move around the pole a little. They tell you to take off layers of clothing during the dance, including your top toward the end, never your bottoms, and then you're done, and you collect anywhere between two and three hundred dollars a night, all for about three hours of work.

"I was working as a part-time waitress job in a diner making about three dollars an hour minimum wage plus tips and barely bringing home seventy-five bucks a night after a full eight hours of really hard, greasy, back-breaking work. And there were some real slimy guys that grabbed at me there. I was told the clientele at Wildcats would be high class since they paid big sums of money to get in, and that the staff didn't allow just anyone in since they wanted to maintain the club's sophisticated reputation. I figured it sounded like a huge step up from where I was.

"I needed the money to continue college. I was actually going here to CSN. I wanted to get a degree in sociology and become a counselor one day. I wanted to help people." Theresa lowered her head slightly, and a small smile played across her lips for a fleeting moment. "When I saw the ad online for Wildcats, I thought it wouldn't hurt to apply. I was too embarrassed to ask around campus to see if anyone else had worked there. Besides the money, they said they'd also provide free room and board if needed. I figured I didn't have anything to lose. I was living with my mom, who was a pill addict and bringing home boyfriends all the time, a few who tried to have their way with me, and I was handing over most of my paycheck for rent, so it looked like I wasn't going to have enough left for college if I stayed. I thought, why not live at Wildcats for free during the summer and save up enough not only for college but also for a place of my own.

"So I interviewed, got the job, and started that weekend. But it was nothing like they said it would be. The very first night I was given plenty of alcohol and the drug Ecstasy, did my dance, and then was shot up with heroin against my will and forced to have sex with a guy whose name I can't even remember." Theresa cleared her throat, the sound echoing throughout the silent auditorium.

"I was shy, and the alcohol and drugs made me feel numb to what I was doing. The second night was like the first, only instead of one guy, there were three. Every day after that I woke up bruised, ashamed, and addicted. I realized that my employer was taking more than half of my paychecks to pay for the drugs they had hooked me on.

"One night, when a customer was particularly rough and hit me in the face, almost breaking my nose and teeth, I swore I'd quit. That next morning I went in to tell Jameel, the manager. I'll never forget the look he gave me. His eyes were filled with loathing and cruelty and rage. He said, 'Tiffany, after all we've done for you, giving you a job, food, and a home, how could you even consider walking out on us? That would be ungrateful. I'll pretend I didn't hear this. You owe us far more than you know for all of the drugs you've been doing.' He took out a folder from a file cabinet, apparently some type of file on me, and read from it. 'It says here that you owe us fifteen hundred dollars for cocaine, heroin, barbiturates, and marijuana you've used over the past two months. I'd say that means that you're going to be working here to pay that off for a long time. And unless you stop doing drugs, I think you might as well decide you're going to work here until we don't need you anymore.'

"When I protested that they got me hooked, he stood—and he's a big guy, as some of you know—and said in this wicked voice that if I ever spoke about leaving again, I would be beaten, and I'd probably have to work the rest of my days as a cleaning woman in the club because I wouldn't look good enough to be around the customers after that."

Some of the college students in the audience visibly shuddered, murmuring among themselves.

Theresa took a deep breath, exhaled, and continued.

"I know it sounds too horrible to be true. Maybe you think I was too weak, or should have found a way out. Believe me, I blame myself every day for walking into the club in the first place. But I can't go back. I can only warn all of you."

A young woman raised her hand and shouted out a question. "So you expect us to believe that it's like that in all these clubs? Maybe you just had a bad experience. I mean, let's face it, unless you were born yesterday, strippers have been around forever, and a lot of them are making good money and even moving on to modeling and movies."

A deep, husky voice from the back of the auditorium spoke out.

"Things have changed." Everyone simultaneously turned to look back for the voice that had made the statement. Their eyes fell on the former stripper known as Candy, who was now standing. "This is what happened to me." She pointed to what used to be her right eye, now sealed shut. Rory had heard she had lost it after an unsuccessful surgery in the hospital. Then she pointed to a jagged pink scar that ran the length of her face, then to her arm, still in a sling. Some girls sitting nearby noticed a gaping hole where three of her front teeth used to be.

"Guess what? I played by their rules. I didn't ask to leave. But when Tiffany . . . I mean Theresa, escaped, they took it out on me.

They broke my arm, they punched out my eye, they took a knife to me—I have other scars you can't see. Maybe this industry didn't used to be so bad. But I'm living proof that it's a whole new ballgame out there now with these Mafia guys running the show, and it's evil.

"I tried to blame Theresa. But I know I only have myself to blame. And really, not even myself. Because they told me the same thing they told her. Of course, we can blame them all we want, but it won't change anything. They've got to be stopped. And I think we're the only ones who can stop them."

Rory watched as Tiffany beamed a smile at her former club mate, her eyes shining with pride and affection.

"Thank you, Connie." Tiffany stood at the podium beaming with pride, tears of gratitude in her eyes, and raised her hand in salute to her tall black friend in the back. "She's absolutely right. If we don't spread the word and stop other girls from going in those doors before it's too late, we're just as guilty as the guys who run the clubs. If we take away the strippers, there won't be any strip joints. If we take away the girls, there won't be any call girls or girls' shows. If we take away the prostitutes, there won't be prostitution. If we don't have any porn stars, there won't be any more pornography.

"That's why we're here today. Let's join together and spread the word. We've got volunteer sign-up sheets in the back. Do it for Connie . . . for Danielle . . . for us all."

CHAPTER TWELVE

- - - - - - - - - -

The 911 call came in at half past midnight.

A thirteen-year-old boy named Juan Ramirez had allegedly killed a neighborhood boy, bashing his skull in with a baseball bat, after smoking the latest local designer drug to hit the streets of Vegas known as Green Tobacco. The boy had reportedly been part of a small gang that had smoked the illegal synthetic drug, disguised as a legal herbal blend, and then turned on the victim, who happened to be black instead of Hispanic like they were, and thus considered "the enemy." When the police arrived on the scene, the other teens fled, managing to escape, but Juan had been caught, bat in hand, dripping blood.

When the police arrived, Juan looked at them, confused. He had been too high and dazed to think to escape, and even if he had tried, he was overweight and probably would have been too sluggish to run fast enough.

The victim was fifteen-year-old Nicholas "Nicky" Brown, the youngest son of a working-class single mom who lived on the outskirts of Las Vegas. He had been alone, playing basketball on a neighborhood court that night, and they had followed him home and attacked him in his front yard.

Neighbors later reported that they heard Nicky's mother wailing into the night for what seemed like hours, mourning her lost son.

The terrible tragedy would have made headlines or the nightly news in most other cities or towns, but not in Vegas, where gangs gathered every day on nearly every street corner, and kids were seen smoking Green Tobacco like cigarettes.

Synthetic drug blends had come and gone for years—bath salts, jewelry cleaners, herbal incense—with names such as "K-2" and "Blaze" and "Spice"—harmless household items until they were laced with a variant of THC, the compound found in marijuana, or synthetic hallucinogens. They were usually sold legally in convenience stores until most were banned as illegal once the FDA investigated them.

But this new synthetic drug Green Tobacco had cropped up specifically in Vegas and was being sold by members of gangs reportedly employed by the ISM. Police had discovered that this new "Green T" was being secretly manufactured right in Sin City itself, and that it was far more potent and powerful that its predecessors had ever been, providing higher highs and wicked lows.

Abuse of the drug often led to vomiting, seizures, hallucinations, high blood pressure, organ damage, loss of consciousness, and extreme acts of violence. Las Vegas hospitals were seeing an increasing number of emergency room visits due to drug overdoses and the brutal acts committed by users, mainly young people between the ages of twelve and twenty-nine.

Many users—and their victims—weren't surviving.

— — — — —

"So the sting was largely a success," Chief Steele said, standing in front of the men eating take-out pizza at their desks in the Condo. "The city has shut down seven of the ten strip clubs along with two major prostitution rings and a few X-rated girls' shows."

"Yeah, I heard the Foo Fighters are coming in concert to take the place of one," John Dade said, scratching his head. "I'm not sure who they are, but I think they're big."

"Big? Heck yeah they're big." Carlos affectionately smacked John on the shoulder. "Hey, can anybody get me tickets? I love the Foos."

"Gentlemen, I'm still talking." The chief shook his head, but he couldn't suppress a wry smile. "As most of you know, seven Mafia members who ran the strip clubs have been arrested so far. Unfortunately, many of the others escaped. Of the seven, only three have been arraigned and are awaiting trial. The others have crackerjack lawyers who got the charges dropped, claiming the raid was illegal."

Steele turned and faced a large screen behind him. The face of an Islamic terrorist wearing a black turban on his head filled the screen—a man in his forties with brown skin, a large hawk nose, a short black beard and mustache, and menacing black eyes.

"For those still unfamiliar, this is the infamous Jameel who was arrested but is one of the leaders with a good attorney. These guys have already bought enough judges in town to purchase their freedom. So Jameel was released and has managed to slip back underground.

"None of the guys arrested have given up any information during their interrogation about the Mafia, much less anyone called the Master. So while Operation No Dice has scored a win as far as cleaning up some of the prostitution and sex trade business, we still haven't made much progress in rooting out the real Mafia leaders, who have just slithered back into their snake pit.

"That's why we're having this little party today. We've got to come up with a new plan."

One of the police officers working the phones shouted out, "Chief, we may have a lead."

Rory, Carlos, and John hurried down to the Sheriff's department to listen in on the interrogation of young Juan.

They were instructed to glean any tidbit of information that might lead them to the source of the drugs that Juan and his gang had acquired. They were hoping the kingpins behind the drug cartel were also ISM members who might lead them closer to finding the nuclear weapon.

Rory stood with the others behind the two-way mirror, realizing he had sat in the same room when he had first come to Las Vegas, wanted for the same alleged terrorist plot he was now helping to investigate.

Life is full of irony, Rory thought, watching as the sheriff's deputy paced menacingly around the teenager, diving in, raising his voice, beating his fist on the table, all an act of intimidation. *Or more accurately, life is full of God's ironic justice.*

The deputy didn't have to work too long or hard at using intimidation tactics. With no lawyer there to guide him, Juan broke down in terrified tears.

Juan had amazingly waived his right to an attorney on the shocking advice of his mother, Isabel Ramirez, who sat with him quietly through the police interrogation.

The thirty-five-year-old Isabel, originally from Puerto Rico, had moved to America with her family when she was ten. A Christian who believed in the Old Testament's teachings that everyone must pay for their sins, she told the police that her son must face up to what he had done, no matter the consequences.

She was called in to sit with Juan in lieu of an attorney. "I don't r-re-remember," the kid blubbered in response to the deputy's questions, tears streaming down his chubby pink cheeks.

The deputy was pacing across the table from where the mother and son sat, and suddenly pulled a bat, streaked with dark blood stains, from behind his back. "You don't remember holding this in your hands and swinging it against the head of that black boy, Nicky Brown, like your gang leader told you to do, to teach him a lesson?"

"N-n-no!" Juan cried. "I swear!"

The deputy laid the bat down hard on the metal table with a crack, making the mother and son jump in their seats. Isabel wrapped her arm around her son protectively, glaring at the deputy, who then produced a plastic bag filled with a used hash pipe and bits of green tobacco leaves.

"How about this? Do you remember smoking this?" The deputy yelled the question.

Rory shuddered involuntarily, feeling pity for the boy.

No words came this time. Juan simply sobbed quietly, nodding his head. Isabel held her son in her arms, rocking him, tears streaming down her cheeks.

The deputy sat across the table from Juan. His tone softened.

"What do you remember, Juan? Tell me from the beginning."

The young teen wiped his tears with his pudgy hands and sniffed, looking to his mom before he started. Isabel nodded, encouraging him to speak. "I was always picked on at school for being fat," the boy stammered, embarrassed. "One day this group of older boys defended me. I was being shoved around, and they got between me and these bullies and punched them out. Then they told me I would never have to put up with that stuff anymore because they were going to be my new friends.

"We had a secret clubhouse, and it was a little scary but mostly really cool. They usually just sat around talking about other clubs who were our enemies, planning how they were going to stomp them out. They asked me and the other younger kids if we wanted to make some money helping them sell tobacco. They said it was legal, and we could make twenty or thirty bucks a night. I knew my mom could really use the money." Juan glanced sheepishly at this mother, who wiped away a stray tear that ran down her face. "So I said sure, as long as it wasn't wrong and I wouldn't get in trouble.

"The night I was arrested, we were just hanging out on the basketball court. Our leader told us young kids that in order to stay in the club, we had to do a special induction thing and smoke some of the tobacco we were selling. That way we would know what we were selling and could talk to our customers about how good it was. I didn't want to, but they said they would kick me out if I didn't." Juan hung his head, ashamed. "I just didn't want to go back to being bullied anymore.

"I remember smoking that nasty stuff and feeling a little sick. And the next thing I know, I feel a shove and see this black kid's face in front of mine, and then it changed into a black rat's face with big sharp teeth, and it was going to bite me . . . and all the kids were screaming, 'kill him, kill him, kill him!' And then I blanked out I guess." Juan started sobbing again. "I never meant to hurt anybody, mister. You've gotta believe me!"

"I do believe you, Juan," the deputy replied gently. "And thank you, Mrs. Ramirez, for your help in this matter. I will let everyone know how you both helped us. But Juan, we're going to need as many names of the gang members as you know." The deputy produced a notepad and pen and pushed it across to Juan.

Isabel nodded, encouraging her son to comply.

Juan was then booked and sent to spend the rest of the night in the police station's holding cell to await his arraignment as an adult the next morning in Clark County District Court on first degree murder charges; under Nevada law, anyone charged with murder, regardless of age, was tried as an adult.

The gospel singer's voice rang out, resonating on the heat wave that sweltered around the funeral crowd gathered at the burial site: "Amazing Grace, how sweet the sound that saved a wretch like me. I once was lost but now am found, was blind but now I see..."

Nicky Brown's mother Claudette shook with sobs in her modest black dress bought on sale at the local Walmart. Her oldest son, Jimmy, barely eighteen years old, held one arm around his mother's frail shoulders and another around his sister Renee.

The local Baptist minister read from the Bible and said a few words of comfort to the grieving family, friends, and fellow parishioners, who numbered nearly two hundred strong.

Claudette came from a religious family of ten and was active in her church, and everyone had turned out to support her and her family.

No one saw Isabel Ramirez walk slowly up to the awning where the Brown family sat. Everyone was focused on listening to the singer belt out the hymn's final words.

When the music ended, the lone Hispanic woman in the largely African American crowd knelt down beside Claudette's chair, placed a hand in her gloved one, looked up into her eyes, and whispered, "I'm so sorry."

Jimmy, who was seated next to his mother, was the first to react to Isabel Ramirez's intrusion. "Wait a minute, how dare you show up here?" Jimmy stood and towered over the woman. Her son had viciously killed Jimmy's brother in cold blood. He felt no compassion for her apology.

But Claudette grabbed her son's forearm, squeezing it hard, stopping him with a silent stare as only a mother can do.

Claudette then turned to face Isabel who remained kneeling, hand in gloved hand, head bent in humble, contrite sorrow, and lifted the face of the woman whose son had murdered her own to gaze into her eyes. And without a word, the two single mothers who had both lost so much embraced.

The only sound was a mockingbird singing through the thick summer air.

While the killing didn't make the news, Nicky Brown's funeral did. Someone had captured the emotional moment in which the two moms embraced, and it went viral.

Rory and his team had been there at the funeral, had seen the video, and had brainstormed that night until they came up with a way to use the case to help their cause.

They planned to start a task force named VAYA con Dios (VAYA standing for Vegas Allied Youth Association). The mission of the adults involved would be to speak out against drugs and gang violence and to work toward providing a club organization alternative for their kids.

According to the plan, the kids could take turns meeting in each other's homes, in church halls and basements, or even outside in parks and fields. They would keep their meetings non-denominational but would open and close with a prayer then break into smaller groups according to their various interests. There was already talk among the kids about forming a punk rock band, an arts and crafts club, a literary arts magazine, an auto mechanics shop, and starting a variety of support groups and twelve-step recovery meetings like Narcotics Anonymous or Alcoholics Anonymous for those with addictions.

This would give the kids something to do, people to hang out with, a place to go, and someplace to belong besides the violent street gangs.

Rory and Carlos agreed to head up the new task force to fight drug abuse and gang warfare among youths, and they asked both Isabel Ramirez and Claudette Brown to speak out like Theresa Brindle had done against prostitution and sex trafficking.

"All it takes is one or two voices to make a difference," Rory had told the two moms during their first meeting at the Condo a few days following the funeral service.

"But the kids won't listen to moms," Claudette Brown argued.

Isabel agreed. "They only listen to each other, and unfortunately, the bad voices are the loudest and most often heard."

"Which is why we've also recruited some kids." Carlos walked over to the door of the conference room and opened it.

Jimmy and Renee Brown stood there, holding hands with Juan's four siblings; they entered the room, grinning at their moms, who looked at them in astonishment. The kids took their moms' hands and led them out of the conference room and out the front door of the Condo.

"We've got a surprise for you," Rory told Claudette and Isabel.

Jimmy opened the door to an amazing sight. Claudette's and Isabel's mouths hung open, their eyes filling with tears as they stood before a never-ending field of kids and young adults of all ages, standing in the night holding candles, forming a sea of light across the front lawn and out into the street.

"Oh, my Lord." Claudette clutched her heart and turned to Isabel, who was equally moved, and the two hugged, weeping tears of joy.

Juan and Nicky's siblings had seen their moms forgive and unite, despite their pain and suffering. Jimmy Brown, being the oldest of the six, had extended the invitation to his sister and the Ramirez children to work together to do something to stop more kids from undergoing Nicky and Juan's fates.

They spread the word among their friends on social media and in their schools, and pretty soon a dozen kids banded together and then fifty, and then more.

Some of the kids had asked their church leaders to join them that evening in what came together as a candlelight prayer vigil for

Nicky Brown and Juan Ramirez. A local Muslim imam, a Catholic priest, a Jewish rabbi and several Protestant ministers led the group in prayers interspersed with singing from a number of talented youth in the crowd.

When everyone was invited to clasp hands, Rory felt a surge of emotions: sympathy for the people of this god-forsaken city, respect for the young people gathered there that night, and profound sadness that he had grown so distant from his own children. Following the service, as he reluctantly let go of Susan's hand, he also felt love and desire swell within him for the policewoman by his side.

The morning following the candlelight vigil, Rory got a call from an anonymous informant.

"Juan Ramirez didn't kill Nicky Brown." The man spoke English with a slight Middle Eastern accent. Rory immediately motioned to John Dade sitting across from him to start a trace on the call.

"And who is this?" Rory asked.

"That's not important. Juan Ramirez didn't kill Nicky Brown. But I know who did."

Rory whipped out a notepad. The anonymous source stated the name of the murderer was Ali Jabar. "I know for a fact that Ali dealt the fatal blow to Nicky's head and then placed the bloody weapon in Juan's hands because the boy was in a drug-induced stupor." Rory quickly recalled that during Juan's interrogation, he had written Ali's name as a member of the underground Mafia. Juan didn't know last names, but there was only one Ali.

"How do you know this, and can you give me more information about the suspect?" Rory saw John and Carlos in his peripheral vision working to trace the call on a nearby monitor, and did his best to keep the caller on the phone as long as possible.

"Ali is fourteen, half black, half Muslim, and he's working with the ISM. That's all of the information I can give you."

"Do you know anything more . . . the names of any ISM leaders he's working with?"

"Goodbye, Mr. Justice." The call ended, just as the location of the caller was about to come up on the screen.

"Agh, we were so close!" John pounded his fist on the desk and removed his headphones.

Carlos instructed the FBI's top technical agent, who had been monitoring and mapping the call on a large computer screen, to get as much data as possible from the recorded call.

Rory held his head in his hands, his thoughts spinning. *This guy called me, and he knew my name. Why me?*

But there wasn't time to think.

Within forty-eight hours, a full-blown police investigation was underway, and Ali Jabar was arrested along with three other boys suspected of aiding and abetting in the killing. The four youths were brought into the Las Vegas Police Department for questioning.

Ali Jabar and two others didn't say a word as they were interrogated, either out of loyalty to or fear of their Islamic terrorist leaders, or maybe both.

But one of the four youths, an eleven-year-old black boy who was a newer member of the gang and wasn't a Muslim nor tied to the ISM, broke down in tears and gave them several names of adults he had heard mentioned during gang meetings, as well as the location of the place where they went to get their drugs to sell.

Armed with new information, the Operation No Dice team planned another sting operation, this time to hit the Mafia where it really hurt—to take down their drug manufacturing facility—and to try once again to find the kingpins behind the entire operation.

They discovered the plant had been right under their noses all along; it was a few blocks down Schuster Street in another old, abandoned warehouse.

With the help of SWAT teams, they raided the warehouse and found nearly one hundred kilos of cocaine, several bags of heroin, and seven hundred kilos of manufactured Green Tobacco, along with cutting tools, drug paraphernalia, and several tons of various raw products that went into making bath salts, incense, and other drug-infused products that had been shipped from Mexico.

The US Drug Enforcement Administration estimated the confiscated drugs had a net value of approximately five hundred million dollars, money that would have eventually gone toward Islamic State terrorism.

Six men of Middle Eastern descent, suspected of being members of the ISM, were arrested. A few were considered leaders in the terrorist organization, but the reported Master was still at large.

It was Susan McAfree's idea to have the emptied warehouse deeded over to VAYA con Dios for use as a new clubhouse for the already rapidly growing kids' organization.

The hot new boy band, Break Out, was scheduled to perform that weekend, and after another OND brainstorming session, Susan called the band's promotional company and asked if the boys could make the concert a fundraiser for the new VAYA clubhouse, to which they eagerly agreed.

Susan received complimentary tickets and asked Rory if he would like to go with her.

"Seriously, a boy band?" Rory teased.

"Okay, I'll ask someone else," Susan retorted.

"All right, I'll go," Rory said, rolling his eyes, secretly thinking *I would go with her if it was Sesame Street Live.*

Rory actually enjoyed the concert, although he didn't like the music. Just seeing Susan dance, sing, and smile made it all worthwhile.

They sat in the third row in the VIP section of the Planet Hollywood resort casino where the concert was held. A few rows had been reserved for all of the police units that had helped in the drug bust together with all of the VAYA volunteers and kids.

At one point during a brief intermission between acts, Claudette Brown and her son Jimmy took the stage to address the crowd, urging kids to stay free from drugs and out of the gangs that sold them. When Isabel Ramirez and her oldest daughter Samantha took the stage with them, and they all held up their clasped hands in a sign of unity, the crowd erupted in deafening cheers.

After the concert, Susan told Rory she had to stop by the Condo to pick up some mail she had left in her desk.

It was dark outside of the warehouse building, the lone streetlight apparently busted by a rock some kid had thrown.

Susan fumbled through her purse for her key-pass card. "It was a lovely night," she said, still searching, and then she finally found the card. When she looked up, her brown eyes locked with Rory's.

Unable to control his emotions, Rory put his hand at the nape of her curly red hair, drew her face to his, and kissed her with tenderness and then abandon as she returned his passion.

A passing car made them aware of their surroundings again, and they pulled apart, laughing nervously.

When they entered the building, Rory followed Susan to her desk and stood waiting in front of it, idly fingering some neatly arranged pencils in a pencil holder, his mind racing, his ears still ringing from the music, adrenaline coursing through his veins from kissing Susan.

He realized with mixed feelings of fear and excitement that he was quite possibly falling in love with this spunky redheaded cop.

But I can't get involved, he reasoned. *I won't let myself, not permanently, anyway. She's my co-worker, and I'm just not the relationship type of guy anymore.*

Susan was hunched over her file drawer, head bent. Finding the folder that contained her bills, she lifted her head, and Rory watched her face freeze and her eyes open wide.

He couldn't see the figure on one of the surveillance camera screens behind him.

Usually the screen simply showed the empty street and sidewalk outside the front entrance. Susan pointed to it, her eyes fixated, and Rory turned around to see a shadowy figure standing just outside the warehouse front door.

Susan hurried over to the computer controls and zoomed the camera lens closer. The screen showed a dark-skinned man dressed in black pants and a black windbreaker with a hood pulled over his head, shielding half his face. His hands were thrust in his pockets, and he was pacing back and forth. He seemed agitated.

Then they heard the front door buzzer ring, the sound so startling and shrill that it made them jump.

CHAPTER THIRTEEN

uick, grab your gun and let's see what he wants." Susan clutched her gun from its holster and led the way to the front door.

"Are you crazy?" Rory hissed, frozen with fear. "What if there are more of them out there?"

"I think we'd have seen them on the other cameras. Besides, he doesn't look armed. Let's call for backup and let him in." Susan picked up her cell phone and called Rodney Steele, informing him of the situation.

She hung up and turned to Rory, who still stood paralyzed, although now with his gun in his hand. He had slowly drawn it out of its holster while Susan was talking, her back turned to him. It felt like it weighed a hundred pounds and Rory fought to keep the hand that held it from shaking uncontrollably. *C'mon man, get a grip, you're trained for this*, he scolded himself internally, taking slow, deep breaths, trying to slow his wildly beating heart.

"The chief said to be very careful; he'll be here in fifteen minutes with Mark Glover, and he'll radio a patrol car to circle the area. He doesn't want too much attention drawn to the Condo, but he does want us to be safe."

"That's a comfort," Rory said sarcastically.

They heard the doorbell loudly ring again.

Susan frowned. "Okay, I can go let him in myself if you'd like."

That did it. Rory felt her words sting, and yet they empowered and emboldened him to act.

"I'm right behind ya." Rory held his gun pointed forward at arm's length, all cop-like, and followed a step behind her. He saw Susan's mouth turn up in a slight smile. Rory wondered if it was a look of amusement at his expense or pride that he was doing his job correctly. She nodded, so he hoped it was the latter.

Taking advantage of the element of surprise, Susan flung the front door open and pointed her gun straight at the man's chest, only a few inches away.

Rory fell right in line and pointed his gun at the man's head. *Oh my God, I am holding a gun to someone's head,* his mind screamed.

The man's dark brown eyes grew wide with surprise and terror. He threw his arms up in a gesture of surrender. Rory didn't know who was more afraid.

Susan pulled the intruder by the jacket through the heavy metal door into the Condo, and Rory slammed it shut.

"Hands behind your back!" Susan shouted, taking charge, her gun still pointed at the man's chest.

The man obeyed, slowly putting his hands behind his back and turning around so that Susan could handcuff him while Rory kept his gun trained on him, holding it as steadily as he could.

Susan kept her gun on him and ordered him to kneel down on the cement floor, telling Rory to keep an eye on the monitors. "We need to make sure this guy came alone, and to know when our back-up arrives."

She's trying to shake him up with that last announcement, Rory realized.

Then she patted him down and, finding no weapons on him, pulled the windbreaker hood back off his head, revealing the man's face. He was Middle Eastern, with brown skin, dark eyes, black hair, and a short, trimmed black beard.

"Are you alone?" she asked sternly.

"Yes." He spoke softly, never taking his eyes from hers.

"What is your name?"

"Rafik Jabar."

Jabar. Rory immediately recalled that was Ali's last name, the kid who was behind bars for shooting Nicky Brown.

Susan remembered too. "Any relation to Ali Jabar?"

"He's my son." For the first time, the man looked down at the floor, emotion creeping into his voice. Suddenly, Rory recalled the voice on the phone just days ago. This was his anonymous caller, here, in person. And his heart started banging again, so hard he thought he could hear it. His eyes left the monitors and he stared at the man in shock. *This could be one of the Islamic State terrorists right here in their midst!* Rory was still holding his gun pointed and suddenly his arm started to quiver out of a combination of fatigue and fear.

"Rory!" Susan yelled his name, snapping him out of his panic. "Is this the same guy you talked to on the phone? Get in here and question him." She kept her gun pointed at Jabar, her eyes never leaving the suspect.

Rory looked uncertainly at Susan for a second.

"You can drop your weapon," she said softly, encouraging him with her voice, her eyes still trained intently on Jabar. "I've got him."

Rory nodded, his whole body feeling relief. He forced himself to refocus. "What are you doing here? How did you find us?" Rory asked Jabar, his voice steady and his words brave despite the pounding in his heart.

"I came to give you information that might help you find the men responsible for all of these crimes . . . and to find the nuclear bomb you seek."

So it really was true. Rory had been having doubts that a nuclear weapon even existed as each day ticked by with no new evidence of any plans. They had made a lot of progress cleaning up the Mafia crime in Sin City, but they hadn't uncovered a shred of evidence about a nuclear weapon. Rory had actually begun to think that the bomb was just a hoax, that his dad had probably written the letter in a state of dementia brought on by his disease and decline.

Rory felt a twinge of relief course through him. Maybe now he wouldn't have to hold his breath all the time wondering if his father made this whole thing up and worrying how he would get over the embarrassment and shame if he was wrong about the bomb.

And then he felt a stab of guilt that his thoughts had meandered this way.

Susan's firm voice broke his reverie.

"Why should we believe you?" she challenged the man kneeling before her.

"Because I have nothing more to lose." Rafik Jabar's voice cracked and he fell forward, sobbing.

Susan looked at Rory, a flicker of compassion in her eyes.

She slowly lowered her gun and motioned for Rory to pull a chair over to Jabar. "Why don't you have a seat, Mr. Jabar?" he said, surprising himself with the kindness in his tone. *This guy could still be an Islamic terrorist,* he reminded himself. Rory cleared his throat and gruffly added, "We'll keep the cuffs on, but you can at least get up off the floor while we question you."

Susan and Rory helped him into the chair and sat facing their temporary hostage, guns in hand but lying on their laps. They sat on either side of him in a triangle, about three feet apart from one another.

"So, Mr. Jabar, why don't you answer my partner's questions," Susan said firmly. "How did you find us?"

Rafik Jabar sat up straight, his cheeks damp, his eyes now fervently bright. "I've been following you since the night Ali was arrested for murder. I tracked you from the concert here tonight."

"So you're the same man that called me and told me Ali and the others were involved in the murder of Juan Ramirez?" Rory asked, stunned.

"Yes."

"But . . . why would you give up your own son?"

"Even though I despise what he's doing, I love my son and I want him to be safe. Believe me, he is more protected behind prison bars than he is working for the ISM. And he needs to be punished for his crime."

"Why did you call *me*? How did you know my name?"

"I asked for someone on the team working on the Juan Ramirez case. I just so happened to get you, Mr. Justice. And using a little due diligence, I followed you after that, which led me to you here and now."

"What more do you know about the Islamic State Mafia?" Susan interjected, knowing they only had a few minutes before chaos ensued with the arrival of the police and FBI agents.

"I know they're running this city and ruining it," Jabar answered solemnly. "They recruited my son to help them sell drugs and start a gang, and . . . then he ended up killing that boy." His eyes filled with tears. "Maybe if my wife . . . his mother . . . had lived, none of this would have happened. I had to work to put food on the table as a single parent. I didn't have a lot of time to spend with the kids, and I guess Ali got in with the wrong crowd. Once I found out what he was involved in, I tried many times to stop him from going out on the streets, but he said he was one of them, the Islamic State. He said I couldn't stop him, and if I didn't watch out, I would end up dead too. That's when I knew I could do nothing to save him, and I had to do the right thing and help whoever was trying to stop them . . . and that brought me to you.

"These men are monsters . . . they're evil," Jabar whispered. "My son told me he actually saw the plans for a nuclear weapon they're building to blow up Las Vegas."

"Where are the plans?" Susan asked.

Just then, the front door burst open, and Chief Steele and Agent Glover stormed in wielding guns.

— — — — — —

Once Susan and Rory apprised the two FBI agents of the situation, they all moved to a conference room in the back of the warehouse. Mark Glover called off the police who had patrolled the streets around the building to make sure no one else was lurking there.

Rafik Jabar told them what he knew: his son had told him he was part of a core militant ISM gang that had recently started gathering in a small conference room in the casino above where the nuclear bomb was being built. They were being addressed by the Master, and were actually reviewing drawings of the nuclear weapon.

"But Ali said he didn't know which casino he was standing in," Rafik said. "The kids were blindfolded going in so they couldn't tell anyone where they were, just in case they had any rats or moles in the group. Ali described seeing a bunch of metal parts and wires and large rolled up paper sheets with diagrams and drawings."

"Now why would the Master tell the plans to a bunch of kids?" Glover cynically wondered out loud.

"Ali told me the Master was talking to his whole troop at the time. There were dozens of soldiers ranging in age from thirteen to fifty-something. My son was proud that he was one of the chosen selected to carry out the plan of Allah, as he put it. It makes me sick." Rafik Jabar shook his head. "This is not the plan of the Allah of our Muslim religion. I'm sure my son was brainwashed, as many of our boys are these days."

"Maybe we need to bring your son in for more questioning, but use, shall we say, tougher methods," Chief Steele tersely suggested, watching Rafik's face to see how he reacted. The air in the room was thick with doubt over whether this was all a ploy, and the elder Jabar was one of the Mafia baiting them somehow.

"That would be a good idea, except I believe he would rather die before he utters even one word to you," Rafik said. "You would be wasting your time. Ali is better off in prison now."

"You told Mr. Justice and Lieutenant McAfree you have kids. Do you have any other sons involved?" Agent Glover asked.

"I have another son and a daughter. My oldest son Ahmad graduated from high school and went to work for some computer company. He moved away after my wife died a little over a year ago, and I haven't heard from him since. He was very close to his mother and became angry at me over her death, as if I had something to do with it. My wife died of a heart attack, and I think Ahmad thought I caused her stress, but that's not true, we loved each other very much. I just think he had to blame it on someone."

"So you're not sure if he's involved in any of this?" Glover asked.

"I honestly don't know," Rafik answered.

"Well, we'll find out. Tell us about your daughter."

"Amber is eighteen and a freshman at DeVry University. She attended that rally you held at the college featuring the girl named Theresa. She came home and said, 'Dad, that could have been me.' She wants to help fight the ISM, and she is heartbroken about what they've done to her brother Ali, turning him into a thug and a murderer. We both want the Master and his troops to be eradicated, even if it means killing every last one of them . . . including Ali, if Allah wills it." Rafik sighed.

Chief Steele called together an operation meeting early the next morning.

He didn't say what the agenda would be, but Rory figured it was important.

Feeling exhausted from the night before, having only gotten a few hours of sleep if that, Rory was the last to arrive at the Condo. He felt everyone's eyes on him as he entered the conference room where the team was seated. He avoided Susan's gaze and took his seat.

"Glad you could make it, Mr. Justice." Chief Steele's tone held a tinge of sarcasm. "Everyone, thank you for your service to date, but as they say in show business, the best—or as may be the case here—the worst is yet to come."

The agents and officers gathered around the table were silent as the chief paced the front of the room, his deep voice resonating with severity. "As you all know, we've had some success at rooting out some of the Mafia members we suspect are behind the various criminal activities here in this city. But the leaders are still at large, and we received word from FBI headquarters that they are directly connected to the Islamic State jihad and terrorist factions in the Middle East.

"The FBI director has now informed Kathleen Tower of our mission and of the potential nuclear threat the Mafia in Vegas has posed as discussed in Howard Justice's letter to John Dade."

Rory and John shot a glance at each other across the conference table.

"I need to remind you all that this threat has been verified as a plausible one based on the interrogation last night of Rafik Jabar, father of Ali Jabar who is incarcerated for the gang-related murder of Juan Ramirez. To recap, Rafik Jabar has confessed that his son is a member of the Islamic State Mafia and an eyewitness to the plans of the ISM to build an underground nuclear bomb. Mr. Jabar and the rest of his family are in protective custody, and he and his daughter are standing by ready to help us as needed.

"Our mission has now been classified as top secret by the president and FBI director. However, our top men in DC have been using our best satellite surveillance tools and espionage tactics and still haven't turned up a thing—which puts the ball in our court.

"President Tower has ordered that our investigation stay localized and confidential so as not to alert the American people and cause a nationwide panic. She has asked our operation to continue to head this up and to do everything it takes to find this alleged nuclear weapon by the early morning hours of D-day, July sixth, just ten days away."

There was no explanation as to how the deadline had been imposed other than that the date had come from "reliable sources," and as usual, no one bothered questioning the formidable FBI chief.

But Rory knew. He looked down at his hands folded in his lap, knowing he was the one responsible for forecasting the bomb detonation date. He shuddered when he remembered his dad's prediction in his dream. A small part of him hoped his dad was right about the facts . . . and a bigger part of him now prayed he was wrong.

"I will need the following members of OND to accompany me this afternoon on a scheduled visit to meet with Las Vegas Mayor Stanley Cooper." Steele kept his gaze forward like a Marine drill sergeant as he rattled off names one by one. "Sheriff Thomas,

Agent Glover, John Dade, and Rory Justice. The rest of you, man the phones, satellite screens, and computer monitors for incoming information. We'll report back here following our meeting to reconvene and plan further."

Susan McAfree raised her hand.

"Do you have a question, Lieutenant?"

Rory snuck a glance in Susan's direction. He knew she was seated diagonally down the table from him, although he hadn't looked her way prior to this moment. She looked totally unintimidated by Chief Steele's gruff reply, and Rory felt a sudden surge of pride for her.

"Yes, Chief, I was wondering if you could please inform the rest of us as to what the meeting with the mayor actually entails."

Rodney Steele paused and stared at Susan, his eyes clouded, as if he was looking through her, apparently contemplating how to answer her.

After a long moment, he finally spoke again. "Yes, Lieutenant, I wasn't going to inform you all so as to endanger as few of us as possible with the knowledge of the plan, but since you have all been so loyal and hard-working, I owe you an answer. The plan is to ask Las Vegas Mayor Stanley Cooper to shut down the casinos in the city temporarily so we can employ an all-out investigation to find the alleged nuclear weapon." Chief Steele waited for the murmur of surprise to die down. "We will have the entire FBI— as many agents and investigators as required—at our disposal when the plan is put into action. And trust me, at that time, I will need every one of you to participate."

Perhaps it's the red hair, Rory guessed, smiling to himself. *Or maybe being the only female gives her an extra boldness.* While the rest of the group murmured and shook their heads in disbelief, Susan was unafraid to voice her concern.

"Chief, pardon my frankness, but what if Mayor Cooper doesn't want to cooperate? What if, as we've been led to believe, he's in the pockets of the Mafia?"

"Then we'll move on to Plan B."

"Which is . . . ?"

She's got a lot of nerve, that one, Rory thought, mustering a cough so he could hide his grin with his hand.

"We don't have one yet. But you, Lieutenant, can start thinking of one."

Mayor Cooper stood from behind his large oak desk to greet the OND entourage. "Come in, gentlemen, welcome to my humble office."

Rory glanced around at the large, glass-ensconced office on the top floor of the towering state-of-the art building overlooking the city, and thought it looked anything but humble.

The mayor's office was in Las Vegas City Hall, the mammoth solar-powered futuristic building downtown on Main Street that had been a subject of controversy when it was built years ago for one hundred and eighty-five million dollars in the height of the last recession.

Even then, before it had recently declared bankruptcy, the city had the highest foreclosure and unemployment rates in the country, with over a third of the homes in foreclosure, and was currently ninety billion dollars in debt.

Rory read that the building had arisen from the pockmarked, poverty-stricken suburbs around it, with its glass façade and solar "trees" and LED display that lit it up at night so it could fit in nicely with the rest of the glittering architecture on the Strip a few miles away. Like the Israelites and the pyramids in Egypt, residents struggling to keep their modest homes and make a meager living witnessed the construction, or in many cases, labored to build the building they called the "Taj Mahal" to house a dwindling government staff that, by the time they moved in, only filled a fifth of the facility.

A brief synopsis of City Hall had been part of the dossier Rory had studied on Las Vegas and its history, government, and prominent players upon taking the job with OND.

But, just like travel agency brochures touting tourist spots, the papers did not come close to describing Las Vegas, City Hall, or Mayor Cooper.

Rory had never been inside the government building until today, and marveled as their tour guide met them at the entrance, told them how the "solar trees" out front helped save energy, took them past the outdoor concert plaza through the lobby with its marble floors and granite counters, and showed off the fitness center and media room with its scores of televisions and computer stations.

It was as if the city was putting on a brave face pretending nothing had changed from the golden days, when nothing was further from the truth.

And the mayor is like the Wizard of Oz, informing us to pay no attention to what's behind the curtain, Rory realized.

Stanley Cooper flashed a perfect white smile that gleamed in his evenly tanned face as he warmly greeted each of the five men who had come for the meeting. He politely tapped his finger on his intercom and, his smile unchanging, asked his secretary to hold his calls.

Chief Steele briefly introduced each of them. Mayor Cooper elegantly waved his hand, bidding them to take a seat on the plush leather sofas and chairs across from his desk.

"So, Mr. Steele, to what do I owe the honor of this visit? My secretary said it was urgent but didn't give me much more information than that. As you are probably aware, I am an extremely busy man and wouldn't usually, um, entertain visitors without a good explanation as to what they wanted, but since you're with the FBI, I am obviously making an exception."

Rory sat at the far right. In less than a minute, he had decided Stanley Cooper was a fake, pompous, greedy politician, and he didn't like him or trust him. If it had been up to him, they would have turned around and walked out, and come up with a Plan B.

But Rodney Steele, tough as his name, was in charge and remained undeterred by the mayor's grandiosity. As the FBI chief briefly recounted the incidents leading up to the formation of Operation No Dice, Mayor Cooper warily looked at each of the players in the story seated before him.

When Steele finished giving the details of their mission, he paused to let the mayor digest it all.

The four of them waited in awkward silence.

"So you expect me to believe that these club owners and casino operators, who just happen to be Muslims, have formed some kind of new Mafia that is running our city?" Stanley Cooper frowned, folding his arms across the front of his expensive suit. The plastic smile returned, but his tone was icy with contempt. "Fellas, come on. Aren't we being a little bigoted? I know some Islamic radicals have caused a bit of trouble in our country in the past, but I believe that's all been handled. Don't you think I would have found out about an organized mob and a nuclear *bomb* in my city by now and done something about it?"

Chief Steele ignored his phony umbrage. "Mayor, with all due respect, the evidence is too strong to refute, and the troubles being caused are stacking up to be worse than ever for our fair city. And now . . . ." Steele turned to Ned Thomas, who handed him a sealed envelope, which he in turn held out across the desk to the mayor, who took it with a skeptical stare. "We need you to read the letter that was mailed to former Sheriff Dade from Mr. Justice and was actually received from Sheriff Thomas."

The sheriff's face burned red under the mayor's scornful stare.

Cooper's wondering why his own man didn't tell him about it, Rory guessed, feeling a new level of respect for Ned Thomas, who hadn't betrayed their operation like Rory had originally suspected he might.

The five OND men sat silently as the mayor put on designer reading glasses and perused the letter. When he was finished, he took off his glasses, rubbed his eyes then looked at them. He wasn't smiling anymore, and his bronzed skin seemed to turn a wan, muddy shade.

"So let's say it's true that this so-called Islamic Mafia exists in Las Vegas," he said slowly. "And let's, for a moment, say we believe this letter is valid too, although I've got to tell you, I'm not sure I believe it yet."

"Oh, Mr. Mayor, you can believe it," Chief Steele interjected. "Our men in DC have verified its veracity. Even the president has seen it and believes in its potential threat."

The mayor's mouth dropped open in shock. "The president . . . of the United States, as in Kathleen Tower?"

"Yes."

"And why am I just being informed of this now?" the mayor asked angrily, looking from Chief Steele to Sheriff Thomas, who looked down, averting his eyes.

"If you want to know the truth, Mayor Cooper, we weren't sure who knew about the Mafia and who didn't, or who might even be . . . working with them."

The mayor jumped from his chair, rising to his full, six-foot-four height, a lock of hair falling out of place across his face, which was red with rage. "Look here, if you're implying…"

"We're not implying anything, Mayor," the FBI chief interjected. "We are simply stating the facts. We were instructed from the top to keep our operation covert. Your own men had no choice but to keep our mission top secret. And we need to instruct you, by orders of the President, to do the same."

Rory heard Ned Thomas sigh with relief.

"So why are you involving me now?"

"We need your help."

The mayor, visibly trying to maintain a modicum of dignity, settled back down into his expensive leather chair to listen, albeit reluctantly.

Chief Steele turned to Mark Glover.

"According to our information, we believe the nuclear weapon is set to detonate on July sixth," Glover stated.

The mayor's eyes grew large with alarm. "That's only ten days away."

"Exactly. While we've been investigating and rooting out some of the Mafia members, and have even incarcerated several, none of them will confess to their knowledge of the weapon. The president wants our local team, led by these men," Mark gestured toward Rodney, John, Ned, and Rory, "to find the bomb with the full support and aid of the FBI. Again, President Tower doesn't want to needlessly send the whole country into a state of panic when there's a slight chance this won't come to fruition."

"So you admit this might all be a hoax?" The mayor gave a small, satisfied, self-righteous smile.

"Yes, but even if there is a slim chance it isn't, we have to do everything in our power to find the alleged bomb and diffuse it. According to the information we've gathered thus far, we believe the weapon is hidden underneath one of the casinos. That's why we need your help. We need to do an investigatory sweep through each of them. It's the only way."

"How do you do that in Las Vegas for crying out loud? You'd have to shut down the casinos!" The mayor indignantly smacked his hand on his desk.

"Precisely."

Mayor Cooper smirked. "Okay, I've heard enough. That's impossible. We can't possibly shut down the casinos. We'd lose a ton of money. Our city can't afford to lose one red cent, especially in the wake of the current recession. You'll have to find another way." He crossed his arms in resolute defiance.

CHAPTER FOURTEEN

T here is no other way." Mark Glover crossed his arms as well.
"So how do you propose we carry this grand scheme out,
gentlemen?" Mayor Cooper asked sardonically.

Mark Glover tipped his ever-present FBI cap to Ned Thomas.

"The Sheriff's department has been working every step of the
way on this case, hand in hand with the FBI, Mayor," Ned Thomas
said proudly. Rory had to try hard to avoid rolling his eyes. "We've
helped them devise a plan. First, we obtained the floor plans of each
of the casino resorts, determining the square footage and special areas
that may be hazardous or hard to access. Some of our officers will be
assigned to the FBI units conducting the investigation since we are
familiar with the lay of the land. The rest will either be assigned to
normal patrol or to the MGM Grand arena for the fight."

"Ah, that's right, we have the big fight coming up." The mayor
tapped his manicured fingers on the desktop, pausing for dramatic
effect. "I almost forgot. Is that just a coincidence that it's the same
day the bomb is supposed to go off?"

"We don't think so," John Dade said. "We think it was orchestrated that way so as many people are in town as possible. That's why we need your help to shut down the casinos in a short amount of time, why this needs to come from the top. If you hold a well-publicized, televised press conference announcing the shutdown, no one will have a choice."

"Now why would I do that? The people will think I've lost my mind. I will never be elected again."

"Or you will later be seen as a hero, the mayor who saved Las Vegas," John declared, sweeping his arms out with a flourish. *He knows how to play this guy*, Rory thought, realizing that John had worked with Stanley Cooper for a long time. *It's all about stroking his ego.*

"And if this bomb never materializes, I'll be known as the mayor who cost Las Vegas millions of dollars, and I'll be lucky I'm not impeached and run out of town."

"And if it does go off, it won't matter because you'll be a dead man." Chief Steele interjected, his voice deadpan.

"But if I can't tell my people about the suspected bomb, what reason would I give? How do I pull this off without being committed for insanity?"

"President Tower has already decided to back you up by declaring a national Responsible Gambling Weekend, a three-day period that will take place each year over the Fourth of July weekend; this year it will be the weekend leading up to July sixth. Just like you, we found out that President Tower gets her fair share of protests from anti-gambling lobbyists. She will announce a new bill encouraging a temporary halt in gambling in observance of anti-gambling rights in response to all of the protests she's received.

Of course, the media will flock to the major gambling meccas like Reno, Atlantic City, and most importantly, Las Vegas. That's when you'll step in to say that even though Las Vegas will have to make some sacrifices, the city will do its patriotic duty by temporarily shutting down the casinos. Since you'll want to be fair, each casino will be closed for several hours in observance of the new federal law. Of course, the plan will be to stagger their closings to impose the smallest financial impact on the city as possible."

The mayor frowned. "Let's just say I agree to enact this legislation," he said. "How long does each casino need to remain closed?"

"We're estimating about four hours each."

"*All* the casinos?"

Chief Steele didn't flinch. "With the manpower we're promised, we're estimating we can shut down the seventy-five casinos five at a time during the seventy-two hour period leading up to the fight."

"So the fight will go on?" the mayor asked slowly, thoughtfully. "At least we'll get some revenue from that I guess, unless you're proposing to stop that too."

"No, unfortunately there's not enough time to cancel it without sounding off the alarms," Mark Glover interjected.

A somber hush enveloped them all as they sat mulling over the magnitude of the plan.

"I'm going to have to think this over of course," Mayor Cooper said, regaining his composure. "I think you'll need to do a little more to convince me there's a bomb before I go shutting down the lifeblood of my city. The more I think about the whole thing, the more preposterous it all sounds. "

Suddenly, the mayor pointed his forefinger at Rory. "By the way, who *is* this guy? He hasn't said anything. Isn't he the one who started this whole thing? Why should we believe him and that letter from his father?"

"Because we've no reason not to," Chief Steele said.

Rory didn't say a word, wondering for the hundredth time how he had become the messenger in this whole twisted game.

The entire media world was focused on Mayor Stanley Cooper's press conference that brilliant July morning. The sun radiated off the glass panes of City Hall, giving the impression that the city was gleaming and perfect. No one could see or know that the vast majority of the Vegas population lived out in the desert in neighborhoods littered with empty beer cans, broken bikes, abandoned cars, and forgotten dreams, sucked dry like the victim of a vampire, a nightly beast that grew ever more evil and hungry for more.

It had been ordained that the king and ruler, Mayor Stanley Cooper, would take the podium, which was raised up on the stage of the outdoor concert plaza like a shrine surrounded by video cameras and microphones so his eminence could be seen and heard.

Crews from all of the major American networks and news stations, as well as the Associated Press and all of the foreign press, surrounded the stage, vying for space.

Rory stood between John and Carlos, and was disappointed that Susan stood on Carlos's other side.

The memory of their kiss seized him when he caught the scent of her perfume on a slight breeze. He suddenly realized he hadn't talked to her since he had kissed her. They had all been consumed by this crazy Mafia case, and time had flashed by so fast lately that he hadn't had much time to think. Plus, if Rory was honest with himself, he hadn't allowed himself to think or feel, stuffing down his emotions when they arose so that they had grown into a blend of anxiety and embarrassment. It now felt as if there was a tangible wall between the two of them. Rory wanted desperately to shatter it.

After the mayor is done . . . he thought, his mind in overdrive, hatching a plan. *I can't take this distance any longer. I miss her. I've got to talk to her . . . hold her in my arms.* His heart ached to be alone with her, if only for a few minutes.

Rory and the other OND members were briefed the night before that Mayor Cooper planned to make an unusual public appearance. They found out that the haughty mayor had been haunted by his own nightmare the night of their visit to his office, and had been somehow humbled by it. Agent Glover informed the team that Stanley Cooper had called Chief Steele into his office again the next day and confessed everything: he had known about the Mafia, and was in fact receiving bribes to keep quiet about the ISM's underground operations. He even admitted that even though he was terrified to play along with the plan to close the casinos and risk the Mafia's retaliation, he was even more afraid not to for fear of being solely responsible for what might happen if he didn't.

Rory sat in shocked silence as Mark Glover outlined the nightmare recounted by the mayor to Chief Steele. He didn't dare look in Mark's direction.

"He said it was as real as if it were actually happening," Agent Glover relayed, keeping his tone steady. But as Rory listened to him, he knew Mark was doing everything in his power to keep his voice from shaking. "Las Vegas was in the aftermath of some type of nuclear holocaust. Mayor Cooper was one of the lone survivors—and he wasn't his well-groomed perfect self, but a sick, ghostly shell of a man who wished he had never lived to tell the tale because he knew he was partly to blame since he had done nothing to prevent it."

My dream, Rory realized, stunned. He finally looked at Mark, who caught his eye for a second, and then rapidly looked away. *He knows it's the same dream, and even he's afraid.*

To the astonishment of the masses assembled and the millions of TV viewers, Mayor Cooper came out of the glass doors of city hall wearing jeans, a T-shirt, work boots, and sunglasses. Wild applause erupted.

The mayor removed his sunglasses, and instead of flashing his trademark smile, he looked sombre as he waved to the crowd from behind the podium. "Ladies and gentlemen," he began in a voice that was uncharacteristically humble. "I am honored to be standing among you today as your mayor and as a concerned citizen of Las Vegas."

He actually sounds sincere, Rory marveled.

"I am dressed this way to show my solidarity with each and every one of you, and to show you that even though I hold a position of authority as your mayor, I am subject to all of you who put me in office. I am no better or worse than any of you, and I am willing to do what it takes to work side by side with all of you to save Las Vegas from decline and possible self-destruction."

A murmur rippled among the assembled crowd, increasing in sound like an oncoming train until Mayor Cooper raised his hands to quiet them.

"Let me explain." He lowered his hands once the buzz tapered off. "Everyone knows Las Vegas is called Sin City. We who are residents have adopted the name, and we've even been proud to wear it like a badge of honor for many years—wearing it all the way to the bank, if you know what I mean.

"But lately, I and other officials in charge have noticed Las Vegas taking on a darker side to the vices that have long been the source of pleasure for people from all over the world. Perhaps the bad is outweighing the good as people get greedier. The rich get richer while the poor get poorer. I believe it's time to start looking at ways Las Vegas can clean up its act and explore more healthy, family friendly, and uplifting sources of entertainment that benefit all citizens.

"As some of you who read or watch the news know, President Tower has declared this weekend the first annual Responsible Gambling Weekend to draw attention to a platform raised by anti-gambling protestors. It is the president's hope that this initiative will inspire the nation to prevent gambling addictions, to help victims and their families, to keep casinos legal in all their business transactions, and to find other solutions to entertaining tourists who visit cities like Las Vegas, Reno, and Atlantic City.

"President Tower has called on our city to be the leader in curtailing gambling during this July fourth weekend to draw attention to this new legislation," the mayor continued. "I believe this is our chance not only to show solidarity with our nation, but to show how Las Vegas is ready to come out of the depths of the current recession with a new and improved image and game plan. With the blessing of your city council, I have made the decision to shut down all of the casinos in Las Vegas this Friday through Sunday . . . ."

A roar surged through the crowd, and Stanley Cooper bowed his head and raised his hands to wait for a modicum of quiet so he could continue.

"We will shut down each casino for four hours in observance of the new bill. We believe this will not cause too great a financial hardship on each of the casino resorts but will make an impact on the public."

Questions were hurled, but Mayor Cooper simply smiled and shook his head. "This is not that difficult to comprehend, so I will not be answering questions from the media at this time," he said matter-of-factly. "I'm sure you are all wondering whether Sunday's big fight between Jay-Jay Moss and Carmen Gallo will be held. The city has consulted with the promotional company running the fight, and together we have decided it was too late in the planning stages when we heard about the president's responsible gambling legislation to discontinue the event without facing potential litigation that could be costly. So the fight will go on."

Applause broke out once again.

"However, in the spirit of the legislation, there will be no on-site betting on the fight, and our city government will do everything possible to ensure this is a family event and a clean and fair fight." Hecklers booed and shouted profanities, pushing and shoving until they were rounded up by security guards standing close by.

It's a good thing we're providing him with twenty-four-hour bodyguards for the next few weeks, Rory thought.

The mayor continued as eloquently as possible amid the chaos. "We are simply asking you to have faith in us as we trust in our nation's leaders. Doing the right thing is never an easy task—but not doing it can turn out to be even more difficult in the long run. One might ask, how can Las Vegas, already in the throes of a recession and on the brink of a depression, afford to shut down our biggest money makers for a few minutes, much less a few hours? But I ask, how can we afford not to? How can we turn a blind eye to the negative consequences of gambling without finding a solution? It is in our best interest to support our president.

"We will adhere to the following schedule when closing down each casino, from the Hotel at Mandalay Bay to the Stratosphere, for four hours each . . . ."

The mayor's words faded in Rory's ears as his mind raced to figure out a way to talk to Susan.

As the crowd was breaking up, Rory saw his opportunity to approach her. Carlos turned to hold back a large man who was angrily shouting at the mayor for daring to close the casinos, wildly shaking his fist. For a moment, there was a space between them, and Rory closed it, taking a step toward her. Even though Susan was dressed in full police uniform, Rory marveled at how gorgeous she was.

He took her hand, not caring who saw them. She looked at him in bewilderment and started to protest, but he cut her off. "Susan, please have dinner with me tonight. I need to see you, to talk to you alone."

She paused, uncertainty in her eyes.

"Please."

"Okay."

And then the crowd moved like a giant wave, and they were separated again.

They met at Alize at the top of the Palms Casino Resort, one of the city's finest restaurants.

Rory had wanted to pick her up, but Susan had insisted they meet. She was on duty that day and needed time to get ready.

He waited nervously in the classic French restaurant, looking out from his table through the fifty-sixth-story windows at the breathtaking view of the city skyline and the mountainous desert beyond. The sun had set, leaving a fiery orange glow in its wake, giving way to the rainbow of lights that flooded Vegas at night. Some might say man had outdone God in their handiwork, the lighted landscape outshining the night sky, with new "stars" being added as the years passed.

But it all faded in comparison to the vision who walked toward him now, Rory thought with a smile.

Susan approached him slowly, shyly yet beguilingly, dressed in a black sequined tea-length sheath that draped over one shoulder and clung to her curves. Her hair was sleekly twisted up along one side, curls cascading down the other onto her bare shoulder like burnished copper.

Rory reminded himself to breathe, to say hello, to pull her chair out for her, all the while thinking, *my God, she is stunning.*

He was glad he had decided to get decked out in his best black suit for the occasion, had gotten a haircut, and bought a new tie.

All of the guys back at the Condo had recommended this as *the* place to impress that special someone. Rory knew dinner would be expensive, but he still had to force himself from reacting when he glanced down at the menu. The prices ranged from thirty dollars for an appetizer to eighty for an entrée, not to mention close to two hundred dollars for a serving of caviar. If left to Rory's preferences, they would have been eating at the diner where his starched shirt wouldn't chafe his neck, he wouldn't feel so awkward, and he wouldn't be worried that he might not have enough money for a plane ticket back home.

But this is a once-in-a-lifetime place with a once-in-a-lifetime woman. That unbidden thought surprised him. Before he had met Susan, Rory had figured he was finished with women. He had always managed to pick the wrong ones. Haley had been a prime example. Many years ago when he had dated his now ex-wife, she too had been beautiful and seemed innocent, virtuous, and loving.

Time and bitter battles over money and how to raise their kids had not only come between them, but in Rory's opinion, they had turned Haley into a selfish, spiteful shrew. In the end, nothing he said or did was ever good enough for her. He knew he was also to blame for the failure of their marriage, and not only because of his affair. He had allowed his ex-wife and his guilt to overpower him, rob him of all hope, all joy, and any relationship with his kids. To survive he had eventually become numb to her and unfortunately, to his children and to life itself.

Rory had dated a few women since his divorce, but he had always maintained a detached air of defensiveness, which they all subsequently detected. It didn't matter how pretty or smart or nice or funny they were. After a time he believed it was just easier to be alone.

Strangely enough, he had never felt lonely—until he met Susan. And even here and now in the city that he felt was the root of evil, or at least all of the evil that had befallen him, he still felt that stone barrier inside crumble a little bit every time he looked into her eyes.

She was pretty, smart, nice, funny and so much more. She was kind and compassionate yet spirited and strong.

"Rory?"

He raised his eyes to meet hers and felt his cheeks flush.

"You were lost in another world. I was wondering what you're going to order. Maybe we should just get a glass of water. I can't believe these prices!" She lowered her voice to a whisper. "Are you sure you want to stay? This dinner would cost me a week's salary!"

Rory smiled. "It's okay, you're worth it. Let's not worry about money or time or our jobs or anything else but enjoying each other. Tonight, you are a princess. Let me treat you like one, like you deserve to be treated."

Now Susan blushed, speechless.

"Ah . . . that's better." Rory suddenly chuckled.

Susan frowned. "What's so funny?"

"I was just remembering how you spoke up at the conference table when you were being excluded from our trip to see the mayor." Rory laughed. "You were pretty outspoken. I was secretly really proud of you." He sighed. "But this is nice too, taking your breath away."

The waiter arrived just in time to ease the romantic tension between them.

They ordered appetizers of seared *foie gras* and cured beef carpaccio and steak tartare, entrees of filet mignon and Chilean sea bass, and then decided to split an order of *crème brulee*.

An easy banter between them continued through dinner, and Rory marveled how, for the first time ever, he felt completely comfortable talking to a woman about any subject, never once running out of things to say.

As they dipped their spoons into the caramelized custard between them, heads bent toward one another, their eyes met, and Rory could feel a palpable electric current between them.

He almost didn't want to speak, to break it, but he knew the waiter would be approaching again soon with the bill.

Here goes. Deep breath. He took her hand in his. "Susan, I think I am falling in love with you."

He watched as her brown eyes darkened, widened. She didn't say a word.

Rory swallowed, and the words he had rehearsed tumbled out of his mouth before he could stop them. "Pretty soon we'll be done with this mission of ours . . . well, one way or another I guess, and either way, I wanted you to know. You don't have to say anything. Of course, if we don't get nuked by the Mafia, I guess I'll eventually be returning home to Ohio, and I was wondering if . . . if you would be willing, maybe, to come back with me."

Rory exhaled, not realizing he had been holding his breath.

Susan slowly laid down her spoon. He wasn't sure if she was shocked or appalled by his outburst, but her words cut him nonetheless. "Rory, I can't leave Las Vegas."

"Okay then." He laid down his napkin and searched frantically for the waiter, who was nowhere to be found.

"Rory, it's not that I don't feel the same way, but…" Susan's voice trailed off in a strained whisper.

Rory felt the wall literally rising, rock by rock, around his heart again.

"Susan, really, you don't need to say anything more. I get the picture. I'm sorry I said what I did. It's obvious you're just saying that now so I'm not completely humiliated."

"I'm telling the truth, and now I'm angry you don't believe that." A red curl came loose across her forehead and she sat up straight, pushing back her chair. "I can't leave this city and all the work I do, that's all I'm saying."

Rory bent forward, trying not to be too loud as they were already drawing attention from a few other diners.

"How can you stay in this . . . this awful place, dealing with these…people day in and day out? Wouldn't you like to settle down, live a normal life, raise a family?"

"I'm not sure what a normal life looks like, and yes, one day I'd like to have a family, but what's wrong with this place and these people?"

"Look around!" Rory's whisper was desperate. He waved his hand and looked to his left, then to his right. "*These* people are all full of themselves. They are the ones who obviously have more money than they know what to do with, who throw it away on lavish dining, drinking, gambling, girls and who knows what else. And then there are the slaves to this city, the victims of it all. We're not like either of them, you and I."

"And that, Rory Justice, is where you're wrong." Susan stood, regal in her anger, threw her napkin on the table, and walked off, leaving Rory facing a perplexed and flustered waiter holding a very large bill out toward him.

— — — — — —

Susan didn't show up the next day at the Condo for the briefing by Chief Steele. D-day, the Friday when the underground FBI sweep of casinos would begin, was only two days away.

Rory called her after the briefing and a few more times that night, but she never answered. He finally left a voice mail.

"Susan, it's Rory. Listen, I'm sorry about how things ended at the restaurant. I guess I was hoping you felt the same way I did, and when it seemed like you didn't, I got all childish and demanding and everything. Anyway, I'm a little concerned you didn't come in to work today. I hope you're okay and not sick or anything. I hope it's not because of me. Please call me."

After he hung up, he berated himself. *I hope it's not because of me. Now she probably thinks you're full of yourself. Maybe she's just not feeling well. You never should have told her you were falling in love. It was too soon. And she obviously doesn't feel the same way.*

But she should at least have the decency to call back and say she's not interested, that it's over, that I should just take a hike. Part of him was angry not only at himself but at her. Here she had gotten all dressed up, let him spend half his paycheck on dinner, led him on really. Maybe she was just like all the rest. He decided not to humiliate himself further by calling again.

But when she didn't show up for work the next day, his anger dissipated, and he was truly concerned.

He approached Mark Glover after the morning meeting. The FBI agent seemed equally perplexed. "I guess you'll have to ask the chief; maybe he knows."

Rory cautiously entered Rodney Steele's office that afternoon.

"Chief, you got a minute?"

The operations leader had his head down studying some papers. He was nearly obscured by stacks of folders that littered his desk. "What's up, Justice? As you can see, I'm literally buried up to my eyeballs."

"I know sir, and I'm sorry to intrude, but, well, it's important. I was wondering if Lieutenant McAfree is okay."

Chief Steele looked up at him, peering over his glasses, his iron-colored eyes boring into his. "And why do you want to know?"

Rory suddenly felt foolish. "I . . . uh, we, Susan and I, have become friends . . . well, I thought, a little more than that actually, and I'm worried about her."

The chief sighed, wearily removed his glasses, and rubbed his eyes with his thumb and forefinger. "Sit down, Mr. Justice."

Rory obediently obliged but wanted desperately to take it all back and head out the door. *This was a huge mistake*, he suddenly realized. The OND team members had all been under strict orders not to fraternize with each other, or anyone else in the FBI or police department for that matter, and now he had just confessed to breaking the rules, jeopardizing not only his future but Susan's career.

"I'm sorry, Chief, I shouldn't have come in here," Rory said, standing again. "If we can just forget I said anything, and I'll just mind my own business . . . ."

"Sit back down and shut up for a minute, Rory." The chief rose, walked around his desk, went to his office door and locked it, then sat in the vacant chair next to Rory's, facing him. "I'm going to talk to you in confidence. I'd appreciate if you don't interrupt me until

I'm finished since I don't have a lot of time for this. You, of course, keep what I'm about to say strictly to yourself. I need you to give me your word." Gray eyes pierced green.

"Of course. I wouldn't do otherwise."

Sitting this close to him, Rory noticed the lines on the chief's weathered face seemed to have grown deeper.

"I have known Lieutenant McAfree for many years and have always thought of her . . . of Susan as a daughter, which is why, when she came to me in distress two days ago, I encouraged her to take some time off, get away for a few days, even though she really didn't want to. She was distraught over her feelings for you."

Rory sucked in his breath and let it out in a deep sigh of relief. *So, she is okay. And maybe she does feel the same.*

"She confided in me that, even though it breaks the rules, you two somehow wound up as more than coworkers, and she doesn't know how to deal with that. She doesn't think she can work side by side with you feeling this way."

The jagged lines across the chief's forehead furrowed into a frown. "She's a good cop, but . . . well, I'm sure if you've gotten this close to her, you've found out she's a bit vulnerable when it comes to men. I hated sending her into that strip club, but she wouldn't take no for an answer when it came to being of service. Of course, when she told me about your, uh . . . relationship, I had half a mind to fire you on the spot, but I knew she would have had a fit if I had done that, so I told her to take a temporary leave for a few days until all of this hopefully blows over."

Rory wanted to ask where she had gone, when she'd be back, but knew better than to pry, so he kept his mouth shut.

The chief rose from his chair, using his only arm to hoist himself up. He moved like a man who was utterly exhausted. This mission had truly taken its toll.

Rory looked at him, waiting for direction, but the chief merely dismissed him.

"Since I gave you your answer, that will be all, Mr. Justice."

Rory stood and turned to leave, but stopped when the chief spoke one last time.

"I'd suggest you not try to reach the lieutenant, Mr. Justice. If we all survive this ordeal, if Las Vegas survives, I think it would be best—for you and for her—if you leave her alone and forget about her."

He probably hates me, Rory thought, frustration and self-pity rising up within him at his helplessness and loss.

CHAPTER FIFTEEN
- - - - - - - - -

T he casino searches began on Friday, July 4, with FBI and police crews working around the clock on the investigation over the entire weekend. Announcements that the casinos were closing were made only an hour prior to each so as not to give tourists and prospective gamblers a game plan to go from open casino to open casino, which would defeat the purpose of the Responsible Gambling Act. More importantly, the FBI didn't want to give the Mafia bosses a heads-up as to which casinos were closing next. Just in case, surveillance teams were set up at each of the casinos to watch for any suspicious entrances or exits.

The fight was set to begin at 8:30 p.m. Pacific Coast Time on Sunday, July 6.

By 4 p.m. on Sunday, all but the last five casinos had been thoroughly searched, including the MGM Grand where the fight was to be held, and no bomb or nuclear weaponry had been discovered.

The entire Condo team was on active duty except for Susan McAfree, who, they were told, was on a voluntary leave of undetermined length.

The FBI search teams had equipped them with the latest smart phones to simultaneously alert them if and when anything was found, and give them directions as to how to proceed.

Rory had never been to a live boxing match, or any other type of fight for that matter. He had never even watched one on television. In fact, he had an aversion to the sport in general. But even he was filled with curious anticipation of what had been billed as "The Fall," and touted as the "Fight of the Millennium" and the "biggest fight of all time." It was definitely the biggest since the 2015 Mayweather-Pacquiao "Fight of the Century."

Celebrities from Hollywood, politics, and the sports world filled the ringside seats, and it was rumored that tickets had sold for as high as three hundred thousand dollars apiece. Every hotel and motel in Vegas was sold out.

Rory's excitement was tainted by his disappointment that Susan wasn't there. He had planned to apologize for whatever it was that ended their dinner date on a bad note, although for the life of him, he wasn't sure exactly what he had said or done wrong.

I guess she thought I was being judgmental, he thought. *Oh, well, it doesn't really matter now. She wants to stay here, and I want to go.* Rory felt a bitter bile rise up in his throat. *I can't believe I told her I was falling in love with her. What an idiot.*

Just then, the wild cheers of the audience snapped him out of his thoughts. Carlos was clapping and stomping like the rest of the audience around them in time to the beat of Queen's song "We Will Rock You" blaring over the loudspeaker.

Rory and Carlos were stationed together in a corner of the MGM Grand Arena, but they could still see the action in the ring. They were one of several pairs of agents set up throughout the arena to make sure nothing ran amok as the bomb squads finished their searches in the other remaining casinos.

A spotlight cut through the crowd and lit the entrance of the heavyweight challenger Carmen Gallo. Touted as the new "Italian Stallion," Gallo had been raised by his young single Italian Catholic mom in the slums of Chicago after his African American father had abused and disgraced her and abandoned them when he was just twelve.

After surviving on the streets by fighting for money, he was discovered by a local, small-time boxing manager. He literally fought his way up the ranks, eventually rising to become the undisputed US Heavyweight Champion.

Gallo entered the ring in his royal blue robe trimmed in gold with matching boxing gloves and shoes.

If the sellout crowd had sounded like thunder when Gallo entered the arena, now the collective sound grew into an explosion as current World Heavyweight Champion Jose Jamal "Jay-Jay" Moss arrived.

The resonating, steady, synthetic beats of the Eminem song "Lose Yourself" were blaring as the "Mexican Fury" sauntered in.

Moss danced down the aisle draped in a black, red-trimmed satin boxing robe, his white teeth flashing in his brown face for the cameras, his black boxing gloves jabbing into the air to the music for effect. He entered the ring, an assistant taking his robe, and held his tattooed, muscled arms above his head, beaming as the crowd roared.

Then a hush fell as an announcer's bass voice boomed out, "A new king shall be crowned tonight . . . one will rise and one will fall. Ladies and gentlemen, welcome to the greatest boxing match of all time, "The Fall," live from the MGM Grand in Las Vegas, Nevada!"

Cheers erupted as the announcer proclaimed, "In this corner, weighing in at two hundred and ten pounds, we have the challenger from Chicago, the new Italian Stallion, US Heavyweight Champion Carmen Gallo!"

Although he was the underdog, the audience applauded with gusto.

"And in this corner, defending his title as the World Heavyweight Champion, weighing in at two hundred and fourteen pounds of action-packed muscle, here is the Mexican Fury, Jose Jamal "Jay-Jay" Moss!"

Everyone stood and cheered amid a deafening roar.

The bell sounded the first round, and Moss entered the middle of the ring fast and furious, throwing and landing the majority of punches.

Toward the end of the fifth round, sweat and blood flew as Moss threw a roundhouse jab that hit just above Gallo's eye, cutting a gash in his forehead.

Rory felt a strange mix of excitement and uneasiness. The exhilaration of the crowd was contagious, but Rory also felt contempt for himself that he was cheering for two men beating each other senseless.

"Is this great or what?" An ecstatic Carlos poked Rory in the ribs good-naturedly.

"Yeah, great," Rory said, trying to force some enthusiasm into his tone.

"I bet on the champ, so he better win," Carlos whispered behind his hand.

"Moss?"

"Who else?"

"How'd you do it? I mean, I thought there was no online betting on this fight."

"I placed a side bet. So far, so good."

The bell rang to start the sixth round. A determined Gallo came out swinging this time and delivered a few quick and hard body hits that knocked Moss into the ropes, where he hung for a few seconds before dazedly turning and regaining focus, his gloves protecting his face.

Gallo rained blows one after another, and Moss barely lasted until the end of the round, which decidedly went to the Italian Stallion.

The seventh through ninth rounds were a different story. Just as his name indicated, the Mexican's rage refueled him. In the ninth round, he delivered a punch to a reeling Gallo that cut open the gash in the Chicago fighter's eye, sending him to the corner so his cutman could make the bleeding stop with Vaseline and a cold ENSWELL tool.

Gallo came back out to the center of the ring looking shaky, his eye a thin line in a baseball-sized swelling around his eye.

"Moss is going to knock him out cold," Carlos said gleefully. Rory didn't bother answering his partner. In fact, he had become a little disgusted at the bloodlust of his coworker, the thousands of others gathered in the arena, and the millions of viewers watching on satellite TV at home, and he was perturbed at himself for feeling the thrill.

Rory suddenly felt queasy and didn't want to watch anymore. Just as he was about to tell Carlos he needed to use the restroom, he felt his phone vibrate in his pocket.

Simultaneously, he and Carlos pulled out their phones and stared at the same text message: *We found it.* Rory and Carlos looked at each other, their eyes locked in a surprised stare.

Then they received a second text. The message simply said: *meet at the Bellagio lobby ASAP.*

They exited the arena, hustling down two flights of steps and through the exit doors into the sultry night air.

Rory thought they should hail a cab, but Carlos told him they could run faster than ride the mile distance to the Bellagio because the streets were far too packed with heavy traffic surrounding the MGM Grand.

"Come on, follow me, I know a shortcut." Carlos, already sprinting ahead, called over his shoulder to Rory.

I need to get in better shape. Rory forced his legs to pump, but as the famous fountains of Bellagio loomed ahead, he slowed to a walk, gulping air into his burning lungs, his legs too heavy to run any farther.

Carlos had long outdistanced him and was nowhere in sight.

They found the bomb but it hasn't gone off yet. That thought sent new adrenaline coursing through his veins, and once again, Rory was running, past the fountains and into the glamorous lobby with its arched marble entrances, eighteen-foot-high multi-colored ceiling, and piano music.

Heaving, sweating, and momentarily bewildered, Rory stopped to breathe and finally noticed Carlos huddled off to the side of the lobby with a tall clean-cut man wearing a dark suit, apparently an FBI agent. The two looked up and motioned him over.

"Last two in the building," the agent said into a two-way radio device, obviously speaking to someone distant, as Rory approached.

Without saying anything further, the agent quickly led them through the lobby into a hallway where they took the elevator to the thirty-sixth floor, the top of the resort hotel, and entered a large conference room surrounded by windows overlooking the twinkling Vegas night skyline. Inside were two dozen top FBI agents and Condo team members, all men.

Rory immediately felt Susan's absence, his heart lurching then sinking like a ship in a storm being buffeted by a huge wave. He had futilely hoped she would at least show up tonight for the "grand finale" of the investigation.

If the bomb went off now, Rory realized he would be devastated not to share his final moments with her. *They found the bomb but it hasn't gone off yet. And here I am alone without the woman I love.*

"Gentlemen, thanks for getting here so fast; let's all have a seat so we can brief you on what we found." Chief Steele spoke in his deep gravelly voice, commanding authority and respect. Everyone took a seat around the massive conference table in the middle of the room, all excitedly talking at once.

Rory's fingers gripped the leather arms of his chair. He felt like he was going to crawl out of his skin with anxiety and anticipation. *They found the bomb but it hasn't gone off yet, and we're all sitting here wasting time.*

Not inclined to verbosity and realizing the tension in the room was thick, the chief got right to the point. "Quiet, please. So . . . we did find the bomb." Suddenly silence pervaded the room. "However, it was already diffused, thank God."

A collective gasp and murmuring ensued, but Chief Steele interrupted. "Please, I still have a lot to go over, so let's try to maintain quiet for now. I realize that's a little hard to believe, but it's true. When our team of experts arrived here in this very hotel, they found the bomb planted underground had been set to detonate at 9 p.m. Yet, the timer had somehow stopped at eight fifty-nine. With only a minute to go, someone or something stopped it from going off and blowing Las Vegas into shreds. If you were there, you would have said it was a miracle."

Many of the men shook their heads in disbelief and wonder, one actually wept with relief, and a few cheered. It was a good thing he was sitting because Rory felt his whole body go limp. He hadn't realized he had been clenching every muscle while he held his breath, hanging on every word.

Rory suddenly felt an unanticipated slow anger boil up inside. He felt like he had been duped somehow, like he had been a pawn in a master chess game, and now the game was over and nobody had won. It had all been played for naught. He felt disappointed, let down, and angry for allowing himself to invest so much time and energy into this craziness . . . for what?

Everyone was talking at once, and Chief Steele and Agent Glover had to bang their hands on the big conference table to get their attention.

"The good news, besides the bomb being miraculously diffused, is that our FBI and SWAT team members caught five leading Islamic Mafia members as they were about to board various international flights out of McCarran International Airport—including their leader, known as the Master. They were arrested and are being interrogated at the Federal Detention Facility here in Las Vegas while awaiting their arraignment. But I can assure you that they will not be going anywhere for a long time. The most important news is that we believe we now have in custody the ringleaders of this whole Mafia organization."

There seemed to be collective sigh of relief in the room.

But Rory felt a sense of letdown rather than relief, and he couldn't figure out why, like a performer on the last night of a really big show who knew it was his last time on stage and had no idea where he'd go from there.

"So, where do we go from here?" Chief Steele asked, as if reading Rory's mind. "This means that for some of you gentlemen, your work on the operation has been successfully completed. Mission accomplished. Congratulations and thank you." With his one arm, the chief couldn't clap so he nodded as if on cue to Agent Glover, who started to applaud. The men around the table did likewise, shaking each other's hands and slapping one another good-naturedly on the back.

When the room quieted once more, Chief Steele continued. "Some of you will be needed to wrap up the investigation. But for tonight, you are officially free to enjoy your victory. You worked hard, so dinner and drinks for the rest of the night are on us. Keep your receipts, gentlemen."

Rory remained in his chair stunned as the guys all jumped out of their chairs, whooping and cheering. Most gathered to make plans to celebrate together, deciding to do a bar crawl from one end of the strip to the other or until sunrise, whichever came first.

John and Carlos, who had sat on either side of Rory, both offered him a ride to the Hotel at Mandalay Bay casino resort at the south end of the Strip where everyone was headed, but he declined, saying he'd meet them there later.

He alone remained after everyone left—except for Rodney Steele and Mark Glover, who stood at the head of the table talking to one another.

Finally, the two men realized Rory was still sitting at the table.

"Rory, why aren't you out celebrating?" Agent Glover asked.

"I'm having a hard time wrapping my head around all of it," Rory said. He didn't feel like celebrating, but he didn't want to tell them that. He was afraid to ask the next question but blurted it out anyway. He wasn't sure which answer he wanted.

"Will I stay on to help with the rest of the investigation, or am I among those who are finished?"

"Uh, well, yes, you can actually pack your things and head out whenever you're ready," the chief said awkwardly. "I'm sure that's a relief, since you didn't seem to like Las Vegas anyway. I'm with you on that by the way. I don't like it either, but it's where I'm stationed, at least for now. Anyway, Rory, thank you, because we couldn't have accomplished any of this without you." Chief Steele shook Rory's hand.

Yeah, right, he thought. *You found a bomb already diffused. What a big joke.* Rory felt ashamed, and his voice caught in his throat. He realized he had been secretly hoping to stay on to feel useful—and to have an excuse to see Susan one more time. He realized they were all self-serving reasons, but he couldn't help how he felt.

And now you're going home.

Home. It had such a hollow sound. *I really don't have much of a life back home anymore. Did I ever?*

He felt caught in a state of limbo, which is why he stayed sitting in his chair.

"Rory, you okay? You really should go out with the guys and celebrate. Mark and I have to head back to the Condo to start a post-op strategy. Do you need a ride somewhere?"

Rory felt like he was in a dense fog; his thoughts were cloudy and distracted, and he really didn't hear what the chief had said.

He shook his head in an effort to clear it.

"What? Oh, sorry, I'm fine. I'm just thinking about all of the plans I have to make to get home, my flight, et cetera." Rory suddenly felt like he wanted to run from the room before they could see through his lie. "You're right, maybe I will go celebrate, at least for a little while."

"You deserve it." Mark Glover approached him and shook his hand. "It's been a pleasure working with you."

"Likewise."

"You sure you don't want to stay and take a job with us in the FBI?" Steele cracked a small smile.

"Nah, not my cup of tea. See you guys."

He left the two FBI agents behind to discuss important wrap-up strategies and headed down to the Bellagio lobby to hail a cab to Mandalay Bay.

As he waited, the nightly fountain show had just begun as it did every half hour. Rory glanced sideways as twelve hundred plus spritzers shot water up to four hundred and sixty feet in the air, illuminated by dazzling white lights, the water dancing in rhythm to the strains of Bach's *1812 Overture*.

Most people would describe it as beautiful, but Rory's vision blurred in his anger and disgust. *Everything beautiful comes at a cost.* Rory realized subconsciously he was thinking about Susan.

Like the strip clubs, drinking, gambling and now, added to the list, boxing and women had done, the luxurious fountain show now also drew out Rory's feelings of animosity toward everything Vegas.

Rory had seen the show on his last trip to Sin City. Now, just like then, he believed the whole thing was just a colossal waste of water.

Here's an eight-and-a-half-acre lake in the middle of the desert using water merely for the pleasure of tourists and passersby when there are people in Africa dying of thirst, where five- and six-year-olds climb muddy mountains for hours just to fight to fill a dirty bucket with a half-gallon of water, fight to keep it, and fight to get it down the mountain so their families don't die of thirst.

And worse still, Rory had learned that the poor people of Vegas who lived in the desert just miles away could barely afford to provide clean water and food to their families, could not afford to keep even the smallest of lawns or grow vegetables due to the water shortage— while millions of dollars were poured into this monstrosity.

Rory felt that gnawing sensation of disdain festering inside him once again.

Mercifully, the cab finally arrived, although Rory didn't really care where he was going.

CHAPTER SIXTEEN

Rory had to search through four of the eight bars at Mandalay before he finally found the guys.

First he donned a parka and mittens to enter Minus 5, the cocktail lounge almost entirely made of cool blue ice—the bar, the furniture, the glasses—and kept to a temperature of minus five degrees. *I thought I had seen it all,* he said to himself wryly.

Then he wandered past the headless Lenin statue into Red Square, the Russian-themed vodka bar, but didn't see anyone he knew.

A trip through Mix Lounge with its amazing view of the strip resulted in the same.

At least I'm seeing the sights, a weary Rory told himself, although he decided to draw the line at touring Shark Reef, the resort's one million gallon indoor aquarium where real sharks, stingrays, and crocodiles resided.

Giving up, he went outside to get some fresh air and to see the famous Mandalay Bay beach and pool. He walked past the huge, crowded beach with its simulated ocean waves and, not wanting to bother looking among the crowd, he slipped away to the slightly quieter poolside Verandah Lounge where he saw John, Carlos, and eight others from the Condo group sipping drinks and eating gourmet pizza.

"Hey, there's my main man," a visibly tipsy Carlos shouted as Rory walked up to the group. "Get my friend Rory a drink, somebody."

A waiter appeared out of nowhere, and Carlos ordered him some type of cocktail called a Goombay Smash. Rory was too tired to argue and gulped the fruity drink down because he was so thirsty by that point.

"We almost gave up on you," John said. His beefy face was a shiny pink from drinking and carrying on. "We just came from doing shots in the Mix Lounge and wanted to get some food in our stomachs—and maybe meet some girls to take up to the Eye Candy Sound Lounge to go dancing." John jerked his thumb toward the window of the Verandah. About a dozen girls in bikinis lounged by the pool. "Looks like it's one of those bachelorette parties."

"John, I thought you were married." Rory was dumbstruck and felt disappointed and alone all over again.

"I am. I'm not saying I'm going to hook up with anybody. I'm just going to keep Carlos here out of trouble."

"Speaking of that, this has been lame so far—let's go have some fun," Carlos said, wobbling on slightly unstable feet.

Rory meekly followed them to Eye Candy lounge, but when they saw that there weren't too many single women there yet, they decided to head to the Hard Rock Café.

They piled in three taxicabs and arrived at the huge, loud, and very rambunctious circular bar in the Hard Rock, ordering rounds of shots and beers and making fun of Rory when he sipped his.

"Drink, drink, drink," they chanted until Rory downed his shot of tequila and chased it with a few gulps of beer. He hated being the center of attention and caved in just to make them stop shouting his name.

Their confidence bolstered by large volumes of alcohol, the men decided to try their luck at the casino.

Rory hated the thought of sitting at a slot machine for hours, but wasn't sure of himself enough to sit and play Texas hold 'em and lose all of his money. He only had about a hundred bucks in his pocket and figured that wouldn't last very long.

Since he had nowhere else to go and he was feeling too intoxicated to resist, he sat down at a roulette table where the buy-in was twenty dollars.

It must have been his lucky night, because ten spins later, he was suddenly three thousand dollars richer.

He had hit half of the time exactly on the number he played, whether it was his age, his father's date of birth, or a number that just felt lucky.

The other half he hit on black or red, odd or even, and once he hit on double zeroes, the biggest of the payouts. The more he won, the more risks Rory took, and the more chips he played.

Carlos sauntered up to the roulette table, took one glance at the large stacks of chips in front of Rory, and whistled.

"Shut up, Carlos, before you get me kicked out," Rory whispered.

"I just can't believe it, man." Carlos motioned for John Dade, who was playing Black Jack and losing miserably, to come over to the table to watch.

Soon some of the other men in their group who had run out of money congregated, and a small crowd formed around the roulette table where Rory was playing.

"Whoa, guys, this is too much for me. I'm going to take my winnings and go before they lock me up somewhere," Rory said under this breath, recalling his gambling experience on the *Voyager* cruise, even though he now knew that wasn't the reason he'd been escorted out of the ship's casino. Still, he remembered that fear all too well.

He stood up, collected his chips, tipped a few to the croupier, and went to the nearest window to cash in. When he turned around, his colleagues were facing him, staring at him.

"What? Are you mad at me for winning?" His words sounded a little slurred in his own ears.

"No, we're thinking we should keep you going," Carlos said in all seriousness.

"What do you mean? I'm exhausted. It's midnight already. I have to pack and catch a flight home tomorrow. I'm going back to my apartment."

"You can't do that, you're winning!" Carlos grabbed Rory by the shirtsleeve.

The group, led by Carlos, decided to venture forth from the Hard Rock to bigger and better casinos and wound up in the high stakes lounge of the Mirage.

By now Rory was feeling the effects of the cocktails and beers he had downed and, with little sense of direction or purpose, followed along. *Besides,* he smiled to himself, *I'm winning.*

As they walked past the hourly volcano show in front of the Mirage, with its fiery projectiles blasting out of the lake, Rory also felt philosophical in his drunken state. *This place is truly like a crazy hell on earth,* he thought. *Of course, a lot of people who voluntarily come here year after year to give in to all of their carnal pleasures without being caught probably think it's more like heaven, like the animals at a zoo all left out of the cages at the same time, free to run wild. Maybe it's just a microcosm of earth magnified so it only appears larger than life . . . but really just human beings and their egos at their most grandiose selves.*

Then he was pulled along by the sleeve again into an elevator and up to the High Limit Lounge.

There were Black Jack, Baccarat, and poker games among the high-stakes tables set up in quieter, plusher private rooms in the lounge, with buy-ins ranging from one hundred to five hundred dollars, and then there were the private tables with limits set at undisclosed higher rates agreed upon between those playing.

Feeling like he had nothing to lose, Rory played stud poker into the early hours of the morning, his Condo associates cheering him on, refueling him with coffee drinks and cocktails. He did know that game—his scouting buddies had taught him how to play on a camping trip once.

He played with five other players for hours, winning nearly all of the hands. It was as if Rory had the Midas touch . . . he couldn't lose. Vegas had taken its toll on Rory the last time he was here. *Now it's payback time,* he thought, the desire for retaliation and redemption firing him on. *May as well leave this city with a bang.*

All but Carlos and John eventually left to go back to their homes and wives and children. Rory had always been the only out-of-towner on the OND team, with no one or nothing to return to every day but his empty apartment.

He told his two Condo friends to go back home at some point, but they protectively insisted on staying.

Finally, four of the six players had called it quits, leaving Rory and one other gentleman named Max sitting at the poker table together. It was 4:00 a.m.

The dealer asked Max and Rory if they wished to keep playing.

Max, short for Maximilian, Rory learned, was of Russian descent, a medium but strongly built blonde about his own age with ice blue eyes and a nose that looked like it had been broken at least once in the past.

"Since the pot has already been divided and the house has received the ante, can we bet among ourselves this time?" Max politely asked the tuxedoed, baby-faced, but quite adept young man who had served as their dealer for the night.

Max had only a few chips in front of him compared to the stacks in front of Rory, who had been winning all night. Rory could only guess how much money lay in front of him. Sixty, maybe even seventy-five thousand dollars.

Now is the time to walk away. It was probably the one coherent thought Rory had had all night, but he remained seated, realizing this man might very well break his kneecaps if he dared to leave now with all of his money.

"Since it's so late, or I guess so early as the case may be, and as you have mentioned you have a long day ahead of you, I propose we play one last hand, winner take all," Max suggested. "Would that be all right with the house?" He looked at the dealer, who nodded, then at Rory for his consent.

Rory looked at Max suspiciously. *What does he have left to bet?*

As if Rory had uttered the question aloud, Max said, "I know I don't have enough chips to bet, but I did just purchase a new Maserati not too long ago. Here . . . ." Max fished the remote key that had the Maserati emblem carved on it out of his pocket. "We can wait and have a nice drink or two while one of your friends takes this key and checks it out. It's parked in the hotel's valet parking lot." He held out the key to John, who took it and agreed to go find the car and report back.

Max and Carlos ordered top-shelf drinks from a waitress nearby and sipped them, waiting for John's return. Rory ordered a Coke.

Fifteen minutes later, John walked back into the private poker room. He nodded at Rory then grinned. "It's amazing—black, beautiful and brand new. I'd say go for it, bud." John handed the key to the dealer then turned toward the young waitress. "Hey, darlin', can you catch me up to these guys and get me a double Scotch?"

Oh my God, Rory said to himself, half in fear, half in prayer, now feeling totally sober. *I shouldn't even still be here. I should have capsized on a cruise ship, sunk in that submarine, wound up in some jail . . . .*

"Okay, one last game, winner take all."

Max toasted him with his double vodka, and Rory obliged then gulped down his Coke, knowing he needed to stay straight and keep his wits about him.

He took a deep breath and looked at his first two cards, an ace of spades and a deuce of clubs, the highest and lowest cards in the deck.

Since there was no betting, the dealer merely had to turn over three cards, but he did so slowly, allowing the players to relish the moment.

Three of diamonds.

Five of diamonds.

His heart doing somersaults, Rory glanced into Max's steel blue eyes and saw the corners of his mouth turn up ever so slightly. *He has a possible flush.*

The dealer, with agonizing precision, dealt the last card.

Four of hearts.

Rory tried to contain his joy, but his heart dropped when he saw Max smile. He was confused for a second. *I've had way too much to drink*, he thought dizzily, and then watched as the Russian triumphantly turned over his cards.

He had a pair of fives and a pair of fours.

A mixture of exhilaration and terror seized Rory, and he almost felt like he was going to vomit. Max looked expectantly at him, his eyes gleaming.

Rory silently turned over his cards, revealing a straight.

Carlos and John, who had been sitting by nervously drinking another two rounds served up by the pretty waitress, jumped up to see the revealed hands and let out a loud holler of delight.

"Yee ha!" John bellowed.

"Dios mio!" Carlos cried.

Rory didn't know how to react. He was too scared to show any emotion at all so he merely watched Max, whose face turned from pink to deep scarlet. Without saying a word, the blonde, muscular Russian stood up from his chair, handed the dealer a hundred dollar bill, firmly shook Rory's hand, and turned and walked briskly out of the room.

The dealer handed Rory the car key. "Congratulations, Mr. Justice."

Rory blinked in shock. "Thank you."

The hotel concierge had sent a valet to fetch the sleek sports car and drive it to the hotel's main entrance where Rory waited with Carlos and John.

Rory drove the car to his apartment, packed his few belongings, and checked the route he would take to drive home: he would head east on I-15 and then connect to I-70 which would lead him across country straight back to Columbus.

After a month and a half, it was high time for him to head out and leave it all behind—the strip clubs, the bars, the booze, the glitz, the gambling, the overindulgence.

He had read somewhere that Las Vegas held more than ten Guinness world records including tallest observation tower, tallest chocolate fountain, biggest birthday cake, biggest gold nugget, biggest bronze statue and biggest casino winnings.

Rory recalled thinking how ridiculous it all was. He had seen beneath the surface of Sin City to the crime, the sex, the drugs, the depravity, the beggars, the bookies, the gangs, and the gambling addicts.

He also had seen a few good souls who lived here, and who were helping others fight the uphill battle of reforming the people and transforming the city into more than a place with too much of everything—into a place where people could live and work in safety. He would never forget John, Carlos, Rodney Steele, Mark Glover—and Susan.

As he stood waiting for his prize to be delivered, Rory forced the ache of already missing them from his heart, mentally placing the last brick into the wall of superiority and condemnation that he had rebuilt around it, blocking out everything else.

He reminded himself that the FBI and the Las Vegas Police Department had used him. Susan had hurt him. And his father had humiliated him, sending him here to supposedly "save" Las Vegas, only to have some type of miraculous act of God occur that required no help on his part. He felt like he had simply been a pawn in some type of cosmic game. Like the fountains and volcanoes, it all seemed like an illusion now.

John and Carlos started whistling and clapping their approval as the car pulled up to the entrance, breaking his reverie. A few passersby joined in the cheering.

When the valet hopped out of the driver's seat and handed the key to Rory, saying, "Here is your car, sir," Rory beamed, shaking his head, still in disbelief.

I really don't need any of them anymore, he decided now, feeling smugly triumphant, taking the keys from the valet driver. *I have seventy-five thousand dollars in my pocket and the fastest, most beautiful car to take me anywhere I want to go. I've got everything I need.*

"You are one lucky son-of-a-gun," John said. "I'm sure gonna miss you."

He shook John's hand, let Carlos give him a hug, and slid into the driver's seat. "Thanks guys, see ya later," he said to both men. And then he waved and drove away. *So long, Las Vegas.*

CHAPTER SEVENTEEN

R ory sang along to the words of "Sweet Caroline" blaring from his car stereo. He was driving ninety miles an hour on the open road, which had a posted speed limit of seventy-five, and yet it only felt like he was driving forty-five in this new miracle machine.

He had noticed with trepidation and delight that the Maserati could go up to two hundred and eighty-five miles an hour.

Rory watched as the sun rose above the distant mountains on the horizon of the brown Mojave Desert floor that stretched endlessly on either side of the two-lane highway. The vast sky changed before his eyes, a red slit of a sun growing into a blood-orange fireball that sent magenta ribbons of light blazing through pink whispers of clouds. It was like a virtual painting, an indigo and scarlet canvas fading to shades of purple, and then to various hues of coral and blue.

He loved this car. He had even named her. Caroline, of course, after an old girlfriend. He had always loved the Neil

Diamond song, and here it played from the XM station on the radio. He turned up the volume until the sound burst from the car's new Bose stereo. His favorite song had never sounded so good. *Come to think of it, I love this car more than I did the girl.* He smiled to himself.

He sighed with contentment, soaking in the rising sun and absentmindedly stroking his hand along the seat next to him, feeling the car's rich, tan leather interior. He drove with the convertible top down, feeling the warming desert breeze whip through his hair. Thankfully, he had remembered to pack sunglasses to protect his eyes.

For the first time in a long time, perhaps in his entire life, Rory felt happy and free.

He also still felt a little intoxicated. He figured it was probably a combination of all of the alcohol in his system, the satisfaction of leaving Las Vegas and all of its trials and tribulations, and the heady feeling of driving so fast in such a powerful vehicle.

Rory was travelling according to his plan, east on I-15, and had gone about sixty miles. To the best of his knowledge, he figured he would probably see signs for the Arizona state line fairly soon, as I-15 wound briefly through a corner of Arizona before entering the state of Utah.

According to his calculations, he would reach Utah in about an hour, and hoped to get breakfast at the first town he saw. He was getting hungry.

He glanced down to change the channel, and during the few seconds it took to look at the names of the songs and artists that flashed on the screen as he flipped through the stations, he didn't see the sharp, softball-sized rock in the road.

Rory suddenly heard the loud pop of the right front tire blowing out, and the Maserati veered sharply to the left. And there, just off the road, was a small, scraggly Joshua tree, which the car hit before careening to a stop in the desert sand about ten feet from the shoulder of the highway.

Fortunately, he wasn't hurt except for a bump and bruise on his left temple where his head hit the windshield when the car lurched to the left and hit the tree. Getting out of the car to assess the damage, Rory saw that the tire was completely flattened down to the rim, and the whole left side of the car was bashed in. He was so angry and bereft that his brand new Caroline was damaged that he felt tears sting his eyes.

Rory tried to start the Maserati again. The key turned in the ignition, but the car didn't start. The blow to the front end must have done some internal damage to the engine. Rory was now upset and infuriated.

He looked around. There was literally nothing and no one in sight, just miles and miles of desert with an occasional Joshua tree dotting the landscape, nothing else but the road and the sun and some reddish-brown mountains in the distance.

He got back in the car and reached for his cell phone on the passenger seat.

Great, he said to himself sarcastically. *I only have five percent of my battery left.*

He thought perhaps he should call 911, but before he did, he realized he should first find the vehicle registration. He opened the glove compartment and searched through a small stack of papers.

There was no registration card. He looked again. *Nothing.*

Rory then decided that calling the cops was probably a very bad idea. First, he had no registration card for this brand spanking new Maserati. *The officer will definitely think I stole it,* he thought. *I mean, look at me, I'd think I stole it if I were a police officer.* Rory looked in the rearview mirror and grimaced at his bloodshot eyes and scruffy face with its beard stubble. He hadn't had time to shave or shower.

Most of all, he thought, it was a bad idea because he might still have alcohol in his system.

Rory had a long enough moment of clarity to realize he was feeling a hangover coming on, taking form as a headache, nausea, and heartburn.

Suddenly his mouth also felt parched, and Rory panicked. In his drunken state, he hadn't thought to bring anything to eat or drink, not even a bottle of water. He had figured he'd stop at the first town.

The sun was now crawling into the sky, its rays growing hotter as it ascended. Rory didn't know it, but today's weather forecast for this part of Nevada called for temperatures in the upper nineties, and a windstorm was headed his way from the south. And there was absolutely no shade or shelter in sight.

Rory tried the key in the ignition again to at least put up the convertible top and ward off the already hot sun. But again, nothing happened.

This was plain bad luck. Rory got out of the car to try to put up the top manually, but it wouldn't budge.

Now Rory started cursing God.

How could He let this happen to me? Rory thought, near tears again as he climbed back into the passenger seat and slumped down onto the warm leather in frustration, already sweating from the effort he had made. *What are You trying to tell me, God?*

Now his head was pounding.

Just as Rory was thinking of whom he could possibly call for help, his cell phone rang. He looked at his phone and couldn't believe the name that appeared, one of the last he ever would have expected.

It was Rick, his son.

Rory stared at the phone for a few seconds before answering, almost missing the call.

"Hello?"

"Dad, it's me, Rick. How are you?"

Rory fought to keep from barking out a sardonic laugh. How am I? I'm just peachy keen Ricky my boy. I'm stuck out in the middle of this god-forsaken desert, my brand new Maserati, the only thing I have left in my life, is ruined, I feel awful, my head is pounding, I'm dying of thirst, and it feels like I'm roasting in an oven. But other than that, I'm just dandy.

"I'm fine. How are you?" *Oh, and my cell phone is about to die.*

"Dad, I'm calling to talk to you about something. Do you have a few minutes?"

Of all times, Rory thought. *God, please let my cell last that long.* "Sure, son, what's up?" Rory wiped beads of sweat from his forehead and closed his eyes to concentrate.

"First, I wanted to tell you that I'm really sorry I haven't been in touch with you for so long. I guess I was so angry at you for leaving mom and us, and kept it bottled up inside for so long . . . but I'm sure there are things Riley and I don't even know about what happened between you two, which you couldn't tell us. And now that I'm old enough and I minister to married couples who struggle, I know it takes two people to mess up a marriage, and I'm working through it."

Rory had to think for a moment to remember how old his son was now. *He turned twenty-three two months ago.* Rory had at least remembered to send him a birthday card.

"Well, thank you, Rick for trying to be more understanding. You're really growing up. It was nice to see you, even if it was at Pop-Pop's funeral."

"Yeah, Dad, that's another thing. I know that had to be rough for you too, and I'm sorry about Pop-Pop . . . about your dad dying. I'm sorry I didn't get to spend more time with him, but Mom . . . well, she pretty much cut us off from the family. I hope to see Gran soon too."

Tears streamed down Rory's face, and he fought hard to keep his voice from cracking. "She would love that. And thank you, son; it's been hard, but time is a great healer."

"I know—I'm finding that out. Being a deacon for the past year has been a real eye opener."

"I'm proud of you."

"Yeah, it's really brought me closer to God. And I guess that's why I've learned to be more forgiving. I wish Riley would come with me to church once in a while, but she's still so angry all the time."

"I'm sorry to hear that, but I'm really glad to hear your good news." Rory felt sadness clutch his heart for his long-lost daughter. She was so much like her mother, so bitter. He would have to remind himself to pray for her.

"But Dad, that's not my big news. I don't know if you know . . . so I hope this doesn't come as a complete shock, but over the past several years that I haven't seen you, I've also realized that I'm gay."

A long, awkward minute of silence followed Rick's announcement. Rory didn't know what to say. He had known, but it still was a shock to his system to actually hear it. He started feeling nauseous all over again and wasn't sure if it was heat, dehydration, or his son's confession. *Probably a combination of the three*, he thought.

"That's okay, Dad, you don't have to say anything." Rick mercifully broke the silence.

"I guess I realized it; I saw something on Facebook. I don't know what to say except I still love you." The words tumbled out as if by rote. *What I really want to say is how my heart is broken, I'm so disappointed, I would wish for almost anything but this for my only son.*

Rory had heard news that most Methodist churches these days accepted homosexual ministers who had already been pre-ordained as long as they remained chaste and single. He wondered if Rick was following those precepts.

As if his son read his mind, Rick said, "I know it's tough for you to hear, given your upbringing and all. But here's the good news. Through my education, training, and ministry, I've realized that even though I'm gay, I don't need to give in to, well, the temptation of acting on it. I have come to believe that I should stay chaste. It's not easy, but I think it's what God wants."

Rory wanted to ask, "So have you given in to the temptation of acting out on your homosexuality in the past?" Ironically, at the same time he wanted to scream, "Stop talking! Too much information, I've heard enough!" Again, he said nothing, not knowing how to respond and not really wanting to know any more details.

So Rick continued. "I've also decided I want to be assigned to a parish that really needs help—somewhere in the US that I think needs ministering the most. I want to come out there to where you are, to Las Vegas."

"How did you know where I am?"

"I talked to Gran and asked where you were. I had already been considering moving to Las Vegas, but finding out you're already there was icing on the cake, as they say. I figured we could make up for lost time and do some stuff together."

How did his mother find out where he was? Oh well, that didn't matter now. Rory was speechless and felt overwhelmed with conflicting emotions…happiness that his son wanted to be with him yet fear that he wouldn't be able to handle his son's lifestyle; anger and guilt because their relationship had been so strained up until this point yet worry that he would hurt his son all over again when he broke the news that he wanted to maintain his single lifestyle and didn't really want to start up another relationship all over again, much less stay in Las Vegas… *I would love to make up for lost time, but there's no way on God's green—or in this case—brown earth that I am going back to Vegas. Sorry, Rick, not even for you.*

While he hesitated, Rory heard his phone give the signal that his battery was going to die any minute, and since his car wouldn't start, he couldn't charge it.

"Rick, listen, I'm really proud of you, and I want to see you too, but right now my phone's about to die, and I need your help. I'm stranded out in the middle of the desert somewhere in Nevada not too far from the Arizona border on I-15."

"Dad, why didn't you just call the police?"

"I can't. Long story."

"Are you okay?"

"I'm fine for a little while, but it's getting hot, and I have nothing to eat or drink, or even any shade."

"I'm sorry . . . here I went off talking all this time. So what do you want me to . . . ?"

And the line went dead.

No transportation, and now no way to communicate. Rory stared at the lifeless cell phone in his hand then threw it onto the back seat.

The windstorm that, unbeknownst to Rory, had been forecast by meteorologists on television that morning, started to gather force.

Rory had reclined his driver's seat and laid back in it, deciding to try to take a nap. He covered his head and face with an extra T-shirt he had grabbed from his suitcase to block the sun. If he fell asleep, he figured, maybe he wouldn't feel so hot and thirsty and hung over.

He felt the shirt ruffle a little in a breeze that blew by, and he ignored it.

Then the shirt actually blew off his face, and Rory sat up, squinting in the blinding white sun.

He sucked in hot, dry air in his already parched mouth and felt grains of sand sting his sunburned face. He looked in the direction in which the wind was blowing and rubbed his eyes to make sure he was seeing correctly.

In the not too far off distance, Rory could see what he believed to be a sandstorm forming. He wasn't sure, as he had never witnessed one before, but he figured if there was such a thing, this was definitely it.

The sky had turned a dull gray as whirls of sand were swirling and collecting like clouds, suspended in mid-air. They grew larger before Rory's eyes as he watched in awe. Within moments, they had formed what looked like a tidal wave of sand, growing in size as it rolled his way.

Rory was dumbstruck for a few minutes, and then realized he had to do something to protect himself. He crawled into the backseat, unzipped his suitcase, and yanked out pants, shirts, socks, underwear. Then he saw what he was searching for—a garment bag he had received with his purchase of a suit coat he had bought on a shopping trip at the mall in the Vegas suburbs.

He placed a pair of his boxer briefs on his head, ripped a T-shirt down the seam and wrapped it scarf-like around his face, and then crawled feet first into the plastic garment bag and zipped it up around himself as best he could. If he stayed scrunched up with his knees bent up in a fetal position, the bag came up around his shoulders and covered him from the neck down.

Rory lay face down on the back seat. He could hear the gale force winds whistle like steam from a kettle, howling as they picked up speed like a freight train. The sand stung him, pounding him hard and loud like hail, and then the storm engulfed him. He kept his eyes and mouth shut, holding his makeshift mask and head covering as tight as he could in his balled up fists under his chin.

He almost felt like he was going to suffocate so he took short, tiny breaths through his nose, trying not to hyperventilate. He prayed as he lay there. *God, just take me. Let me just die here. I'm no longer useful to anyone. I did my job. Or rather, You did Your job. I knew You would save Las Vegas. I should have followed my first inclination and kept running as far away as possible from this whole miserable mission. It's brought nothing but heartache and humiliation. I never asked for this assignment. So now that neither You nor Las Vegas nor anyone else needs me, and now that I have nothing left to live for, just let me die as quickly and painlessly as possible.*

He eventually lost track of time and felt light-headed and drowsy, unable to breathe. Finally, mercifully, he passed out, the sandstorm still raging.

Rory saw his dad walking toward him out of the gray-brown haze that obscured everything but his shadowy figure.

Howard Justice walked toward him out of the sandstorm as if nothing had happened to him—just like Rory remembered him before he got sick with his lung disease. As his father's shadow loomed closer, it became outlined, surrounded by a glowing white light.

Rory sat up as his father approached the dust-covered, tree-dented, flat-tired Maserati. His dad was dressed in his business suit and shiny shoes as if he were going to work at the FBI, just like he used to do when Rory was in his teens and twenties, but he shook his head, a look of dismay on his face.

"This wasn't my fault," Rory said defensively, already figuring his dad was disappointed that he had been in an accident.

"That's not why I'm looking at you this way."

"Then what's the matter, Dad?"

"Maybe you can tell me, son."

"What do you mean?"

"For starters, why were you just wishing that God would strike you dead? Do you really believe your life is that bad?"

"Yes . . . I mean no . . . well, I just felt like I have nothing more to live for, and I might as well die in this horrible sandstorm than live through it somehow."

"Really? Hmmm . . . you have nothing to live for?"

"Well, I did have this great car I'm sitting in, but look at it. It's ruined. It's nothing but a piece of junk now."

"It must have meant a lot to you, huh?"

"I loved that car. I won it from this Russian guy playing poker. It was so cool—I was so cool, the guys thought I was some kind of poker shark or King Midas or something. I couldn't lose. It was awesome. I drove off into the night not caring about anything but feeling the night wind and driving fast and watching the sunrise. I felt free from everything and everyone I left behind in that miserable city—which by the way, you made me try to save . . . thanks a lot, Dad."

His father just stood leaning against the dented passenger door, listening intently, resting his chin on his hand, occasionally nodding in understanding. He let Rory's sarcastic comment slide by without a change in expression, obviously not offended by it.

"And then all of this happened," Rory continued. "I never get a break. I came out here to this city I literally detest since it was your wish, and I did my part, and I won this great car only to have it turn into a broken-down piece of junk."

"Kind of like some of the people back there, huh?"

"I don't catch your drift."

"Well, you went out to Vegas and met some real losers, as you call them—prostitutes, homeless people, gang members, junkies—broken down pieces of junk."

"Very funny, Dad."

"I'm not trying to be funny, Rory. I'm dead serious. No pun intended. I just find it very discouraging that you seem much more upset about a little car falling apart than you did about any of the people in Las Vegas. And to say you have nothing to live for . . . how very sad. What about your children? What about your son who just called you and asked you to spend time with him?"

"Well . . . ." Rory didn't know what to say to that. He still felt unhappy about the fact that his son was gay. Besides, he was simply not going back to Las Vegas.

"Let me tell you a story," Howard Justice said.

CHAPTER EIGHTEEN

R ory's father opened the passenger door and climbed into the front seat of the dirty, beat-up Maserati. Rory tried not to roll his eyes and summoned all the patience he had left within him to sit back and listen.

"There was this guy—a white man—who grew up in a small town of people who were also white. He was raised being told that people who weren't white were not equal, were inferior in fact, especially colored or black people. He was taught that they weren't to be trusted, that they were criminals, that they would rob you blind, rape your women, or stab you in the back if you let them. He never saw any black kids in his school or even in his neighborhood, so he believed what he heard about them, and he was afraid of them.

"It was ingrained in him that white people always had to be on the lookout, on guard, and stay a step ahead of them. That meant teaching them a lesson sometimes . . . like burning crosses on their lawns. And when they did something bad, like steal something, it meant they got a public beating to scare the others in hopes they wouldn't try any funny business again. That small boy grew into a teenager and then a young man who hated blacks, mostly because he was afraid of them.

"Then one day he was working his first week on the job as a town police officer when he saw a sight he would never forget. A young girl, probably about seventeen, was walking home from school, taking a short-cut through a field, when two white guys, maybe about nineteen or twenty, jumped out from some bushes and attacked her. They threw her book bag on the ground, then they threw her down screaming, ripped her sweater, pinned her, and while one was the lookout, the other jumped on top of her, and was going to rape her.

"Just then a black teenager walked by. If he had been acting in his own best interests, he would have walked on by and ignored what was happening, minding his own business. Instead, he pulled the guy off the girl, and when the other lunged at him, the black teenager punched him in the face.

"What happened next would have been brutal if the young white cop hadn't driven by at that precise time, put on his siren, and sent the white guys running. The black teen had been roughed up and had a cut lip, a swollen eye, and a few bruised ribs. The girl was crying hysterically and shaking so badly she couldn't talk, while the black boy stood by silently, his good eye wide with terror.

"Since the boy and the girl remained quiet, the officer had to discern for himself what had taken place. He could either arrest the black teenager for assault, which would be the easy way out, or he could chase the young white men and arrest them for attempted rape. He knew that it would be a tough investigation, and even if they were arrested and found guilty of the crime, it probably wouldn't serve any purpose. The district attorney who would eventually try the case would only have the word of a black teenage boy and a girl who had a known reputation for hanging out after hours and being on the loose side, versus the two young white men who happened to be former high school football stars and from very prominent families.

"The officer decided to do the right thing anyway. He conducted an investigation and arrested the white boys."

"That police officer was you, wasn't it, Dad?" Rory remembered the stories he had eventually been told about the Ku Klux Klan in Rising Sun, and that his dad had worked as a cop when he was small.

"Yep. And it was by far the hardest thing I ever had to do. I wanted badly to just look the other way. Here I was trying to save this black boy who was a total stranger. He wasn't even from our town, but was just visiting some relatives with his aunt that day. I wasn't totally sure what had happened in the incident, but my gut told me the black boy was innocent.

"Of course I knew I would be ridiculed for my decision, maybe even lose my job over it, and definitely be shunned by half the town, including my own parents. But most of all I was afraid of putting my wife and two young sons in jeopardy."

"Did any of that happen?"

"It all happened, and more. Most of my family and friends disowned me and the police department took away my badge so I had no job. I had your mom take you boys with her to your grandmother's house about a half hour away in Pennsylvania."

"Oh, yeah, I remember when we stayed for a few weeks at Grandmom's. I just thought you were busy with your job and it was kind of like a summer vacation."

"The KKK tried to burn our house down, but I stopped the fire before it got out of hand. There were many days during the police investigation and trial when I just wanted to escape Rising Sun and never return. Luckily, I was befriended by my parish minister who kept telling me to have faith, to keep praying and it would all be ok in the long run. And he was right."

"What happened next?"

"The white boys got their day in court, the girl testified, a jury found the boys guilty of attempted rape, and they got six months of jail time."

"What about the black boy? What happened to him?"

Rory's dad shook his head. "He was hanged late one night in a barn before the trial took place. No one was ever arrested for it."

"So what did you do after that?"

"I stayed in Rising Sun long enough to testify at the trial and sentencing, then I packed up our belongings, sold the house, and we moved closer to DC in Bethesda, which at the time was just a sleepy little suburb. It had a big Jewish population and was much more tolerant of minorities since the Jews had also been victimized by the KKK and were sympathetic to blacks. I eventually got a job with the Maryland State Police, then the FBI, and the rest is history."

"Wow." Rory was flabbergasted.

He also realized that his father was telling him this story to teach him something, to convey a message of some sort. And he had a hunch that it had to do with him and Las Vegas.

"You think I should go back there, don't you, Dad?"

His father shrugged his shoulders and gently smiled. "That decision is yours alone to make, son. Most times, we can't see if we made the right decision until many years later, looking back. And then we can usually see if it was God-directed or not. Looking back on my decision to go after those white football players, I see now that God put me in that exact place at that exact time for a specific reason. Or there were several reasons—to bring a tiny piece of justice to a very prejudiced little town, to make a man out of me, to lead me to my future career as an FBI investigator, or maybe all of the above. I also know now that in calling me to help try to save that girl and that black boy, he was also saving me."

"What do you mean?"

"Saving me from being the fearful, judgmental, self-centered, close-minded man I had become."

And then, much the way he had appeared out of nowhere, his father was gone.

Rory felt a hand on his shoulder, shaking him, trying to wake him.

He was still lying face down on the rear seat of the Maserati, most of his body hunched in the plastic garment bag, which was buried beneath a half inch of sand.

He could barely breathe. Sand had managed to sneak into the crevices of his neck, ears, nose, and eyes, which he could only open into slits. He took a shallow breath through his mouth, which was so parched that he couldn't make his swollen tongue move to lick his dry, cracked lips. He also came to with a piercing headache. It was as if knives were being stuck into his skull.

Rory vaguely heard a woman's muffled voice call his name as if from a distance.

It was definitely a familiar voice. And then he knew. It was Susan.

A man's voice joined in. *John Dade?* "I think he's waking up, but he's definitely dehydrated and suffering from heat exposure. I'll call 911. They'll send a Medivac chopper."

Rory felt cool fingertips touch his neck. "They better. His pulse is elevated. He definitely has hyperthermia, and may have heat stroke."

"Let's get some water into him." After John hung up from the call, he and Susan rolled Rory over and unzipped him from the black plastic bag that had soaked up the sun and was acting like an oven-roasting bag.

Rory felt like he was in a fog. His vision was blurred and he tried to speak, to thank Susan and John, but the words just wouldn't form in his dry mouth and throat. He was so tired; all he wanted was to fall back asleep. His eyes closed again and his head bobbed forward.

"We've got to keep him awake," John said.

Suddenly, Rory felt cool water trickling over his face, his eyes, and into his mouth. He couldn't swallow and gagged at first, then managed to feel a few drops wet his cracked tongue. In a few moments, he was drinking and felt like he couldn't guzzle fast enough.

"Slow down, partner," John said soothingly.

He could finally see the beautiful face of Susan hovering over him, feel her wiping the dirt and sweat from his face with a cool, damp cloth.

She smiled at him. Looking into her big brown compassionate eyes, he wanted to cry, but had no tears in him to do so.

With some effort since he was dead weight, Susan and John hoisted Rory from the back of the Maserati out and into the rear seat of the air-conditioned police cruiser.

Rory could faintly hear the whirring beat of a helicopter approaching.

"They're going to have to land a mile away so they don't start another sandstorm. We'll have to meet them. Let's go."

It was a bumpy ride through the desert, but in just a few minutes, they arrived where the chopper sat waiting. Rory was safely positioned in the back of the helicopter. Intravenous fluids and an oxygen mask were administered by the two Medivac personnel inside, and once John and Susan had driven far enough away, the chopper was airborne, en route to Sunrise Hospital in Vegas.

Rory's body temperature had reached one hundred and six degrees at the height of the sandstorm. He was diagnosed with heat stroke, which could have been fatal if not for the just-in-time intervention of John and Susan.

Once in the hospital, his temperature was gradually lowered, his fluids were replenished, and he was left to rest. When Rory awoke lying in a hospital bed, he didn't know where he was at first. But then his memory slowly kicked into gear.

The first person to greet him was Susan, as if she had never left his side.

Rory smiled, feeling shy and embarrassed.

"Hi, sleepyhead," she said, arising from the chair where she was seated in his private hospital room, waiting for him to wake up. She walked over to his bedside and took one of his hands in hers.

"You're lucky, you know."

"I know." Rory could barely recognize his own voice. It was so scratchy it sounded like he had been a chain smoker for forty years. His throat was still a little sore, but at least he could make his tongue and lips work again. "Thank you."

"You're welcome. Here comes someone else you might want to thank."

John Dade walked into the room, filling the doorframe with his bulk, carrying two coffees in paper cups.

"Well, there's the famous gambler come back from the dead."

Rory winced, recalling his escapades from the night before. He couldn't look at Susan, fearing she had heard the worst.

John set down the cups of coffee, walked to the other side of Rory's bed, and shook his hand. "We're glad you made it, partner. I don't know how I would have ever explained this to your mother." *Always the jokester*, Rory thought with a smile.

"Thank you, John, for saving my life."

"Ah, glad to help. But the guy you really need to thank is your son Rick. He called the police department just in time. Actually, he's on a jet making his way here as we speak. He should be arriving sometime this evening to visit you."

"My son is on his way here?" Rory rasped. *I'm thankful he made that phone call to John and Susan, but he really doesn't need to fly all the way out here just to see me . . . unless . . . .* Rory recalled their conversation about Rick's ministry and his desire to move to Las Vegas. Even though he would love to see his son, he still didn't want Rick moving to Vegas any more than he wanted to stay himself.

"Isn't that a good thing?" Susan asked, and Rory sensed a trace of consternation in her tone.

"Uh, yes, of course. It's just that . . . ."

"You're not planning to stay, are you?" It was more a statement than a question. Rory noticed a slight but irrefutable note of irritation in her voice.

"I'm not sure." *That isn't exactly a lie*, Rory thought. "I may stay for a little while."

A nurse walked in to check Rory's vital signs and to replace the bags of intravenous fluids that hung by his bed.

"I guess we'll just be going," Susan said abruptly. She shook Rory's hand as if he was some stranger she was visiting for the first time. "Good luck, Rory, it was nice to see you again."

Even John looked at Susan with surprise. As she headed for the door, John asked her to please wait in the hall, saying he wanted to talk to Rory about something.

When the nurse left and the two men were alone, John whispered, "What's that all about?"

"Long story." Rory pointed to his throat, indicating it was still feeling a little raw.

"Ah, girl troubles?" John pulled up a chair to chat. Rory wanted to roll over and ignore him but instead, just shrugged his shoulders.

Whatever, he thought. *She's got too much of a temper for me. Who knows what she's thinking? Besides, the truth is that I'm not staying any longer than I have to.*

John laid a big hand on Rory's shoulder, like his dad would have done. "I've known Susan for a long time. I'm pretty sure she likes you, a lot, enough to be annoyed that you can't wait to get out of town again, even though she won't admit it. She is one strong, classy lady. And of course she's beautiful to boot. So what's the problem? Don't you like her too? I thought I knew you by now. You've kinda become like a son to me, and I was hoping I could talk to you like your dad might do if he were still here. Of course I don't mean to ever take his place or anything."

"That's okay, John," Rory forced the words out. "I know what you mean, and I appreciate all you're trying to do. And you're right. Susan is a wonderful woman. I was attracted to her too."

"Was? So you're not now?"

"Yes, I am . . . but . . . she won't leave Las Vegas, and I can't stay. So what's the point?"

John looked puzzled and sad. "What about your son? What are you going to tell him?"

"I don't know. We never really finished our conversation because the phone went dead. I never promised him anything—or her, for that matter."

John slowly rose from his chair and shook Rory's hand. "I will miss you."

The huge ex-sheriff ambled out of Rory's hospital room without looking back, softly closing the door behind him.

CHAPTER NINETEEN

His son arrived at the hospital just after Rory drifted off to sleep that evening. Rick stayed through the night and morning with his father, holding his hand and praying for him.

The next day Rick found a cheap, sparsely furnished, two-bedroom apartment for the two of them in Paradise, a suburb just southeast of the city. It was available on a month-to-month rental basis.

Rory was released from the hospital that night and was too weak to protest the living arrangements when Rick came to get him and told him he would be staying with him in his new apartment. Rick told Rory that he didn't have to stay beyond his recuperation, which the ER doctor had said was expected to last only a few days, as long as he got plenty of rest and fluids.

While Rory followed that prescription over the next few days, napping, watching movies, and reading, Rick was mostly out and about, away from the apartment.

On their second evening together, while they were eating Chinese take-out at the small dinette in their little kitchen, Rory questioned his son about where he had gone for the day. Rick just said he was "checking out" Las Vegas since he had never been to Sin City before. "Okay, I'm also seeing if it's where I want to stay," he added when Rory glanced at him skeptically.

I hope he's not counting on me to stay too, Rory thought.

As if he could read his mind, Rick said, "I know, dad, you'll probably head back to Ohio soon. But that's okay. I'm just glad we're having some time together."

Day four landed on a Friday. Since he was feeling back to normal, Rory decided to stay through the weekend to spend a few quality days with Rick. Besides, he didn't really have a job to go back to anyway.

"But I still think I'll be leaving eventually," he warned his son as they split a veggie omelet for breakfast. Much to Rory's chagrin, Rick had become a vegetarian. *Although that's nothing compared to the whole gay thing*, Rory thought when his son went grocery shopping for the two of them and revealed his eating habits while filling the refrigerator. "I really can't see myself living or working here. I just need to decide where I *can* see myself ending up."

Rory was pretty sure he didn't want to go back to Columbus, and especially not back to his old ad agency job, even if there was an open position. He just didn't know where he wanted to be or what he wanted to do.

He had mostly enjoyed the past three days of virtual isolation, actually. But he felt that if he left without spending more time with his son, he might eventually regret it.

Seeing Rick's face light up when he told him he'd be staying at least through the weekend told him it was the right decision.

"So what do you want to do and where do you want to go this weekend?" Rick asked after they had finished breakfast, and each had showered and shaved.

"I have no idea," Rory said. "I was going to ask you the same thing. It really doesn't matter to me. How about if you decide?"

"Are you sure?"

"Absolutely." *I couldn't care less when it comes to Las Vegas*, Rory thought. *I've already seen far too much.*

"Okay, in that case, I do have a few places in mind that I'd like you to visit with me."

"Hmm . . . so where to?"

"You'll see. I'll surprise you."

"Rick, you know I hate surprises."

"I know, Dad, but just trust me."

Rory wasn't sure if he did or even could trust anyone ever again. Still, this was his son. *How bad could it be?*

Rick had bought a used Volkswagen at a car lot while he had been gallivanting around the city. The two climbed in, and Rick drove into the city and parked in front of a Goodwill thrift shop.

"Stop number one," Rick said, getting out of the Beetle.

"Here?" Rory looked both ways down the street. Besides the Goodwill and a few rundown vacant buildings, there was only a car wash a block away and a convenience store across the street. They were just on the outskirts of Vegas and could see the skyscraping Stratosphere thrill ride and amusement park at the far end of the Strip about a mile away.

"Yep. Don't forget, trust me." He led Rory into the store. The clerk at the counter, an elderly black woman, greeted Rick like he was her grandson.

"Ricky, good to see you, where you been?" She came around from behind the counter and gave Rick a hug.

"Delores, I'd like you to meet my father, Rory Justice."

"It's a pleasure." The plump woman with black curls that grayed into crispy ringlets smiled warmly, her brown eyes twinkling with genuine mirth.

Rory looked with shock at both of them, unable to fathom how his son could possibly have gotten to know a total stranger in Vegas so well after only a few days. Realizing he was staring and being rude, he forced a smile and took the elderly woman's outstretched hand in his. "Nice to meet you."

"Delores, is it all right if I take my dad into the back?"

"Of course, I'll mind the store."

The back? Rory felt uneasiness creep over him like a prickly cold sweat. But he had no choice but to follow Rick, who led him briskly single file through narrow aisles lined with racks of clothes to the back of the store and through a steel door. They walked into a large warehouse. *What is my son getting me into now?*

Seated at various long tables were about two dozen teenagers sorting piles of clothes. Within moments of seeing Rick enter, they all came up and took turns hugging or high-fiving him.

Rick introduced Rory to them, and explained to his father that the teens were members of a Christian youth organization called Young Life. They were volunteering their time to help with Goodwill's recycling efforts. Goodwill took all of the clothes and other items that were too damaged to be sold in the outlet, bundled them up, and sent them off, usually to third world countries, to be recycled for use as raw materials.

"Nothing's wasted around here," Rick said.

"How do they all know you?" Rory whispered when they were leaving after saying their goodbyes.

Back outside the steel door and in the showroom, Rick paused and told his father how he had contacted the Young Life director shortly after they had settled into the apartment. He had signed up to be a leader.

Rory noticed some of the teen volunteers had called out "see you Sunday!" as they bade farewell. He figured his son must be meeting with them again on Sunday.

Their next stop was at the local homeless shelter downtown.

Rick asked Rory if he would like to help serve the midday hot meal.

Not really, Rory thought, but figured he couldn't very well say no to the request without coming across as a huge jerk.

So he donned an apron once his son introduced him to the other volunteers and shelter workers, and soon was dishing out roast beef, mashed potatoes, and gravy.

Two hours later, after lunch had been served, the volunteers ate, and then they all washed pots and pans and tidied up. When Rory and Rick said goodbye to the others, two shelter workers also said they would see both of them on Sunday.

They're just mistaken, thinking I'm coming to the Young Life meeting, Rory thought, shrugging it off. He felt tired and sweaty, yet strangely content as he sat once again in the passenger seat of the VW, too tired to question his son what was happening on Sunday.

"I've never done anything like that before," Rory said as they drove off. "It was nice how they all said thank you and seemed really grateful. I actually enjoyed helping."

Rick smiled. "I figured you might," he said with a gleam in his eyes. "And they always need volunteers."

"Yes, well, maybe I can do it wherever it is that I move to next."

Rick's eyes clouded with a little sadness. "That would be nice, Dad."

Next they stopped at a place that looked vaguely familiar to Rory.

The VW pulled up in front of an industrial building that bore a sign that read Vegas Allied Youth Association, with smaller lettering underneath that Rory recognized: VAYA con Dios.

"I know this place!" Rory stepped out of the car onto the curb out front and told Rick with a touch of pride how the organization had resulted from the grass roots efforts begun by the Brown and Ramirez families, borne out of the pain of their loss and strife due to gang violence and drug abuse.

"I know," Rick said.

Rory was surprised at his son's comment.

"How do you know that?"

"Because I did my homework. The Young Life folks told me I could probably find some volunteers down here for a small choir or band to eventually sing at my church services. They told me that the same local FBI and police team they had seen on the news that had worked on the bomb scare and helped rid the city of the Mafia had also helped make VAYA a reality. I knew you were part of that team. I'm very proud of you, Dad. "

Rory felt himself blush a little, but brushed off the compliment. He had only been a tiny part of the equation. Actually, as he recalled, Susan had come up with the idea to use the abandoned warehouse . . . *Susan*. Just thinking her name was painful.

He missed her with an ache that was palpable, that hurt like a vise gripping his chest. He quickly changed the subject, forcing the vision of her face from his mind.

"So you're going to hold a church service soon?"

"Sunday, to be exact."

So that was it. "Where?"

"Well, I'm filling in at a brand new local non-denominational church here. I'm really nervous, actually, since I've only been preaching for a few months back home. And it's not exactly your typical church."

"Why, what do you mean?"

"On my second day here, I heard this parish had burned down so I called to see if they needed help. I guess I just felt the spirit move me. Next thing you know, they asked if I could give Sunday's sermon and help them start over again. They are going to congregate at the Two Hearts Wedding Chapel. They're allowing us to use the space until we find a permanent home. We're paying top dollar so the chapel didn't mind losing a few weddings for a couple of Sundays. I'm really nervous actually. I just hope some people show up."

"Would you like me to come?" The words were out of Rory's mouth before he could take them back.

Besides his dad's funeral, Rory hadn't been to a church service in twenty years. The divorce and losing his kids and working at a job he hated and feeling like all that life had dealt him was a bunch of hard knocks had hardened his heart toward anything spiritual or religious. He still believed in God, but after so many of his prayers had been unanswered, he rarely prayed anymore. And when he had prayed lately, his prayers had been more of the foxhole type, like on the cruise ship and the submarine when he prayed "Lord, get me out of this mess," or caught on the run with Tiffany in Wildcats when he prayed, "Lord, please don't let us die," and of course, just recently, in the Nevada desert, when he was in despair and prayed, "Lord, just take me. I have nothing to live for."

So why he had just volunteered to attend a church service was beyond his comprehension.

But Rick's face lit up even brighter than it had when Rory had agreed to spend the weekend with him. "That would mean a lot, Dad."

Too late now, Rory chided himself. *I'll just sit in the back and leave early if it gets to be too much. Then I'll book my flight to wherever.*

The tiny chapel overflowed with people that Sunday morning—young mothers with infants, teenagers and young people in their twenties, homeless men, addicts looking hungover—the poor, the outcast, the downtrodden, those on the fringes of society.

It turned out that all the while Rory had lazily lain on the couch in their shared apartment watching television and playing video games, Rick had literally pounded the pavement on a mission to gather people to come to the first service of the fledgling new church called Kingdom Rising.

He couldn't offer them money or jobs or a cure for their diseases and addictions; he only offered hope and a better way to live if they attended for just one hour a week.

Some arrived out of curiosity. Some came because there was the draw of free coffee and cookies, proclaimed on the fliers Rick and some Young Life helpers handed out on the Vegas street corners.

And others, like Rory, came out of a sense of guilt and obligation.

Rory didn't know at the time that he would come to believe every single one of them would leave that service feeling like Rick had upheld his end of the bargain.

The handsome young minister walked out to the altar at the front of the cheesy little wedding chapel as the youth band he had recruited played a contemporary Christian rock song. Pastor Rick was dressed in a navy suit with a white shirt and tie. Rory admired how handsome his son looked, and half held his breath hoping he would do well, whatever that entailed.

After he prayed a blessing over them all, Rick read a passage from the Gospel of Luke, chapter seventeen, about the ten lepers being cleansed by Jesus.

"Now one of them, when he saw that he had been healed, turned back, glorifying God with a loud voice, and he fell on his face at His feet, giving thanks to Him. And he was a Samaritan. Then Jesus answered and said, 'Were there not ten cleansed? But the nine—where are they? Was no one found who returned to give glory to God except this foreigner?' And He said to him, 'Stand up and go; your faith has made you well.' Now having been questioned by the Pharisees as to when the kingdom of God was coming, He answered them and said, 'The kingdom of God is not coming with signs to be observed; nor will

they say, 'Look, here it is!' or 'There it is!' For behold, the kingdom of God is in your midst.'"

After he finished reading, Rick reverently closed the Bible, gently laid it on the lectern where he stood, and folded his hands for a moment, seemingly lost in thought.

"So what is Luke saying?" he finally asked, addressing the audience assembled before him. Some fidgeted or were falling asleep in their chairs, and Rory wanted to shout at them from the front row, "Pay attention, he's my son!" but he didn't want to be disruptive.

"What is Jesus saying?" Rick asked again to those who were listening. "I'd like to share with you my thoughts. First of all, I believe we're all lepers—unclean in some way. We've all made mistakes, and while it may not always show on the outside, most of us are damaged in some way—sick, sinful, sad, and suffering on the inside. Most of you wouldn't be sitting here today if you weren't."

Just look around the room at this bunch, Rory thought, trying unsuccessfully to put his judgmental attitude aside.

"But I also know we can be healed." Rick walked over to the small, makeshift altar and lifted a wooden cross about a foot tall, held it in his hands for a few moments carefully and lovingly, then held it up for all to see.

"All we have to do is believe we *can* be. Believe there is a God who loves us enough to make it happen." He laid the cross back down on the altar and walked around front to stand among the motley congregation.

"Yet most of us don't believe there is someone who loves us that much. Nothing good ever happens to us, and we think we're not worth it, or we refuse to believe it, or if we do believe, we're just plain angry at God that things aren't going our way."

Rory felt the jab of his son's last comment prick his heart a little, but he made an effort to pay attention, trying not to get lost in his own self-absorbed thoughts.

"And if something good does happen and we actually believe our prayers have been answered, at least temporarily, we quickly forget just days or sometimes hours later, becoming like the nine lepers who had been healed but weren't grateful."

Rory thought about the way he had become so bitter and angry at God, enough to just want Him to end his life, all because his beloved car had crashed and he had been caught in a sandstorm. *A car that I won in a game of chance, that I didn't even earn.*

It dawned on him that if the events of the morning he crashed hadn't unfolded the way they had, he wouldn't be sitting here listening to his son preach right now.

Unexpectedly, Rory felt an overwhelming urge to weep. It took everything in him to hold back the tears that welled in his eyes. Gratitude filled him, and he whispered a silent prayer of thanks.

"I also believe Jesus is telling us to look around because the kingdom is right here, right now, and we are the people to uncover it, to build it, to make it shine. If we don't, no one will. We need to help each other. Look around you. Look to your right and left. Introduce yourselves. I'll give you a minute."

Rory wanted desperately to do anything but look around. He was afraid, but stiffly turned to his right and shook the dry, withered hand of an elderly man, crooked with arthritis, leaning on a cane and smiling at him through wrinkled, rheumy eyes. Rory could smell the alcohol on his breath.

This could be me in thirty years, Rory suddenly thought. *An old alcoholic, all alone.*

Then he turned to his left and shook hands with a young man who looked Indian or Arab. He was handsome, probably around nineteen or twenty years old.

Rory was puzzled at first as to why the young man was in a Christian church, since he thought most Arabs were Muslims. *Of course, it is non-denominational,* he thought. *Still . . .* Rory felt a wave of unease rush through him, realizing it was prejudice seeping through him like poison.

He swallowed his pride and introduced himself.

"I'm Rory Justice."

"Father of Pastor Rick?" The young man flashed him a beaming smile. "You must be very proud," he said with an Arab accent. "And you must be a very good father."

"Why, thank you. And what is your name?"

"I am Ahmad Jabar."

A wave of panic washed over Rory. *Ahmad Jabar.*

Could it be a coincidence? Is he sitting next to me on purpose? Rory glanced around quickly but didn't notice any other Middle Easterners.

He was afraid to ask the young man his next question but felt too curious to hold back.

"You wouldn't happen to be related to Rafik or Ali?" Rory asked hesitantly, suddenly fearing for his life, but daring to look squarely into the young man's intense dark brown eyes.

"Yes, I am Ali's brother and Rafik's son."

Rory's voice caught in his throat, and he couldn't speak for a few moments. He took a deep breath and said, "You also must be very proud of your father."

Ahmad beamed a smile at Rory and put both arms around him, hugging him tightly. The tears that stung Rory's eyes fell onto his shirt, and he sniffed back a sob.

Rick held up his hands as a signal they were to finish their introductions and resume the service. Rory fought to contain his emotions once more and stood looking straight ahead.

"We need to help each other—believe in the good, uplift one another's spirits, teach each other the right way, be good examples," Rick continued. "We are all important, all the children of God. We need to look past one another's skin colors or nationalities, religions or social status. Jesus loved all the people He met and ministered to—especially the lepers and sinners—because they were the ones who needed the most help and had the best chance of reaching out for it in their desperation. We are the ones. We are the kingdom, right here, right now, because God has brought us to this place, in this time, with these people. And as the song says, 'we're all we got'."

Rory felt Ahmad Jabar's hand touch his left shoulder in a comforting gesture.

And as the youth group broke out once again in song, Rory sat in his chair, put his face in his hands, and wept.

Rick said a final prayer over the congregation then welcomed everyone to have cookies and coffee. He stood at the back of the chapel where he warmly bade farewell to each person as he or she exited.

Rory alone stayed, sitting in the pew, head in hands. He was all cried out, but he couldn't bring himself to face anyone.

When the last person had left, Rick sat down next to his dad.

"Want to talk?" he offered softly.

Rory raised his head. He could feel his eyes were swollen, but at least he had no tears left in him. He felt embarrassed to be crying in front of his son like this.

"You did a good job up there, Rick." Rory smiled weakly.

"Dad, why are you crying?"

"Oh, I don't know, I guess because I was so proud of you."

"Dad, that's not why. I think you need to let go of this . . . this stuff you've held bottled up inside for so long. You know how Christians talk about being saved? Dad, do you believe you've been saved?"

"Oh, Rick, let's not talk about that. Let's talk about how great you did up there!" Rory forced a big grin. "You were amazing."

"Please, Dad. It all doesn't mean anything when my own father is sitting here feeling this way. I want to help. Do you believe you've been saved?"

Rory looked into the shining green eyes of his son, so innocent, so kind.

"I don't know what that even means."

"Being saved means believing your sins have been completely forgiven, and starting anew in that faith."

Rory sat for a moment thinking *that's it?* But he couldn't bring himself to answer the question.

"Dad?"

"I guess I've never really thought about it that way before. I always thought I had to be baptized in a lake or go to confession or something. I honestly don't know."

"Have you forgiven everyone who has ever hurt you?"

Rory thought about that for a minute. He certainly hadn't forgiven his ex-wife Haley. He hadn't forgiven his co-workers or his boss at AdExecs. And he most certainly could not forgive the Islamic State Mafia and all of the other low-lifes of Las Vegas who had taken advantage of other people and caused him to have to come out here and experience all of this suffering. He hadn't even forgiven Susan for ditching him.

"Have you forgiven yourself?" Rick asked gently.

For what? Rory thought instantly. *Where was I to blame in any of this?* And suddenly, memories flooded back like a tidal wave: having an affair with a call girl right here in this city and keeping it a secret for so long; leaving his wife and children, blaming them for all of his misery; wasting all those years just getting by in life, working at a job he despised with people he loathed; escaping his father's deathbed request by hopping on a cruise ship; dismissing the one woman he had ever truly loved because she wouldn't conform to his plan; hating Las Vegas, the world, and everyone in it; and most of all, hating himself and hating the God who put him here.

And the tears he thought had all dried up fell once more.

"No," he said, his voice choked with grief.

"Let's do it now then." Rick took his dad's hands in his own, closed his eyes, and bowed his head. Rory did the same.

"Father, please allow your grace and forgiving spirit to wash through my father, cleansing him of all the pain and anger he has stored up inside. Help him to forgive others and himself so that he can be saved through Your Son Jesus Christ, can believe in You, and start his life anew. Amen."

Rory inhaled and felt a deep, cleansing breath fill him, touching him deep down inside. Suddenly he felt renewed. *I guess this is what it means to be born again*, he thought, and he smiled.

He opened his eyes, and there in front of him, smiling too, was this amazing man that he, Rory Justice, had raised, but whom, he just now realized, God had brought into this world for His own special purpose.

And I guess He has a purpose for me too. He smiled inwardly. *I've been trying to run away from it all this time. I didn't stop long enough to listen.*

"I need your help, Dad," Rick said, and Rory had a hunch he was about to find out what he was supposed to do.

EPILOGUE
- - - - -

The clean-shaven young man dressed in slacks, a collared shirt and a blazer stood to the right in the lobby of Caesar's Palace so as not to interfere with the hotel guests checking in and out.

Yet he was strategically standing in a place where tourists and guests would pass by coming in or going out of the resort's casinos or main tower of meeting rooms and hotel suites.

He was unobtrusively handing out pamphlets to those who stopped long enough to take one, smiling a greeting but not saying much besides an occasional "hello" or "have a nice day." His name was Tim.

A small group of five middle-aged men, all dressed in expensive suits, walked by the young man holding out his pamphlets that night. It was 6 p.m., and they were headed out to party after attending a long day of conference sessions. One of them stopped to check his watch and his pocket for his keys right next to Tim, who smiled politely and handed him a brochure.

The man called to his buddies to wait a second, took the brochure from Tim, and gazed down at it.

"Ha!" He shouted obnoxiously to no one in particular, although loudly enough for the rest of the group waiting for him to hear. "What is this garbage?"

Tim stood by and said nothing as the man, who had obviously already had a few too many drinks at a happy hour, ranted on.

"This guy is handing out Christian stuff. He must be one of those Bible thumpers, or maybe he's just gay. Here I thought I was gonna get a coupon for free drinks at one of the nightclubs or better yet, info on how to find the hottest women in town. Vegas is going downhill fast. From what I hear, there aren't even any really good strip clubs left, you know, the kind where you can get some action." He swung his hips forward to show what he meant as his compatriots circled around him to take him with them.

"Come on, Chad." One of the guys in the group took the loud-mouthed man's arm, coaxing him away from Tim. "We'll find one."

Rory watched the scene unfold from behind one of the marble columns in the hotel lobby. He had arrived minutes ago carrying a box of brochures to give to Tim to replenish his stock.

He recognized Chad and two of the other guys in the group from AdExecs. He wanted to stay hidden behind the column but decided he needed to say something after all.

Rory walked up to them just as Chad made a show of ripping the brochure into pieces and throwing the tiny bits into the air like confetti while calling back over his shoulder in Tim's direction, "Hey, here's what I think of your gay Bible crap!"

"Excuse me, that wasn't very nice Chad." Rory had walked quickly right up to the group and now stood inches away from his target.

"I'm sorry, do I know you? Rory? Rory Justice?"

It took a minute for Chad to recognize his former colleague. Rory had grown his hair a little longer and now had a mustache and short beard. *They probably think I turned into some kind of hippie.* Rory suppressed a grin. "Yes, it's me. And I actually help pay for those brochures you just ripped up. I think you owe young Tim over there an apology. He was only doing his job."

Chad's eyes grew into slits as he peered condescendingly at Tim, who was standing in the same spot, his mouth hanging open a bit.

"Hey, I'm sorry." Chad huffed in an insincere tone then turned back to Rory. "So what's gotten into you, man? What happened to the ad exec I used to know? What are you, some Jesus freak now?" Chad threw a pretend punch at Rory's ribs.

"I'm working for my son's new church, Kingdom Rising. He moved out here to Las Vegas and became a minister, and since I had won a ton of money out here in the casinos recently, I decided to stay and help him out and volunteer. I don't really need to work anymore."

Rory couldn't help throw that last dig in, and watched with guilty pleasure as Chad's face registered surprise and a hint of jealousy, which he tried to hide.

"By the way, it's non-denominational and full of sinners of all nationalities, ages, races, shapes, and sizes. We can always hold more." Rory felt like he was on a roll and couldn't stop.

Chad now looked indignant. One of his friends in the group whom Rory didn't know called out to rescue him, seeing his anger rising. "Hey, Chad, are you coming or what? We're gonna leave without you."

"I'm coming." Chad didn't bother to shake Rory's hand as he turned to go. "Well, good luck with all that. See ya."

Rory heard him turn to his buddy just as the door was closing behind them and say, "What a chump!"

Rory waited for them to disappear then walked over to the entrance, set his box on the floor, and joined Tim to pick up the torn pieces of paper. After they were done cleaning up, Rory gave Tim a hug and shook his hand.

"You did great keeping your cool," he told the young man. "It was all I could do not to punch that guy in the mouth. I never did like that dude."

When Tim looked at him quizzically, Rory explained. "I actually used to work with him at an advertising agency in Ohio called AdExecs. He was a punk then and is still a troublemaker today, it seems. Of course, I wasn't much better myself back then." Rory looked at his watch and saw it was after six. "Come on, I'll give you a lift back to the church. It's quitting time."

After he dropped Tim off in the church parking lot, Rory went inside.

His son had entrusted him with one of three keys to the building. The other two went to Rick and the church's maintenance director.

Rory was supposed to meet his son here at seven to grab a late dinner. Since he was early, he decided to take advantage of the quiet for a little while.

As he flipped on the light switch to the front vestibule, Rory marveled once again at how beautiful the church had turned out to be and how ironic it was that it had formerly been a seedy, run-down strip club.

Incandescent light flooded the cream-colored, high-ceilinged lobby, which opened to a side office. Rory went into the office, laid his box of brochures and keys on the desk, and went back into the foyer and through the stained wood doors that served as the entrance to the main chapel.

It was amazing what several coats of paint, some nice lighting, new carpeting and the installation of several rows of pews and an altar could do.

What had once been known as the dance floor of Shady's topless bar was now the sanctuary of Kingdom Rising. The place had been gutted of its dance poles and long bars and neon signs. A beautiful chapel decorated in earth tones and wood accents with seating for about two hundred now filled the space, radiating serenity, warmth, and light.

Rory entered the church and sat in the back pew. He reflected back on how his life had twisted in a different direction ever since that Sunday morning one year ago in the Two Hearts Wedding Chapel.

Father and son had left the little chapel together that day and gone home to their apartment to talk over their plan into the late hours of the night.

Rory decided he would stay in Vegas to help Rick build Kingdom Rising. He ended up donating fifty thousand dollars of his gambling winnings to the fledgling church, which helped pay for rent, utilities, and other expenses to hold services at the Two Hearts Wedding Chapel until they could find a permanent place.

He also put his ad agency experience to work, promoting Kingdom Rising and its message of hope as well as a schedule of services through print advertising, publicity, pamphlets, internet ads, and social media. Soon the word spread, and the little chapel was overflowing.

Rory co-signed the bank loan to help Rick buy Shady's and renovate it, and soon, his son was preaching from the beautiful church Rory stood in today.

He reminisced about the first day he and Rick had walked into the empty former nightclub, which reeked of stale beer, cigarettes, and sweat. Rick had stood right in the middle of the dark, dank room and smiled, then shouted, "Alleluia! Thank you Jesus!" It was like he had walked into a big Baptist church instead of a bankrupt strip joint.

That was about three months after Rory was saved and decided to stay in Vegas. "You've got to be kidding," Rory had still said skeptically. "Surely you're not going to buy this place?"

"It's perfect!" Rick had exclaimed. "I can just envision what it will become."

Rory was joyful in helping Rick follow his dream and achieve his mission, but he still felt a small empty ache inside.

He knew he was missing something, or rather . . . someone to share it with.

The morning after he had sat in the attorney's office with Rick signing the loan papers for Kingdom Rising, Rory had felt an overwhelming urge to see Susan.

Fortunately, he didn't have to search too far to find her. He found out she had gone back to work at the Las Vegas Police Department SVU.

Rory had told Rick where he was going, and asked his help in selecting an outfit. Rick suggested he wear something casual yet stylish, like new jeans and a white button down shirt.

He had decided to surprise her, hoping beyond hope that she would be there.

It was mid-morning on an early November Tuesday. Rory stopped at a florist along the way and picked up a half-dozen white roses. He would have bought her a dozen red roses, but after talking to the florist, realized that might look too presumptuous and overwhelming.

Walking up to the police station entrance, Rory hesitated on the steps just outside the door, flowers in his trembling hands, his heart beating like a frantic drum.

He had never felt so anxious, so panicked in his entire life, including the time on the cruise ship in the storm and as a prisoner in the submarine submerged hundreds of feet in the deep with no way out.

What if she's not here? Or worse yet, what if she is, and she refuses to see me or talk to me? What if she laughs at me, yells at me, throws the flowers in the trash?

Rory summoned his courage and said a prayer. *God, please keep her heart open, if it's Your Will.* He took a deep breath and entered the station.

She was sitting at her desk, her chin resting in her cupped hand, staring down at some paperwork, and didn't see him walk in.

Carlos, who was standing chatting with another officer on the opposite side of the room, did see him, however, and his mouth dropped open. Rory held his finger to his lips, silencing his old

Condo partner, who smiled and glanced toward Susan but didn't say a word.

Rory slowly, quietly walked up to her desk, and was only two feet away when she sensed a presence and looked up. Shock registered in her big brown eyes as she sat up straight and just stared at him.

He brought the flowers, which he had been holding behind his back, out in front of him and held them forward across the desk with a sheepish grin.

She took the flowers and smiled, and Rory felt his crazy heart melt inside him.

"You were right, by the way," he said bashfully.

She didn't say a word, but Rory saw the question in her eyes.

"I decided to stay here in Vegas." He paused to see her reaction, and his heart sang when the corners of her mouth turned up slightly, and a mischievous "I told you so" gleam lit up her eyes.

"I guess my son Rick needed my help, and I couldn't say no." He grinned slyly. "Turns out maybe I can be useful, and the folks here aren't so bad after all."

Susan stood up and crossed her arms indignantly, a frown on her face, and Rory felt flustered and confused. *Uh-oh*, he thought, *here it comes. She didn't get that I was joking.*

"You've been here three months and you haven't called me?" Susan raised her voice, but her tone seemed only mildly perturbed, and Rory felt relief sweep through him.

She cares where I've been and that I haven't called her!

"I'm sorry, I didn't . . . uh . . . I wasn't sure where . . . or how you felt and . . . ." He let his words trail off, uncertain how to finish.

She smiled and Rory exhaled with relief. "That's okay, I'm sorry too. I didn't exactly end things well with you either." She looked down at the flowers she was still holding. "These are beautiful. Thank you, Rory."

Hearing her say his name was the most wonderful sound in the world, and he wanted to cry from the happiness that filled him.

And in an instant, the past was seemingly forgotten as she put the flowers down, came around the desk and put her arms around him, hugging him tight.

Rory hugged her back, shutting his eyes, drinking in her familiar sweet scent, forgetting everything else around them, and feeling like the luckiest man in the world just to hold her for this moment. Then he looked into her eyes, which sparkled with joy, and kissed her.

Carlos loudly cleared his throat, reminding them he and the other officer were still in the room. "We're still here! Go get a room."

"Shut up, you!" Rory shot back, noticing Susan blush. They broke from their embrace, but he didn't mind that it was an awkward moment. She had hugged him and kissed him back, and all was right with the world.

Shortly after Rory's reunion with Susan and Carlos, he received a very special piece of mail. It was an envelope addressed to him from the office of the President of the United States. Inside, on the president's official stationery, was a formal letter of commendation for his heroic efforts on the FBI Las Vegas Operation and an invitation, embossed with the presidential seal, to a ceremony in his honor to award him with the Presidential Medal of Freedom. The ceremony was to take place in two months on January 6, celebrating the six-month anniversary of the day when the nuclear bomb was diffused and the ISM leaders were arrested and brought into captivity.

Rory was among fifteen people involved with Operation No Dice to be awarded with the Medal of Freedom that evening in the East Room of the White House. President Tower took the podium to address the crowd, and one by one, the inductees were called by name to receive the nation's highest civilian award. They included Mayor Stanley Cooper, FBI Chief Rodney Steele, Special Agent Mark Glover, Las Vegas Police Sheriff Ned Thomas, former Sheriff John Dade, Sergeant Carlos Fuentes, SVU Lieutenant Susan McAfree, and Rory Justice.

"On behalf of myself, my husband, Paul, and the entire nation, I welcome you all to the White House." President Tower addressed the assembly of press corps members, inductees, friends, and family. "We set aside this time to celebrate people who have made America wiser, stronger, safer, and freer. This medal is the highest honor bestowed on individuals who have made especially meritorious contributions to the security or national interests of the United States.

"We thank all of them for the gifts they have given to us: outstanding displays of human courage, indomitable spirit, and selfless bravery that have benefitted thousands, if not millions of Americans."

President Tower briefly introduced each of the recipients before they received their awards. The applause was loudest when the last recipient took the stage—Rafik Jabar.

"Mr. Jabar risked his life and those of his family members to do the right thing and report findings that paved the way for our FBI team and police force to find the nuclear weapon planted by the Islamic State Mafia in Las Vegas," the president noted. "He looked beyond the borders of race and religion to see what makes American citizens of integrity the same: the desire to do good and not evil."

These last remarks were met with a standing ovation.

A black-tie dinner at the American History Museum followed the White House ceremony. Rory had invited his mom and his son Rick to attend with him but made sure he sat next to Susan, who was dressed in an elegant royal blue sheath that set off the fiery ringlets that cascaded on her shoulders.

Susan was accompanied at the dinner by Theresa Brindle, Claudette Brown, and Isabel Ramirez. It warmed Rory's heart to see them there and to realize how thoughtful Susan was to invite them.

As everyone was chatting after dinner, Rory noticed Rick talking with Ahmed Jabar and his sister Amber, and felt a mix of emotions course through him.

Flashes popped and Rory briefly thought how attractive a couple Rick and the beautiful Amber would have made had his son not been . . . *but then life is life, and we all have a destiny ordained by God to discover and fulfill,* Rory mused, dismissing the what-ifs from his mind. Pride suddenly enveloped him as the father of this extraordinary young man. *How sad it would be to limit our potential and purpose in life to what society, or our parents for that matter, deem appropriate.*

Rory sat as the dusk fell and the only light in the church was the soft amber glow of the sconces on either side of the altar. While the temperatures remained fairly constant in Vegas, the night still came early in October.

He reminisced about how he came to stay for over a year now in a place he originally despised and vowed never to step foot in again, and how he came to be here in the first place. He recalled the letter from his father, and the visits his dad had made in his dreams.

Rory suddenly had an epiphany: he hadn't experienced one of those dreams since he had made the decision to stay here. He smiled to himself. Even though his dad hadn't appeared recently, Rory still talked to him occasionally, usually right here in church.

Sometimes he could see his dad smiling down at him.

You won, Rory said now to his dad, smiling to himself, looking up toward the church's vaulted ceiling. *And I won.*

Rory put his hand in his pants pocket and pulled out the small ring box. He opened it, gazing for the hundredth time at the gold band with the round, half-carat diamond set perfectly in it. It sparkled even in the dim lighting.

I hope she likes it, Rory told his dad. *I hope she says yes.*

Rory was planning to pop the question the following evening. He and Susan had a dinner date at an out-of-the-way little Italian café they had come to love. This time he was planning to give her two dozen red roses.

They had been seeing each other since he had surprised her that morning at the police station.

He was sure she loved him. She had told him so. And he was committed to her, to marrying her, to living here in Las Vegas with her, come what may.

The irony wasn't lost on Rory—getting married in Las Vegas. If anyone had told him a year ago that he'd be marrying a woman he met in Vegas, a cop no less, right here in Sin City, he'd have laughed out loud and said the notion was insane.

I guess God can seem a little crazy like that if you let Him steer the ship, Rory thought. *If I had done things my way, I'd be sitting in my little apartment in Ohio in my own small world, dying a little each day from boredom and loneliness. And that would truly be insanity.*

Just then, he heard his son enter the big front door of the church and saw Rick walking up the aisle toward him.

"Sorry I'm late, Dad." Rick sat down next to Rory. "But I've got great news. We just got the loan approved for our second church on the south end of the Strip. It's time for you to step up marketing efforts again. And when we fill that one, we'll build another, and . . . ."

"So I guess I have some job security now?" Rory teased his son. "Will I ever get to retire, though?"

"Probably not, but then, why would you want to?"

"Can I at least take a week off soon?"

"Well, I guess that will be okay as long as you come back. You're not thinking about going on another cruise are you?"

"Nah. But I may need time off for my honeymoon." Rory watched Rick's expression, waiting for his words to register.

Rick looked at him with surprise.

Rory pulled out the ring box again and opened it.

"Dad, that's fantastic!" Rick grinned then hugged him.

"There's just one problem."

"What's that?"

"I'm not sure whether to ask you to be my best man or our minister." Rory smiled.

"I would be honored to do either," Rick said, tears in his eyes.

"Thanks, Rick, for everything."

Father and son stood and headed out for dinner, Rick leading the way.

Rory stopped and turned back to face the sanctuary. "Thank you, Dad," he whispered. "Oh yeah, and thank you too, God."

CPSIA information can be obtained at www.ICGtesting.com
Printed in the USA
BVOW02s0509200616

452419BV00001B/1/P